The
Exiled

Christopher Charles

MULHOLLAND
BOOKS
HODDER

First published in Great Britain in 2016 by Mulholland Books
An imprint of Hodder & Stoughton
An Hachette UK company

1

A CIP catalogue record for this title is available from the British Library

Trade paperback ISBN 978 1 473 61197 9
eBook ISBN 978 1 473 61196 2

Printed and bound by Clays Ltd, St Ives plc

Hodder & Stoughton policy is to use papers that are natural, renewable
and recyclable products and made from wood grown in sustainable
forests. The logging and manufacturing processes are expected to
conform to the environmental regulations of the country of origin.

Hodder & Stoughton Ltd
Carmelite House
50 Victoria Embankment
London EC47 0DZ

www.hodder.co.uk

For John Coyne

The Exiled

1

The Wilkins ranch covered a thousand acres of piñon-dotted slopes rolling into mountains capped year-round with snow. Raney drove the access road, crossed a dry creek bed, crested a hill, and came out in the clearing Bay had described. The sheriff was leaning against his squad car, smoking a cigarillo and watching the lab techs unload their van.

"Sheriff Bay," Raney called. "It's been a while."

"You're all they sent?" Bay said.

"Budget cuts. Not enough bodies to justify the manpower."

"This oughta help."

Bay pointed to a clapboard shed on the far side of the clearing.

"Scene's under there," he said. "We kept our distance with the vehicles."

They started across, Raney a hundred pounds leaner and a foot shorter than Bay, sleek in his blazer and jeans, his black ankle boots a compromise between city and country; Bay towering in his Stetson, his sheriff's belt tugging his pants below the waistline.

"Beautiful country," Raney said.

"You hold that thought."

"Bad?"

"This one's right out of your past life."

"Narcotics?"

"That's part of it."

The shed was no bigger than an outhouse. The door had been torn from its hinges and dumped in a strip of broom sage.

"Your work?" Raney asked.

"Someone done it for us."

Raney leaned inside, discovered an open trapdoor and an extension ladder descending into a concrete bunker.

"We took up the false floor," Bay said. "And put in some lights down there. Otherwise, it's like we found it. Coyotes must have caught the smell. You can see where they clawed at the boards."

He handed Raney a surgical mask and a pair of latex gloves.

"You coming?" Raney asked.

"I've looked all I care to. The one by the ladder is Jack Wilkins. I've known him and his wife forty years. He owns—owned—this place. Never saw the Hispanics before today."

"All right," Raney said.

The stench cut through his mask before he'd reached the bottom rung. Battery-powered lamps lit the space like a photographer's studio. He stood for a moment, taking stock. It was a large and solid room, built to be lived in once the bomb dropped, then repurposed sometime after the Wall fell. At the center was a cutting table lined with razor blades, clear Baggies, a wooden salad bowl brimming with a gray, granular substance. The floor was covered end to end in uncooked grains of rice. Empty burlap sacks lay in a heap near the table.

Three dead: Wilkins sprawled faceup near the exit; two Hispanics—one male, one female—slumped against the far wall. Wilkins with a hole in his chest and his throat slit wide, blood and rice mixing to form a claylike halo above his head. His right hand clutched at the trigger guard of a break-action shotgun. His left eye had been gouged, the eyeball partially dislodged. Long scratches disappeared into his white beard. There were half a dozen shell casings scattered around his feet.

Raney crossed the bunker, rice cracking under his heels. Wilkins's fellow deceased were young and shared similar broad features. Siblings, maybe twins. The girl had been shot in the stomach, her throat cut with the same stroke that finished Wilkins. She died pressing a balled-up T-shirt to her wound. Her blouse and underwear were torn, one breast exposed, bite marks around the nipple. She wore a short denim skirt, no leggings, sandals with a thick heel. Toenails striped the colors of the Mexican flag. A faded contusion on her left cheek, lipstick smeared, short white hairs mixed with the blood under her fingernails. Raney knelt as close as he could without disrupting the scene, looked for bruising on her thighs, found none.

I hope you were spared that much, he thought.

Her brother, the apparent knifeman, lay bare-chested beside her. His physique put him somewhere between seventeen and twenty. He'd OD'd, hemorrhaged internally, bled out through his eyes, mouth, ears. The syringe had fallen from his right arm. A Glock 18, a metal spoon, a Bic lighter, and a sprung stiletto lay in a pond of blood between the bodies. The brother's pockets were turned out, as though someone had thought to save Raney the trouble.

Traces of white powder spotted the cutting table. Raney crouched down, sniffed. Cocaine, pure enough to step on several times over. Eighteen years clean, and still he felt a surge, the slight tingle of a phantom limb. He peeled off a glove, dipped his pinkie in the salad bowl, touched the tip of his finger to his tongue. Baby laxative. He spit hard into his sleeve. He looked more closely at the bowl, spotted a plastic edge poking through the surface. He pulled it free, brushed it off. A full dimebag. Sifting through the bowl with the blade of his penknife, he discovered two more bags. He wrapped these in a handkerchief, buried the handkerchief in his blazer pocket. He left the third bag for the lab techs to find.

The shipment was gone. Judging by the empty sacks, Raney estimated ten kilos, maybe more.

He stood on a chair, surveyed the blood trails. They told a confused story: the most he could determine on his own was that no one had died instantly, that people had moved and/or been moved after their wounds were inflicted.

Fact: they'd been locked down here for days before they died (proof: quantity of urine and excrement stewing in a bucket at the back of the room). Fact: Jack lost an eye assaulting the girl. Fact: Jack shot the girl (to avenge his lost eye?).

Scenario: the brother either fell asleep, was coldcocked by Wilkins, or faded into a drug nod. Wilkins attacked the girl. The girl fought back. Wilkins shot her. The blast or its echo woke the brother, who shot Wilkins, then slit his throat (some kind of signature?). Brother tended to sister. When it was clear she wouldn't live, he euthanized her. Probability: she begged for it.

Raney climbed back out of the bunker, stopped to inspect the trapdoor. It was forged of a heavy metal and coated with tin; one hasp on the interior, another on the exterior. An open padlock with the key inside lay on the ground a few feet away. Raney saw now where the remaining shells had gone: Wilkins had been firing into the underside of the door, looking to blast his way free.

Bay hovered a few yards from the shed, rolling a fresh cigarette.

"Well?" he asked.

"Wilkins had a side business."

"Figures. He always was a shit rancher. You see a single cow on your way up here?"

Bay kicked at the dirt. Raney stared at a spot somewhere above the tree line.

"Where's the widow?"

"Mavis? At the house. I got my deputy with her."

"I'd like to talk to her."

"She's shook up, Wes."

"I guess she would be."

"What do you think happened?"

"They were trapped. They turned on one another. Then someone came back for the supply."

"How long you figure they been down there?"

"Hard to say. The dry and dark would have slowed the decomp. A while, I'd guess. Whoever locked them in wouldn't risk coming back early."

"Goddamn," Bay said.

Raney searched the clearing. Apart from his sedan and Bay's squad car there was only the county van.

"Their vehicle is gone," he said.

"The Mexies'?"

Raney nodded.

"Probably burned to shit in a ditch somewhere."

"Probably."

"This how it was in New York?" Bay asked.

Raney shrugged, shifted his gaze back to the mountains.

2

They drove in tandem down the dirt road cutting through Wilkins's property. Bay was right: not a cow anywhere. Raney slowed to a crawl at the creek bed. Bay flashed his lights. Raney glanced in the rearview mirror, saw Bay smiling.

The house came in and out of focus between the trees. An adobe, well maintained, a garden of wildflowers out back. Mrs. Wilkins owned and ran the town's crafts store. She fancied herself a painter. The shop doubled as a café, and she had a guest artist giving after-school lessons in a side room. Jack kept to himself. The couple had been married forty years. Jack and Mavis. Their names ran together. That was as much as Bay had told him.

He parked beside the sheriff's squad car on the gravel between the house and road. Bay started for the front door. Raney held him back.

"Let's have a look first," he said.

There was a stand-alone garage a few yards distant. Raney walked over, tried the side door, found it unlocked. Bay followed him in. Fishing tackle and camping gear crowded the rafters; there were two cars on the floor, one a decade-old station wagon, the other covered with a thick plastic tarp. Raney peeled the tarp back, unveiled a gold-colored Jaguar, gleaming, fresh off the lot. Bay whistled, placed a palm on the hood.

"Cool," he said.

"Wilkins come by any money lately?" Raney asked.

"Not that I know of. But then he wouldn't have told me."

They started toward the house.

"I'll take lead," Raney said.

"Okay, but remember—Mavis has lived her entire adult life in the middle of nowhere."

"So?"

"Keep the fight fair."

"How much have you told her?"

"Didn't have to tell her anything," Bay said. "She went down there herself before she called us. She saw what you saw."

"That's a start. How was she when you got here?"

"Disoriented. It was her who called nine-one-one, but she seemed startled, like she'd forgot we were coming. Then she just went quiet."

"I'd like to hear that nine-one-one call," Raney said.

Deputy Manning let them in, a lanky twenty-year-old who tried like hell to hide his pimples under a cream three shades darker than his skin.

"How is she?" Bay asked.

"She ain't saying one way or the other."

Manning looked at Raney—excited, as though meeting a celebrity.

"Detective Raney, right? From New York? More people per square block than in all of this county. You must find it dull as dirt out here."

"Not today, son," Raney said.

Manning blanched, pointed.

"She's in the kitchen," he said.

Mavis was sitting at the table, breaking the stems from a bushel of green beans. She didn't look up.

"Do you mind if we join you for a moment?" Bay said.

"I figured you might."

Raney took the seat opposite her; Bay sat between them at the head of the table. Mavis kept her hands busy, her eyes on her work. She was in her early sixties, like Bay, but elegant, with high cheekbones and Grace Kelly eyes, a classic beauty who must have made Jack enemies along the way. It seemed to Raney that she knew this interview would be coming sooner or later but had banked on later. The vegetables were a prop, part of a performance she hadn't had time to rehearse: the meek housewife who couldn't pull herself from her chores even on the day she found her husband shot to death. Raney studied her and thought: She knew. With that car in the garage. With them driving right past the house. She had to know.

"Mavis," Bay said, "this is Detective Wes Raney. He covers the county's homicides. I've worked with him before. He's good people."

"I wish I was pleased to meet you," she said.

"I understand," Raney said. "I'll try to make this quick. I just have a few questions."

"Of course," she said. "I'll help as best I can."

"We appreciate that," Bay said.

"How long have you and your husband lived in this house?" Raney asked.

"Forty-one years. Or it would have been next month."

"And when did you build the bunker?"

"The year we bought the place. 1961. That summer. There was an army base not far from here. Jack said it was a surefire target. He was worried we wouldn't have the thing done in time."

"Jack built it himself?"

"Mostly. He hired day laborers now and then."

"It's a good-size shelter."

"We were planning to have kids. I used to say to Jack, 'If the world's ending, why bother?'"

"Did you get any use out of it?"

"The shelter?"

"Yes."

"We stayed down there quite a few times, mostly for drills, but once for real, when the tornado came. We had it fixed up nice then, with canned goods and furniture and magazines and a spare mandolin for Jack. It's the last instrument you would have thought Jack played, but he was damn good."

"There's one thing I'm curious about," Raney said. "Why put locks on both sides of the door?"

"You don't want squatters going in when you aren't there, and you don't want them going in when you are there."

"Smart. When did you stop thinking of it as a shelter?"

"When Jack stopped believing the bombs would come. I hadn't set foot in that hole for years."

"You mean before this morning?"

"Yes."

"So you saw what happened? You know what your husband was doing down there?"

"I have an idea."

"How long have you known?"

"That he was mixed up with Mexicans? Since this morning."

"Still, can I ask why you didn't call sooner?"

"What are you talking about? I called Bay right off."

"But the scene down there isn't fresh. It's been a week at least. Why didn't you report your husband missing?"

"I didn't think he was missing. Jack said he was going on a fishing trip."

"Who with?"

"Himself. He went everywhere by himself. Isn't that so, Sheriff?"

"He wasn't shy in his own company," Bay said.

"Why did you decide to look for him in the bunker?"

"You're going to embarrass me now," she said. "Sometimes, after we'd had a fight, he'd hole up out there. After a while, it became the one place I wasn't allowed to go. Jack was peculiar about it. Like I said, he'd never been away that long. I thought maybe he'd gone down there and hurt himself somehow. Maybe he'd had a heart attack."

"If you thought he was hiding from you, ten days seems like a long time not to look."

"I told you," Mavis said. "I thought he'd gone fishing."

"But his poles, his tackle box, his bucket are all there in the garage."

"I wouldn't notice that sort of thing."

"Really?"

"Really. Bay, where is this going?"

13

"What's your question, Raney?"

"Your husband owned a cattle ranch with no cattle on it. You manage an art supply store in a town of fewer than two thousand people. But there's a brand-new Jaguar in the garage and an add-on to the back of your home. Where did you think the money was coming from?"

"Jack ran into an inheritance."

"Who from?"

"A cousin."

"We can check that."

"It's what he told me."

"When did he run into this inheritance?"

"Last year."

"When last year?"

"It was fall."

"Early or late?"

"I don't remember."

"How much?"

"He didn't tell me."

"And you didn't ask?"

"I'm tired. My husband is dead."

"And you never noticed a truck driving past your house in the middle of the night? Never noticed Jack getting up and going out?"

"No. Please, I can't do this right now."

"He bought a car for himself. Did he buy anything for you?"

Mavis hid her face in her hands.

"Go!" she screamed.

Raney stayed put. Bay tugged his arm.

"All right, Mrs. Wilkins. But we're going to have to look around. The warrant is signed, if you want to see it."

"That's fine."

"I'm sorry again for your loss," Raney said.

"You never said sorry a first time."

Bay leaned forward, touched Mavis's shoulder. Raney thought he saw the big man's eyes linger a moment too long.

3

Their search of the house turned up nothing—no drugs, no ledger, no hint of who Wilkins bought from or sold to—nothing but the portrait of a relationship that had long since become something less than a marriage. Crafts magazines on the nightstand in her bedroom; potboilers on the nightstand in his. In one room, a small arsenal behind a display case, taxidermied bobcats and mountain goats ranging the walls; in another, an outsized loom, an easel holding up a half-finished painting of a wild iris, a picture window framing a hummingbird feeder, Navajo rugs on the floor. His and hers, alternating throughout the house. But what struck Raney was the unflagging sense that the home belonged to Mr. and Mrs. Wilkins and no one else. He could find no evidence that Jack and Mavis knew anyone but Jack and Mavis—no photos or postcards magnetically pinned to the fridge, no calendar to keep track of the occasional luncheon, no inscriptions in any of the books he thumbed through. Somehow, this absence seemed in keeping with a pervasive, almost obscene cleanliness. When the lab techs got here they'd be lucky to find a dust mite, let alone a wayward fingerprint. Each room felt like a diorama, a reenactment painstakingly assembled by an anthropologist and then freeze-dried for the edification of future generations.

He found Bay pacing outside, kicking at the gravel, smoking, swearing with every exhale.

"This ain't right," he said. "It ain't like rousting meth heads or busting up bar fights. I've known Mavis going on forty years."

Mavis, Raney thought. A matronly name. Almost an alibi in itself. Bay seemed to read his mind.

"You can't really think . . ."

Raney shrugged.

"Death by padlock," he said. "The new woman's crime. Cleaner than poison."

"She couldn't have known they'd kill each other," Bay said.

"No."

"So she left them down there to starve to death? While she went on about her business?"

"Somebody did. She's the only one who could have been certain they'd stay down there. Anyone else would have worried the wife might find them."

"I know her," Bay said. "Mavis ain't one to take life for granted. Hers or anyone else's. It don't figure."

"Neither does half of what she said."

Bay quit pacing, slumped down on the trunk of his car.

"What about the missing coke? No way a lady her size hauls however many bricks out of that bunker and then drives off with them."

"I agree. Either someone put her up to it or someone helped

her afterward. Or both. We need to figure out who. And we need a handle on Jack's business plan. He gets a package from Mexico, steps on it, and then what? Was he selling to locals, or did he run it up to Albuquerque? Or Denver?"

"The reservation, maybe? There's money up there now with the casino. There's money all up in these hills. Everything from big-time ranchers to Hollywood types looking for quiet."

"ID'ing the Mexicans might give us a clue."

"Goddamn," Bay said. "It just don't make sense. I've known her forty years."

"Jack knew her longer."

"You're talking like it's fact," Bay said. "You ain't proved a damn thing."

"I know. You're right. So point me in a direction."

"What kind of direction?"

"Who was Jack close to?"

"Nobody. Jack was a sulker. It's true what Mavis said—he went everywhere alone."

"All right, what about Mavis?"

Bay thought it over.

"Clara, that gal working in the shop. They say Mavis is like a mother to her."

"I'll go have a word," Raney said. "One other thing."

"What's that?"

"Keep Junior posted outside the house. In a big shiny squad car."

"Junior? The kid's half narcoleptic."

"Rotate him, then."

"I don't have anyone to rotate him with," Bay said. "You worried Mavis might run?"

"I'm more worried about who might come looking. Somebody got double-crossed."

Bay shook his head.

"Shit," he said. "This is the day the lord hath made. He can have a do-over if he wants it."

"Just the one?"

Bay sniggered.

"Where've they got you bunking?"

"Hotel on Main."

"That old brothel? The county spares no expense. They shoulda put you up at the casino. All you can eat, breakfast through dinner."

Bay pointed to an adobe castle near the top of the foothills. Raney wondered how he'd missed it.

He drove a winding descent toward town. It was July, nearing 7:00 p.m., the sun sharper here than it would be at noon back East. He spotted a clutch of mule deer grazing in a paddock alongside a lone Appaloosa. Bay had called the area a desert, but it wasn't the type of desert you saw in the movies: it wasn't deserted, wasn't desolate. Birds didn't drop from the sky, dead of heatstroke. There were mountains and trees and a dozen types of grass. The world changed with every jump in altitude. It sometimes rained in the spring, and in the winter it snowed often. Death was everywhere. Raney never went for a hike without coming across bones, skulls, now and again a full skeleton, rarely a fresh kill. But death here seemed governed by natural law. What happened in that bunker belonged to another place. It was urban, something from what Bay had called Raney's past life, something that would have made sense in the basement of a Lower East Side tenement but here was out of joint, a reminder that men fail to act naturally no matter the setting.

4

Raney stood outside a shabby ring, tugging at the skirt, watching one of Dunham's stable pummel a three-hundred-pound Italian kid from Bay Ridge. Timed rounds, no referee. Fifty dollars to fight, a thousand back if you won. Now and again a seasoned street punk might land a shot worth mentioning, but Dunham's boys were topflight amateurs. One even made alternate at the Olympics.

Dunham himself sat perched on a stool at the far side of the ring, suede jacket hanging to his thighs, a thick gel holding every hair in place. He was tall, angular—a gaunt face on a muscular body. The sports pages would have called him wiry. According to an informant, the show went some way toward assuaging the grief Dunham felt when his own boxing career ended with a bullet to the right forearm and a three-year stint at Rikers.

In his deposition, the informant claimed that Roy Meno— dealer, extortionist, racketeer, murderer, and Dunham's uncle by marriage—wanted Dunham dead. Dunham was a liability, likely to start a war because he couldn't keep his hands off someone's girl or because he woke up mad at the sun. That and he talked too much. Not about business: he was just the type who couldn't stay conscious without running his mouth. So Meno isolated him, gave him a bar to manage on Staten Island, far from the hub. And to hedge his bets, the CI said, Meno sent Dunham out on any job likely to get him killed. It was playing with house money. If Dunham didn't come back, so much the better. Until then, Meno made the most of Dunham's skill set. Rival dealers were turning up dead across the five boroughs; the extorted were paying on time.

"If I was you all," the informant said, "I wouldn't worry about Dunham. It's like the chemical that makes fear was sucked from his brain. Meno's right: sooner or later, he'll take care of himself."

Meanwhile, Dunham was chafing on the other side of the Verrazano. Word was he needed someone to talk to, someone to laugh at his jokes and generally ease the pain of exile. Raney was young enough to play lackey, able enough to keep pace. So when his lieutenant, who felt about Raney much as Meno felt about Dunham, learned that his junior detective was a three-time Golden Glover, he saw an opportunity. Raney agreed. It sounded like a quick path out of the buy-busts that kept the same faces rotating through the squad's holding cell.

The fat kid from Bay Ridge made it to the third round, in part because his opponent—Manny "the Cobra" Martinez, a moniker that didn't hold up if you considered the fighter's squat, snub-nosed physique—was too short to hit him in the face, and in part because the kid, who hadn't put a mark on

Manny, knew how to guard his midsection. When the bell sounded for the fourth, Manny came out looking fed up. He ducked a slow-motion right, then beat on the kid's spleen until he buckled and fell. It took four men to haul him away. Manny pranced around the ring. The crowd jeered: the house would only cover bets *against* its fighters.

Raney was up. He climbed into the ring, pulled off his T-shirt, heard the crowd buzz, saw people rush to place their bets. The emcee announced him as Mike Dixon.

"And who will challenge the challenger?"

A fighter called Spike jumped the ropes. He had three inches and twenty pounds on Raney. Powerful upper body, stick legs, soft middle. A spiderweb tattoo circling his neck.

A fellow undercover shouted up to Raney:

"Don't get caught with anything stupid."

The kind of advice a mother might give. Still, it was sound. Raney hadn't been hit with a bare fist since junior high.

"Remember, gentlemen," the emcee said. "No kicking."

For this play with Dunham to work, Raney couldn't just put his opponent down: he had to humiliate him, make him look as threatening as a middle-aged man staring out the window of a commuter train. "I want blood," Lieutenant Hutchinson said. "Make his eyes look like two rainbow-colored water blisters. That's how you get Dunham's attention."

He held back early, bobbing and weaving, sizing up Spike's defense: straight as a board, hands by his sides. Raney danced, jabbed, ducked. Midway through the round he launched two quick lefts just above the belt line. The second landed clean. Spike gave him a sad, man-child look, then stepped hard on Raney's lead foot and knocked him off center with a looping blow to the chest. Raney teetered into the ropes. Spike charged.

Raney sidestepped, connected with a straight jab that nearly sent Spike bolting into the crowd. Spike found his footing, spun back around. Raney went to work, staggering the bigger man with a bull's-eye uppercut, blackening his right eye with a four-punch combination. End of round 1.

"Nice, kid," the undercover called. "Keep working the body."

Raney charged back out at the bell, swung hard and missed, swung and missed again. Round-2 Spike was light on his toes, held his hands high: a resurrection of the fighter he'd been before Dunham's off-book brawls turned him sloppy. He countered Raney with a left cross to the temple. Raney backpedaled, shook it off. Spike smiled.

"Come on, kid. Get after him."

Spike was boxing now, measuring distance with his jab, moving his head from side to side.

Take what he gives you, Raney thought.

Spike came at him with a body-head combination. Raney picked the shots off, moved inside, doubled Spike up with a hook to the liver. The big man dropped to his knees, spit blood on the canvas. Raney hovered, taunting him, demanding that he get up. He waited for the ten count, then realized it wasn't coming.

"He's not down," the undercover shouted. "He's not down!"

Raney heard, but too late. Spike caught him with a roundhouse flush to the hip. Raney stumbled, felt his right leg go dead. Spike made it to his feet. The bell rang.

Round 3:

Spike's right eye was swollen shut, his teeth dripping blood. Raney dragged his right leg behind him, waved his opponent forward, daring him to stand toe-to-toe. Spike obliged. Raney dodged a sweeping left, tagged Spike's good eye, splintered his cheekbone with a double right cross. Spike toppled, his feet twitching on the canvas. No round 4.

The gamblers collected their money. Raney wrapped a handkerchief around the knuckles of his right hand, watched the fabric swell with blood. The ring girl—Dunham's cousin, a well-proportioned blonde who had done time for solicitation—climbed onto the canvas and passed Raney an envelope.

"Nice job, babe," she said, kissing him on the cheek. The undercover hooted.

Dunham's boys regained their swagger in the final two fights—one a first-round KO, the other a slow meting out of punishment that had Dunham off his stool for the first time all night.

"That's right," he shouted. "Give the janitor some fucking work."

Raney lingered by the door, waiting for the crowd to clear. The fighters queued up. Dunham doled out wads of cash without counting the bills. Spike was absent, lying on an ICU gurney somewhere, spinning a tale about the punks who jumped him. It was the Cobra who spotted Raney.

"You got a lucky draw, kid," he said.

"Maybe," Raney said.

"No maybe about it. Come back next week and ask for Cobra."

"I'll do that."

"It'll be the biggest fucking mistake you ever made."

"Why wait?" Raney said. "We got the ring right there."

Dunham guffawed.

"Tough guy," Cobra said.

He was backing down. Dunham smelled it, too.

"Hey, Cobra," he said. "It took you four rounds to get rid of the Pillsbury fucking Doughboy. Why don't you crawl back to whatever crab-infested snatch you're screwing this week and have her rub ointments on your boo-boos? And make sure your balls drop before I see you again."

Cobra scanned the room for any dignity he might salvage, then turned and skulked off. Dunham looked hard at Raney.

"What's up, kid? The envelope short?"

"No, sir," Raney said.

"Sir? The kid's old school. What's your name again?"

"Mike Dixon."

"Deadly Dixon. I like it. Deadly Dixon with the mean right cross. You should use that. What can I do you for, Deadly?"

"I was hoping we could talk."

"So talk."

"In private."

"You want to give confession? You've come to the wrong guy, Deadly."

"I've got something to offer."

"No shit? You don't hear that ten times a day. All right, I'm curious. Fellas, your pockets are full. One of you pat this kid down and then all of you get the fuck out."

Raney assumed the position while a heavyweight pawed him from shoulders to socks.

"Clean."

When they were alone, Raney took the envelope from his pocket and held it out to Dunham.

"What's this?"

"I'm giving it back," Raney said. "And then I want you to give it back to me. As a salary."

"Salary?"

"I've been out four months. I tried going straight. Dock work. Construction. I drove a gypsy cab for a week. I even bused tables out in Sheepshead Bay. It ain't me."

"What were you in for?"

"Possession of a firearm. They found my piece but not the kilo taped up under the tire well."

"Why come to me?" Dunham said. "How do you even know who the fuck I am?"

"Everyone knows who you are."

"Then everyone knows I work alone."

"I hear the jobs are getting bigger. I figured you might want some extra muscle."

"So tonight was an audition?"

"Something like that."

"Clever. You're a clever boy, Deadly."

Dunham squared up on his stool.

"I tell you what," he said. "Hit me. Right here."

He pounded his chest.

"One shot. If you can knock me off this stool, then we'll talk."

"Mr. Dunham . . ."

"It's Joey. One shot. Take it or turn around and walk the fuck out."

Raney took it. Dunham lay on the floor in a fetal position, laughing and slapping at the concrete. Raney extended a hand. Dunham waved it off, stood, drew a Glock from his waistband and pressed the muzzle to Raney's forehead. Raney held still.

"You and me," Dunham said.

He stepped back, slid the gun to the center of the ring, slipped out of his suede jacket, folded it over the ropes. He looked like a Greek statue crammed into a wifebeater. Raney moved away, his hands raised.

"I don't want . . ."

"What? You afraid if you draw blood I'll kill you? How's this? You don't draw blood, I'll kill you."

Dunham rushed him, caught him with a shoulder to the sternum. Raney landed on his back, gulping air.

"Protect yourself at all times, Deadly. Already I'm disappointed."

Dunham took up the stool, flung it full force. Raney kicked it away, managed to get to his feet before Dunham charged again. Raney pivoted, caught Dunham with a knee to the chest, grabbed his arm and threw him to the floor. Dunham started to rise. Raney kicked him in the ribs, jumped on his back, wrapped an arm around his throat. Dunham reached behind, found an ear, and pulled. Raney bit back a scream; his grip slackened. An elbow to the jaw sent him spinning.

They stood bent over, gasping, Dunham bleeding from the nose, Raney from the mouth. Dunham's hair jutted out in all directions. There was a long pause before Dunham lunged, swinging wildly, overreaching, grazing Raney's head with his forearm, leaving himself wide open. A long volley to the stomach put Dunham on his knees. He reached out, grabbed Raney's ankles and pulled. Raney landed on his tailbone, felt a seismic pain rocket down his legs. They lay on the floor, sucking in air, each waiting to see if the other would get up.

"Enough," Dunham said, pressing on his chest, pushing the words out. "You passed the first test."

Raney sat up, coughed, wiped blood from his mouth.

"What's the second test?"

"Be at my bar Friday night. Eight o'clock."

"All right."

"And come heavy."

He stayed up past sunrise. Sophia stayed up with him, listening, stroking his hair, fretting over his injuries. He told her what he could.

"This is my way in," he said. "No more glorified street cop."

"Seems glamorous," Sophia said. "Wes, let me take you to the ER. Lord knows where you might be bleeding inside."

"I've had worse," he said.

"You're being ridiculous."

"I'm fine."

"Oh, really?"

She kissed his neck, started to climb on top of him. Her leg brushed his ribs. He yelped, pushed her away. She sat up, mock-pouting, tugging at her T-shirt where it clung to her thighs.

"What, you're not in the mood?"

She pulled the elastic from her ponytail, shook out her hair, twirled a long strand around one finger.

"You're being mean," Raney said.

"You never took a beating this bad in the amateurs."

"They weren't allowed to hit me with chairs."

"So what's next? What's the reward for putting yourself through this?"

"Now I start making cases," he said. "No more harassing junkies. No more hanging out all night in Port Authority men's rooms, asking anyone who needs a bath if they want to cop. I'm going above the street. And I'll be reporting straight to the DA. In practice, I'll have more power than my desk-jockey lieutenant."

"Power?" Sophia said. "Listen to you."

"Your father will be proud."

"Don't worry so much about my father."

Raney nodded to the portrait Sophia kept on her dresser of retired captain Ed Ferguson decked out in formal blues.

"People still talk about him," Raney said.

"I know. No one liked him, but everyone respected him."

"The Bruno case made him a legend."

"Is that what you're after? A legacy?"

"I just want to make cases," Raney said.

"Liar. You're exactly like my father."

"You knew I was a cop when we met."

"I like my clichés big and glaring."

"We should work that into our vows."

"Done," she said.

She switched off the light, set her arm slowly across his chest. Raney lay there, eyes open, listening to her breathe.

5

The sign on the glass door read CLOSED, but there was a woman unpacking merchandise at the far end of a slim aisle. Raney searched for a bell, then rapped on the glass with his knuckles. The woman ignored him. He rapped harder, stood back and waited. The sun was setting over the western range, casting all of Main Street in a violet shadow. Raney wished he had his camera.

"I'm sorry," she said, "but we close at six."

Raney held up his badge. She was older than he'd imagined, past thirty, with red hair that flowed to her hips and a single cluster of freckles at the bridge of her nose. She appeared fit in a way that suggested running or mountain biking, wore a bevy of rings—turquoise, silver, lapis lazuli—but none that linked her to anyone else. Pretty, stylish, unbetrothed: the combination made her exotic in this part of the world.

"Can I help you?" she asked.

"You haven't heard?" Raney said.

"Heard what?"

"Do you mind if I come in?"

"I'm in the middle of inventory."

"It's important."

The store, unlike Mavis's home, appeared crowded and chaotic, but the chaos was organized: a deliberate color scheme drew the customer's eye clockwise around the room, from the faded umber of a landscape painting to the burning sienna of a Navajo headdress. In between were metal shelving units running front to back, crammed with colored pencils, tubes of oil paint, sketch pads, stretched and unstretched canvases, barrels of yarn. To the right of the entrance was a small coffee bar and a varnished wooden bench.

"There's been an incident, Ms. . . ."

"Remler," she said. "But call me Clara."

"Clara. How long have you worked for Mrs. Wilkins?"

"Almost three years."

"I hear you consider her a friend as well as an employer."

"That's right. What's this about? What incident?"

"I'm sorry to have to tell you that Jack Wilkins is dead."

"Dead? How?"

"Ms. . . . Clara, I investigate murders."

She stepped back, dropped onto the bench, then leaped straight up.

"What am I doing?" she said. "I need to see Mavis."

Raney took her arm, tugged her gently back down.

"You'd better wait. Forensics won't have finished yet."

"Tell me what happened," she said.

"I will. But first I need to ask a few questions."

"Was it a break-in?"

"That's part of it. Let me——"

"Just tell me that Mavis is okay. Tell me she's okay, and I'll answer all the questions you want."

"She's fine."

"Thank God. I never liked her living out there, alone with that man. Jesus, what am I saying? He's dead."

Unlike her employer, Clara seemed genuinely flustered—not hysterical, but lost, as though waiting for a single emotion to settle in.

"It's all right," Raney said. "Take a moment. Can I get you something? Water? Tea?"

"I'd love an ice water," she said. "That's very kind of you."

Raney stepped behind the bar. Clara watched him scoop ice into a glass.

"I thought you were supposed to shake me to my senses," she said.

"I don't have a partner to play good cop."

"So you're playing?"

"No," he said. "I'm not playing."

She sat cradling her glass, drawing deep breaths, taking an occasional swallow.

"All right," she said. "I'm ready now."

Raney told himself to go slow.

"It seems you weren't fond of Jack."

"I'm sorry, this sounds awful, but there was nothing to be fond of. I'm sure there was once, but not now. I never saw the man without a beer in his hand. He'd have these fits of rage. He'd criticize Mavis. Her cooking. The way she dressed. He'd ridicule her painting. In front of me or anybody else. Then he'd apologize in this cloying, sniveling way that would go on and on. It was horrible to watch."

An angle Raney should have anticipated: Jack dipping into his own supply, disguising his habit with alcohol.

"Did he ever hit her?"

"Not that I know of."

"Why do you think she stayed with him?"

"Like I said, there must have been another Jack, one she hoped he'd turn back into."

Raney remembered the divide in the Wilkinses' home. He remembered Bay's long glance.

"And in the meantime?" he asked.

"The meantime?"

"Mrs. Wilkins is an attractive woman. I hear she has companions."

Clara blanched.

"There's just the one that I know of," she said. "And that ended a year ago."

"Tell me about him."

"He wasn't much better than Jack. He used to be an airline pilot, then he made a small fortune in real estate. But he gambles. He started asking Mavis for loans. Small loans at first, but the amount kept growing."

"What's his name?"

"Bob. Bob Sims."

"Do you know where he lives?"

"No, but I know where you can find him. Up on the hill. At the casino."

"Describe him."

"Average height. Midsixties. No one would call him slender. Wears a jet-black toupee that's too small for his head. And he dresses the way Europeans think Americans dress—button-down Hawaiian shirts, the louder the better. And cowboy boots with a snakeskin design."

"You'd make a good cop," Raney said.

"I doubt it."

"You're sure there's been nobody else?"

"She was talking with a guy online. A schoolteacher up in Albuquerque. I don't think they ever met face-to-face."

"Thank you. You've been a big help."

"I'm glad," she said. "Now tell me."

He told her. The bunker. The bodies. The missing coke. He left out the padlock, the fact that they'd been caged down there, maybe for weeks.

Clara stood, slammed her glass on the counter.

"Jesus fucking Christ," she said. "The danger he must have put her in."

Did Raney catch a hint of acting? He pushed the thought away, then wondered why he was pushing it away.

"One more question: Did Mavis ever say anything about Jack's side business?"

"No," she said. "I had no idea. And I'm sure Mavis didn't, either."

Raney left his card on the coffee bar.

"If you think of anything else," he said.

He turned to let himself out, found an older woman poised to ring the bell. A skinny, redheaded boy—five, maybe six—gripped her free hand. Raney looked back at Clara.

"My son," she said. "And Mrs. Hardin, his tutor."

Raney unlocked the door, held it open.

"Obliged," Mrs. Hardin said.

As they moved past, the boy reached out, ran an index finger across Raney's badge.

"A lawman," Mrs. Hardin said. "What do you think about that, Daniel?"

Daniel answered with a series of swift and fluid gestures, second nature to him, mesmeric to Raney—as though the boy were performing a flash ballet with his hands.

"He wants to know why you wear the badge on your belt and not your chest."

Raney pulled it off, thumbed the clip.

"So dum-dums like me don't stab ourselves," he said.

Daniel signed again.

"He's asking if it's real."

"Of course it's real," Clara said. "How about a hug for your mother?"

She crouched, arms spread. Daniel ran, leaped, knocked her off balance.

"Show some restraint, child," Mrs. Hardin said.

Raney excused himself, slipped outside.

6

The dinner crowd was gone, the diner nearly empty. He took a booth in the back, between the decorative jukebox and the hallway leading to the bathrooms. The waitress on duty looked like she'd spent the first fifty years of her life smoking cigarettes while standing under a hot sun. She came walking slowly toward him, backlit by the open door.

"Where you from, darling?" she asked.

He'd been out West almost two decades and still the locals knew at a glance. It was freeing, in a way: Raney could make up any past he liked.

"I have a place near the Arizona border," he said. "Just outside the Gila Forest."

"That ain't what I asked."

He smiled.

"New York, originally. What about you?"

"Drifted west all the way from Granby, Texas. There ain't too many places this town improves upon, but Granby makes the cut. Anyway, what can I get you?"

"Roast chicken and a full pot of coffee," Raney said. "I'll be working late tonight."

"You bet. I'll brew some fresh."

He pulled out a small pad and pencil, drew a rough map of the crime scene, placing stick-figure gender symbols where the victims/perpetrators lay. He imagined their last hours, their last moments, starting with Jack. Did the husband suspect the wife? He must have, but he must also have believed she did it to frighten him, teach him a lesson. Soon he'd hear the door lift open, look up to see her frowning down. Was the rape, or attempted rape, which had likely started as a play for something consensual, a kind of vengeance, something Jack could present Mavis with when she came to her senses: *Look what you drove me to?* If Mavis had meant to teach him a lesson, then the attempt failed all the way around. Jack's last moments were too brutal, too ugly for any epiphany. He'd died as the worst possible version of himself.

The waitress brought Raney's coffee.

"I made it extra strong," she said. "If this don't keep you awake, nothing will."

"I appreciate it."

He poured a cup, drank it straight, trying to burn away the craving sparked by that one small taste. He poured a second cup, loaded it with sugar.

He turned his thoughts to the dead boy: a postpubescent mule-cum-murderer, not born for his job but raised in it. Jack, old enough to be his grandfather, was a dabbler by comparison. Did Wilkins mark the boy's first kill? Maybe, but he had seen men killed, known their killers. He was better prepared for death than

Jack. Overdose or suicide? The balance tilted in favor of suicide: he'd avenged his sister but failed to protect her. If someone opened that door, it would either be to arrest him or execute him. If no one came, death by needle beat starvation.

Finally, the girl. It was the bruise on her cheek that stayed with Raney, a mark of innocence, made by the kind of backhand any girl is susceptible to in a thousand different situations, the crime fathers fight hardest to protect their daughters against. A connection he couldn't help but make: Ella, his own daughter, was the same age as Jack's victim. Raney felt an ache he'd become deft at suppressing. He wanted to call Sophia, demand to know that the daughter he'd never met was happy and safe. Was she dating anyone? Had she applied for college? But phoning would make for his worst betrayal yet. To Sophia, he was a member of the walking dead, and he would not allow himself to haunt her at this late date.

The waitress set half a roast chicken and a side of greens on the table.

"Anything else, darling?" she asked.

Raney shook his head.

"No thank you," he said. "I've got enough here for a small army."

He watched her walk away, thought: And what are your secrets, darling? What have you done besides survive?

7

The casino was polished, upscale, every surface bright, gleaming. A maze of slot machines on one side; a floor-to-ceiling bank of TV sets behind the roulette tables; a bar in the back with metallic-blue chandeliers and stools that looked like Bakelite eggcups. A cordoned-off seating area faced a glass wall overlooking the valley. At 10:00 p.m. on a weeknight, the place was just under half full.

Raney stalked the blackjack tables, studying the patrons. There was no shortage of fat men in gaudy shirts, but only one wore a jet-black toupee with the edges peeling back. He sat alone, losing consecutive rounds to the dealer, a young Navajo woman in a severely starched shirt and bow tie. She handled the cards mechanically, her mind somewhere in a future that didn't include Bob Sims.

Raney had no authority here. The slightest gaffe and they could escort him out on the grounds that he was bothering the clientele. He drifted back among the slot machines, took a notepad and pen from inside his blazer, wrote:

Meet me at the bar. Urgent.

He tore the paper from the pad, folded it in thirds, then returned to the tables. He waited for the croupier to collect Sims's latest stack of chips before tapping him on the shoulder.

"Bob?"

Raney smiled, put on his most pleasant voice; Sims let his irritation show.

"Do I know you?"

"You know Mavis Wilkins. She asked me to give this to you."

He handed over the message, winked at the croupier. She didn't seem to notice.

"Am I getting served?" Sims asked. "Don't tell me Mavis is pregnant."

They were seated at the table farthest from the bar. The glass wall gave onto a black vista dotted with stars and electric lights. Raney brushed back his blazer, let his badge show.

"Can I buy you a drink?" he said.

"I thought cops weren't supposed to drink."

"Up here, I'm just a citizen. This is a courtesy call. I have news I thought you should hear in person. News I wish I didn't have to share."

The barman came for their order. He was upwards of fifty, had the heft of a pro weight lifter, smiled like he'd never known an unkind thought.

"Your pleasure, gentlemen?"

"Vodka collins," Sims said. "With extra lime."

"And a Jim Beam, please. Neat."

"Coming right up."

Raney watched him walk off, half-stepping to a jazz tune that was barely audible over the electric racket of the slot machines. Some people are just happy, he thought. Circumstance has nothing to do with it.

"So what's your news?" Sims asked.

"Jack Wilkins is dead. Someone shot him and then cut his throat."

He was abrupt, trying to get a rise, hoping Sims's reaction would tell him something: that he knew or didn't know, was inclined to lie or tell the truth. Sims said nothing, showed nothing—just sat there massaging his temples, filing through a list of questions, uncertain which to ask first. When the barman returned with their drinks, Sims pounced on his. Raney heard ice bouncing off his teeth. After a while, Sims said:

"Jesus. What about Mavis?"

"She wasn't hurt."

"When?"

"We don't know. We found them this morning."

"Them?"

"There were two other victims, a boy and a girl. Late teens, early twenties."

"Who?"

"We're pretty sure they're Mexican."

"Mexican?" Sims said. "Jack didn't know any Mexicans. He hardly knew any whites."

"Whether he knew them or not, they died a few yards apart."

"Where was this?"

"On the property."

Sims ran a hand over his mouth.

"Shit," he said. "I drive by there twice a day."

He was making the right expressions, saying the right words, but he was distracted, vacillating between this new reality he couldn't ignore and the table he could just make out from where they sat. Raney understood the addiction, if not the vice.

"I need to ask you a few questions," he said.

"What can *I* tell you?"

"I understand you had a relationship with Mavis."

"We saw each other for a while, but that ended a year ago."

"Still, we have to look at all angles. You had an affair with a woman whose husband turned up in a triple homicide. And since it was a robbery-homicide, your motive rates high."

"What's that supposed to mean?"

"I haven't looked into your finances, but I think it's safe to say that a man who spends his nights in a place like this has liquidity problems."

"You kidding me? Everyone should have my liquidity problems. I did damn good in my day. What I drop here is nothing. It's charity."

"Charity?"

"You should have seen this place pre-casino. You couldn't even call it a shantytown. Now it's all new developments. Cute little bungalows with wood floors and solid plumbing. If the casino went bust, they'd be right back where they were."

"And where would you be?"

"What does that have to do with Wilkins?"

"Nothing," Raney said. "So if someone told me you'd asked Mavis for loans, they'd be—"

"Full of shit. Check with Mavis. Every dinner was on me."

Was he lying? Or had Mavis lied to Clara? Or Clara to Raney?

"Let me ask you something else. What do you know about Jack's side business?"

"Side business?"

42

"Careful now. No one has an affair because they want to keep their spouse's secrets."

"Mavis and I talked, but I don't know anything about a side business."

"The killer took off with a heavy stash of coke."

Sims sniggered.

"Jack Wilkins couldn't manage a booth at a flea market, and you want me to believe he was some kind of drug dealer?"

"It's the one thing I know for sure. My only question is whether or not Mavis was involved."

"I can answer that one. No."

"You're positive?"

"Positive."

"How?"

"Look, Jack was using, not selling. That was the secret Mavis didn't keep. Nothing about any drug enterprise."

"What did she tell you, exactly?"

"That she hated what it did to him. She was planning some kind of intervention when we split. I don't know if she went through with it, but if she did it didn't stick."

"Hypothetically speaking, let's say Jack was selling—"

"He wasn't."

"Say he was. If he sold locally, who would know about it?"

"Everyone would know about it. Just like everyone knows where I spend my nights. The country out here goes on forever, but the towns don't come any smaller."

"What do people know about Mavis?"

Sims poled at a lime with his straw.

"They know I wasn't the first," he said. "And they know I probably wasn't the last, either. Mavis did her loving and leaving on the side."

"And Jack?"

"Knew but didn't care. Sex was something twisted for him. He couldn't get off unless he paid for it."

"Prostitutes?"

"Yeah. That's where he went 'fishing.' In Nevada. The person who tells you Jack was a good guy is the one who has something to hide. He was the kind of son of a bitch that's born, not made."

"So I've gathered. Is Mavis with anyone now?"

"I honestly don't know."

"Okay," Raney said. "I'll let you get back to it. Here's my card. If you think of anything, call me."

Sims stood.

"You know, I'm sorry about Jack. Despite what I said before."

"I'll pass that on."

"Better not."

Raney sat sipping his whiskey, staring out the glass wall. The town was lit up in the distance, and there were lights scattered around the valley below. One pocket of light seemed particularly incandescent, as though a film crew were shooting a night scene. Raney raised his glass to the lab rats.

8

Detective Raney," the receptionist said. "We were wondering when you would get here."

She sounded happy to see him, even relieved, as though they'd known each other a long while, or as though he were the hotel's most loyal customer.

"I had stops to make on the way."

"Of course."

She didn't ask for details, didn't seem the least bit curious. The one advantage to a crime scene buried in the hills: the media hadn't caught wind.

"The room is all paid for. Top floor in the back, like you asked. I just need your John Hancock."

She handed Raney a pen.

"Oh, and you have a visitor."

"A visitor?"

"Sheriff Bay. I told him he could wait in your room. I hope that's okay."

"How long has he been up there?"

"About an hour."

"I hope there's a TV."

"There is, but it's busted. We put flowers on it. Makes the place homey."

Bay was lying prone on the bed, arms folded across his paunch, feet dangling. He hadn't bothered to turn on the lights. Raney fumbled for a switch.

"Nice of you to take your shoes off," he said.

"There wasn't anyplace else for me to sit," Bay said. "These rooms were built just big enough for a bed and a nightstand, for reasons that should be obvious. The current owner bought it as a fixer-upper but never fixed it up."

"Keeps the rates low."

"I suppose. You know I have a guesthouse out at my place. Free of charge. Or we could bill the county, if that'd make you feel better."

"Maybe next time."

"Suit yourself."

"To what do I owe the pleasure, Sheriff?"

Bay pointed to an unopened bottle of Scotch and two shot glasses balanced on the windowsill behind the bed.

"A housewarming," he said.

"Sheriff Bay, you just might be the kindest man I know."

Raney maneuvered his suitcase into a narrow space between the bed and wall, set his holster on the nightstand, kicked off his shoes. Bay passed him a glass.

"I don't remember you being this hospitable the last time I came around," Raney said.

"I brought you something else, too."

Bay pulled a manila folder from under the pillow beside him.

"Interpol came back fast with those prints," he said.

Bay tossed him the folder. Raney set his glass on the TV next to a vase of fake orchids. He opened the file, skimmed the top page, paraphrased aloud.

"Cartel kids. Twins. Ramon and Luisa Gonzalez. Low-level border hoppers, picked up twice apiece for possession with intent, released both times thanks to a big-name lawyer neither of them could possibly afford."

Raney paused, turned the page.

"But their uncle could," he said.

"Their uncle?"

"Sergio Gonzalez, capo in the Nuevo Milenio cartel. I remember him as a lieutenant from my narco days. Ran a pipeline all the way up to Montreal. He must have gone into business for himself. That doesn't happen without a body count."

"What did Jack get himself mixed up in?" Bay said.

"Nothing he has to worry about now."

"That's kind of cold, even from you."

"He killed that girl. He raped her first, or tried to."

"Yeah, I know," Bay said. "Jack never was worth much. God rest his soul."

Raney drained his glass, reached out for another.

"You mind if I ask you a question?"

"What's that?"

"Why are you here?"

"To give you that file," Bay said.

"You live forty miles out of town and you waited here an hour to give me information I couldn't possibly do anything with until morning?"

Bay set his glass down.

"You're right," he said. "I've got a confession to make."

"Should I Mirandize you?"

"This ain't a joke, Raney."

He waited for Bay to say more.

"I should have told you earlier."

"Told me what?"

"I had no business sitting in on that interview."

Raney smiled, tapped at a plastic flower with his index finger.

"You, too, Bay?" he said. "Mavis is all right, but she must have more than meets the eye."

"It's not the kind of thing I'm inclined to do on a good day. I don't want to make excuses, but Jack never did treat her right. Not since the day they met."

"Then why didn't she leave him?"

Bay shrugged.

"I wish I could say."

"How long ago?"

"Thirty-plus years. And we've been nothing more than cordial since."

"Relax, Bay. She probably doesn't remember."

"Don't be an ass."

"I'm kidding," Raney said. "Besides, my skeletons could eat yours for breakfast. Still, you shouldn't have been in the room. It's not like she confessed, so I don't think it can hurt us at trial. But you'll have to keep your distance."

"It's a little early for you to be talking about trial."

"Maybe."

"But you don't think so?"

"No."

Bay rubbed his stubble with the backs of his fingers.

"You're out on a long limb with this one, Raney."

"She knew about the drugs. She told one of her latest boy-friends that Jack was using."

"Doesn't mean she knew he was selling."

"The one is a stretch without the other. She's involved, Bay. You're right, though: there was more to the job than she could have handled alone."

"So what's next?"

"We need to focus on the missing coke. I'll take another go at Mavis in the morning. I know some things now that I didn't know when we started."

"You might bring Junior a cup of coffee. An Americano, with just a little cream. I wasn't kidding about the narcolepsy."

Bay stood, stretched out his arms. "Let's end this day," he said.

"Sounds good. Thanks again for the hooch."

"Don't mention it. But I would like to hear about those skeletons sometime."

Alone, Raney walked into the bathroom, dug his handkerchief from his pocket, set both dimebags on the vanity. He stared down at them, feeling more curiosity than craving. It made no difference how many addicts and dealers wound up brain-dead or bankrupt, died in jail or the gutter. Everyone who snorted a line managed to believe they were the exception.

As if by instinct, he lifted one of the bags, tapped half its contents into the toilet, watched the granules swirl and vanish. He hid what was left in a pair of socks at the bottom of his suitcase.

9

"Y ou look like you got your ass kicked," Dunham said. "Funny thing is, so do I."

He was standing outside, wearing the same suede jacket, smoking a joint under the bright light of a streetlamp, flanked by sullen-looking bouncers.

"I'm most of the way healed," Raney said.

"Yeah, me too. You find the place all right?"

Raney nodded.

"They got me buried out here. But fuck 'em, I made lemonade. This bar was a beer-and-shots dive when I showed up. Two hundred grand later and you'd think you were in the Village. People dress up to eat here now. Even the citizens of Staten Island deserve a nice place."

The interior wasn't what Raney expected. He'd imagined a dropped ceiling, dartboards, duct-taped bar stools, a scattering of middle-aged drunks. What he found was more supper club than saloon: polished wood floors, tacky but expensive chandeliers, cloth table runners, candles floating in ceramic bowls, a jazz trio playing on a platform stage. He stood with Dunham at the back of the room, Dunham tapping his foot, scatting under his breath.

"I pay them in blow," he said. "It's the only way to get them out here."

"They sound legit," Raney said.

"In another life, I'd have been a sax player," Dunham said. "I've got every record Coltrane made. Hard to picture, right? Boxing and music are the only two things I give a shit about. So how did I end up the prodigal errand boy, banished to a trash heap?"

"Seems like you're doing all right."

"There are worse ways to fail. I could be making change in a tollbooth. They say those people earn good money, but I'd lose my shit with the fumes and the honking."

There was a shift in the music; Dunham let loose a hard round of applause. People at the tables turned to look.

"The schmucks out here don't know to clap after a solo," Dunham said. "Come on, I'll show you around."

He led Raney into a small but state-of-the-art kitchen, introduced him to a short, round man in an apron and a puffy chef's hat. Raney wondered if Dunham made him wear the hat.

"This guy is topflight gourmet. He's a chef, you know? Not a cook, a chef. His name's Benny, but I call him Pierre. Guys named Benny twirl pizza dough in the air. Pierre, give our friend Deadly something to taste. A spoonful of your chowder, maybe."

Benny found a spare ladle, dipped it into a vat, handed it to Raney.

"Salt pork and bay leaves," he said. "That's the key."

"I buy him everything he asks for," Dunham said. "Only the highest-quality ingredients."

"Mostly everything," Benny said.

"Pierre, don't start with me."

"This is fucking delicious," Raney said.

"See, I told you," Dunham said.

Benny made a small bow.

"All right," Dunham said. "We've got one more stop on our tour. Thank you, Pierre. You're a prince among peasants."

Dunham pushed Raney back through the double doors, steered him down a hallway behind the stage.

"Don't take this wrong, but I want to show you the john."

He knocked, then opened the door marked GENTS.

"I keep meaning to order one of those EMPLOYEES MUST WASH HANDS signs."

He gave Raney a moment to take it in. The room was a nearly uninterrupted mosaic of small encaustic tiles. They covered the walls, the ceiling, the base of the toilet, the sink. Raney found no principle guiding their arrangement, no pattern or color scheme. Like taking a shit inside the mind of a madman, he thought.

"I've never seen anything like it."

"The work relaxes me," Dunham said. "I had a guidance counselor in junior high who told me my personality type 'couldn't be left to its own devices.' She wanted to bus me to a school for exceptional children. I never knew if that meant gifted or retarded. I paid a kid from the hood to slash her tires. I had him do it with witnesses around so no one could say it was me. She knew, though. She never brought up the exceptional thing again."

Dunham switched off the light.

"Now let's take a little ride," he said.

Back in the main room, he blew kisses to the musicians.

They drove over the Goethals into Jersey.

"Where we going?" Raney asked.

"Someone whose name you don't need to know is venturing into the real estate business. He bought himself a row of crack houses. Brownstones. Nice homes in their day, whenever the fuck that was. This person wants to make them nice again, but he needs certain individuals to vacate first. These individuals are being disagreeable. Our job is to make them agreeable. You got your piece?"

"Yeah."

"Good. We're talking about rousting some half-dead tweakers, so a couple of fear-of-God shots and a pair of baseball bats oughta do. Normally I'd say go for the kneecaps, but we want them to walk away. Tweaker bones break easy."

The informant was right: Dunham talked nonstop, talked in overlapping words, as though there were a backlog of sentences stacked vertically in his mind, one sliding off the other. He talked about last week's fight at the Garden, about his own amateur career, about the warehouse matches, about traffic, about the chemical stench that flooded parts of north Jersey, about his predilection for strippers and the virtues of fucking them in the shower. He shouted over the local jazz station, smoked without dropping a syllable. The constant stream made Raney's job easy. He didn't have to spin stories about Dixon's childhood, didn't have to account for his bit upstate. He just listened.

They pulled off the Turnpike, rolled through a low-end suburban neighborhood, came out in a ghetto with crews mixing on every corner.

"This is our block right here."

He cut the music. A corner kid spotted them, put down the paper bag he'd been sucking from, and shouted, "Five-O." A half dozen runners scattered from in front of a bank of pay phones. Dunham laughed himself to tears.

" 'They startle easily, but they'll be back, and in greater numbers,' " he said. "You recognize that? That's from *Star Wars*. Goddamn, the little shitheads think I'm a cop."

"It's the threads," Raney said.

Dunham tugged at his jacket collar.

"No narco could afford this."

"He could if he was dirty."

"You're saying I look like a dirty cop?"

"Isn't that a good thing?"

"Yeah, I guess so."

Dunham slowed the car, pointed to a sagging brownstone near the middle of the street.

"That's her."

The front door was sitting off its hinges, propped against the frame. The windows were boarded over, the boards tagged with graffiti.

"So how do we play it?"

"We'll go in from around back. Otherwise the corner boys might get curious. These fiends are their bread and butter."

He coasted down the alley with the headlights off. Chain-link fencing lined both sides. Trash spilled from one yard to the next: three-legged chairs, rusted bicycle frames, cracked kiddie pools. Nothing of value. Nothing that could be scrapped or traded.

A pit bull almost impaled itself trying to get at them.

"What a beauty," Dunham said. "A damn shame. I'd have her eating from my hand inside of a week."

"I'd like to see it."

"I'm shit with people, but animals love me. That's how I know I'm not a sociopath. I never killed any bunnies when I was little."

The back of the house looked even worse than the front. An electrical cord ran up to the second floor and through the only window that remained intact. What had once been a porch was now rubble. The fence was torn out, the yard crowded with shopping carts.

"They're waiting for the new Ford model," Dunham said.

He cut the lights, switched off the engine. The alley went dark.

"I've got two ski masks in the glove compartment. Put one on."

Dunham reached behind him, took a pair of aluminum bats off the backseat.

"Remember," he said. "The idea is to fuck a few of these skels up so bad the whole block scatters."

"Looks like most of them left already."

"We need them all to leave."

Dunham glanced up and down the alley. Raney stood beside him, felt something greater than adrenaline take hold—power laced with fear, an almost giddy anticipation.

"Christ," Dunham said. "We're about to make some shitty lives a whole lot shittier."

They flipped a shopping cart, climbed up through what had been the porch door, and entered a gutted kitchen—appliances gone, sink gone, electrical wire torn from the sockets. A narrow hallway connected the front and back of the house. Two rooms on the left, staircase on the right. Light flickered through bare door frames. A slow and droning conversation seemed to come from nowhere in particular.

"You want the front or back?" Dunham asked.

"Front."

Front gave him a chance to clear the room before Dunham could survey his work.

"All right," Dunham whispered. "If the upstairs junkies slip past us, who gives a shit? We're looking to send a message. Just make sure it's a clear message."

Dunham pulled the Glock from his waistband. "Fear-of-God time," he said.

He fired three rounds into the floor. Raney jetted, suppressed a *Hands, hands, show me your fucking hands.* Inside, three skels huddled around a garden-pail fire. Skel 1 was tied off, a needle jutting from his bicep. Skels 2 and 3 were roasting marshmallows on chopsticks, calm, as though the sound of Dunham's Glock had died in the kitchen. Raney spotted a fourth lying under the front window, wrapped in blankets. The Boy Scout skels saw him, dropped their sticks, stood with their hands folded behind their heads. Glassine eyes sunk deep in sallow faces; no meat and hardly any bone. Impossible to guess an age, to say if they were twenty-five or fifty. Their friend was weaving through a heavy nod. Raney fired at the floor near his feet. The man raised himself up, fell face-forward, jerked back when the flames licked his forehead.

"Get him out of here," Raney hissed.

He tucked the gun back in his waistband, lifted the bat over his head, swung at the empty vials scattered across the floor.

"This is your fucking eviction notice."

"Jesus, man. We wasn't hurting nobody, we just . . ."

Raney palmed the handle of his gun.

"You ain't hearing me. Run, motherfucker. You don't live here anymore."

They hobbled off, dragging their friend between them, protesting in a flatlined drawl Raney couldn't decipher. He started for the man in the blanket, stopped at the sound of Dunham's voice echoing from the other room.

"Did everyone here just shit themselves at once?"

Raney heard what sounded like a body hurled against a wall,

then a woman screaming. He stepped into the hallway, wondering how he would play it if Dunham went too far, wondering what *too far* meant. A pair of eyes gleamed down from the top of the stairs. Raney waved the man on, raised his hands as a sign of peace. A small militia of junkies came barreling down the staircase, tripping, bouncing off the remains of an oak banister.

Dunham:

"So you're a hero now? You'd bash her head in yourself if I gave you a dimebag to do it."

He let loose another round. The woman lost her voice, started dry-heaving.

"What? I didn't touch you."

Two more shots followed by a scattering through the hall, one of the junkies yelling, "Fuck, fuck, fuck," another gripping his head, blood spilling through his fingers. Then Dunham smacking the woman around, taunting her: "It must be easier to suck dick with no teeth." Enjoying himself. Raney thought: One day soon, I'm going to put this fucker down. He fired into the stairs, hoping to draw Dunham's attention. The woman went quiet. Raney stepped back into the front room, emptied the pail onto the floor and stomped out the flames.

Dunham appeared in the doorway, dragging a female skel by the hair, dangling her an inch off the ground. Her coat was three months out of season, her feet bare.

"Jesus, Deadly," he said, nodding at the man in the corner. "You missed one."

"I was getting to him," Raney said.

"He must reek like sewage under all those blankets. Come on, let's finish this."

Raney walked over, jostled the man with his foot. Nothing. He pressed the barrel of his bat against the man's temple.

"Get the fuck up. Now."

Nothing. A hard kick to the ribs. The man didn't stir. Raney turned to Dunham.

"I think he's dead."

"Take out your piece and make sure."

"What?"

"You heard me."

Raney felt the bat being pulled from his hand, looked down, saw a long blade swing for his thigh.

"Holy shit," Dunham said. "It's alive."

Raney jumped back, reached for his gun, but the man was on top of him.

"Gonna cut you, motherfucker."

Raney backpedaled, his hands up, the man following, slicing hard and fast, Dunham laughing, his female skel begging to be let go.

"Handle this, Deadly," Dunham called. "Come on, handle it."

The man drew his arm back and lunged. Raney slipped him, saw the knife stick in the wall, saw the man struggling to jerk it free. Raney kicked his feet out from under him, jumped on his chest, pummeled him unconscious. He stood, breathing hard, burying his face in the crux of one arm.

"Nice, Deadly! Nice."

Dunham stepped forward, jerking the woman with him.

"This guy a friend of yours, darling?"

She shook her head.

"He's no skel," Raney said.

"Sure he is. He sobered up inside is all. Look at him—he's still got his yard muscle."

"His eyes were burning red."

"Do me a favor," Dunham said. "Take a couple of steps back."

"What?"

Dunham tossed his bat, pulled out his gun. The woman went limp. Dunham shook her.

"Now, darling," he said. "There's some good news. You're gonna live to see your next fix. But I want you to watch this very carefully, and then I want you to tell all your friends from the neighborhood what happened here tonight. You understand?"

She nodded, spit dangling from her lips.

Dunham shot the man twice in the face.

"You think you can remember that, angel?"

He let her drop, knocked her backward with his heel, belly-laughed as she crawled through the doorway and down the steps.

They pulled into a dark and empty aisle at the end of a Turnpike rest stop. Dunham beat his fists against the steering wheel, unleashed a victory howl.

"Goddamn, that feels good," he said. "I mean, tell me your blood's not pumping. Tell me you aren't more alive now than you were when you woke up this morning. Where do you go after something like that? What do you do? Fuck a stripper? Lift some weights? It's like one minute you're swimming with sharks and the next you're in a coma. So how do you hold on to that feeling? You know what I mean?"

"I think so."

"Tell me something—do you sleep?"

"Everyone sleeps."

"Okay, but I mean, do you just lie down and shut off? Head hits the pillow and that's it?"

"Most nights."

"You're lucky. Not me. I'm afraid if I fall asleep I won't wake back up. It's a thing. There's a name for it. I've had it since I was a kid. Since before I can remember. So I take pills. And then those pills stop working, so I have to find different pills. It's like a game. Sometimes I mix the pills with booze. But sometimes I don't want to sleep. There's a feeling I want to keep. I want to stay up with it all night long. You hear me?"

"I hear you."

"So let's keep this feeling."

He pulled a small, clear Baggie of white powder from his jacket pocket.

"Peruvian shit. The stuff out of Mexico will make your brain fizzle."

He dug his wallet from his jeans, spread an assortment of licenses and credit cards on the dashboard.

"Try some," he said. "You look tired. I need you to keep up. You did good tonight. We're going to be great friends."

They met at District Attorney Stone's apartment on West 96th Street, far from any courthouse or precinct station. Stone ordered lunch from a Thai place, gave Raney the tour while they waited for the food to arrive. A long and lean two-bedroom, an art collection in its early stages—small modernist canvases that reminded Raney of Dunham's bathroom. Stone's home office was decorated in laminated news articles chronicling his successes, everything from maximum sentences for street-level dealers to a 120-year bit for a serial killer preying on Columbia undergrads. The *Times* described him as "a man whose small stature belies his ferocity." He was known for apoplectic cross-examinations, for crowding the witness stand while spewing out harangues. Op-ed after op-ed called him heroic; one called him a legend at forty. Still, he hadn't touched anything the size of Meno's organization. Raney saw himself in the middle of a pitched battle between two giants who would only meet face-to-face once Stone had already won.

Raney told him everything over a heaping plate of noodles—from the weed outside the club to the killing in the crack house to the coke in the car. Stone rolled his cloth napkin between his fists as though it were a snowball.

"How are you holding up?" he asked.

"I had a man murdered at my feet, and I've broken just about every law I'm sworn to uphold."

"Apart from that."

"Hungover."

"Sometimes justice has to work backwards."

Raney sniggered.

"Listen to me," Stone said. "Everything you did was to protect yourself and your cover. There's a bigger picture here."

"Bigger than homicide?"

"Bigger than a single homicide, yes."

"Okay, but why not arrest Dunham now? Threaten him with life twice over. Get him to turn witness. There's bad blood between him and Meno."

"Because we don't know enough yet."

"Meno ordered the job."

"You can't be sure. You said so yourself: Dunham wouldn't give a name."

"He killed a man," Raney said.

"A man you beat unconscious. How do you think that will play in court?"

"He came at me with a knife."

"You came at him with a baseball bat and a gun."

"Yeah, but I'm the good guy."

"The man was still defending himself."

"So what's the endgame here? Why am I doing this?"

"We want to dismantle Meno's organization. Top to bottom. We want to cripple it so severely that no one rises up to take his place. This isn't about putting a Band-Aid on a bullet wound."

"A dead junkie is a bullet wound?"

"For now. We're building a case. He'll be a part of that case. He'll get his day in court."

"And in the meantime I keep playing accessory?"

"If things continue at this pace, it won't be long. I promise you."

He rented a room in Fort Hamilton, just across the bridge from Dunham's club. He told Sophia it was for her protection. He repeated the DA's words: *It won't be long.* Sophia looked at him as though she knew better, as though she saw the end in the beginning.

10

Raney pulled the curtain back, watched the contrails of an airplane fade into a sky that was just starting to brighten. It would be an hour before the diner opened. He splashed water on his face, then noticed for the first time that the bathroom, with its claw-foot tub and double sink, was at least as big as the room he'd slept in. The lore about the place being a brothel for pioneer soldier boys seemed more likely: they'd simplified the conversion by making every other room a bath. The building suffered as much from lack of imagination as from neglect.

He dressed, walked past the empty reception desk and out to his car. There was something his father used to say, something he'd forgotten for a long while and then remembered: *Find what makes you glad you're alive and do it before the world's in your face. A day is no good unless you get out in front of it.* Back in New York, that meant rounds on the heavy bag and a circuit in the weight room. Then mornings became the dead time in which he slept off one fix in order to make way for the next. Now he spent the early hours of the day walking the trails behind his cabin, climbing a thousand feet before reversing direction. When he first arrived in New Mexico, he brought a gun with him every time he stepped outside. Now he brought a camera. City life had been an accident of birth, one he'd corrected with a brutality that he could only put behind him by thinking of his life as part 1 and part 2.

There was national land on the other side of the reservation. He parked at the first trailhead he came to, zipped up his nylon jacket and strapped his camera around his neck. He set his stopwatch for thirty minutes, hiked up into a juniper-piñon savanna, pausing to photograph whatever might not be there if he followed the trail a second time: a Steller's jay pecking at juniper berries, a tuft of fur where a small animal had brushed against a prickly pear. When the stopwatch sounded, he sat for a moment, breathing in the altitude—a thin air he found invigorating though it made most people nod off.

On the drive back he thought again of Luisa Gonzalez. No one would come forward to claim her body. She'd be buried by the county in an unmarked grave. If anyone cared enough, they'd hold a service for her and her brother back in Mexico. Her uncle would call her loyal, disciplined. The priest would recommend her soul to heaven. The people who'd raised her to be murdered in that bunker would glorify her death, make her a martyr to local children. Raney saw himself standing among them, saw his guilt reflected in theirs. He'd brought a child into a world split between people who cause pain and people who endure it, and then he'd left. He offered her nothing—no guidance, no love. What place, he wondered, did she see for herself now?

He sat in a corner booth with a cup of black coffee, poring over the Gonzalez file. He imagined sharing the contents with Mavis, setting the twins' mug shots on the kitchen table, asking if she knew whose kin it was that died in a bunker on her property. With nothing else to go on, he'd cast Uncle Gonzalez in the role of bad cop. *His blood died down there,* Raney would say. *His sister's children. He may not know where they are now, but he damn well knows where they were headed last time he saw them.* When vengeance came, he'd tell Mavis, it wouldn't be swift. He'd prompt her imagination with true-crime descriptions of tire fires, of people buried to their necks and left to burn or bait scorpions in the Mexican desert. Gonzalez had an army at his disposal. And what did Raney have? The protection of the state and federal governments, if she chose to cooperate.

He continued rehearsing over an egg-white omelet, scripting and rescripting Mavis's reaction. She wasn't Dunham, wasn't Meno, but she wasn't one to flinch, either. Her performance yesterday afternoon may not have been nuanced, but it didn't have to be: for the time being all she needed was conviction. She needed to stick with the same lie she'd been telling for forty years no matter how transparent it now seemed. Jack didn't build a shed with a false floor to escape the apocalypse; he built it because he thought they might have to hide, wait someone out. Jack and Mavis had been on the run.

"Good morning, Detective Raney," Clara said.

Her eye shadow clashed with her skin tone; the straps of her tank top hung at odd angles. She stood behind the coffee bar, looking like a bleary version of the woman he'd met a little more than twelve hours ago. Daniel sat on the floor a few feet away, filling in a coloring book, crayons scattered around him. He lifted his head briefly, then let it drop: invisible as well as silent. But listening, Raney thought.

"Are you holding up okay?" he asked.

"I spent last night with Mavis, at the ranch."

"How was she?"

"Inconsolable. Not for Jack or for herself, but for the girl. For what Jack had done to the girl. She kept repeating, 'It should have been me.' Over and over again. Sobbing. I didn't know what to do. I kept wondering if I should call a doctor, but then I thought that was just an excuse to leave the room."

"All you could do was be there."

"It didn't feel like much."

"It never does."

"What can I get you, Detective?"

"An Americano. Large, with a little bit of cream, please."

"You wouldn't happen to be buying for a certain deputy?"

"This *is* a small town," Raney said.

"These things are going to ruin his stomach."

Raney watched her tamp down the espresso, line up the shot glasses. She moved quickly, her fingers graceful. Raney knelt beside Daniel, in part to keep himself from staring. The coloring book was desert-themed. Daniel was rendering a saguaro in purple, no trace of color beyond the thick black lines. Again, as if by instinct, the boy's fingers reached for Raney's badge. Raney unhooked it, handed it over. Daniel weighed it in his palm, then set it on the page below the cactus and began tracing its outline in silver.

"You know, a paper shield is just as good as the real thing," Raney said.

Daniel tapped his forehead with one finger: *I'm not stupid.*

"Who knows?" Raney said. "Maybe you'll be Detective Remler one day."

He clipped his badge back in place, stood. Daniel grabbed his pants leg.

"Hey, there, kiddo," Clara said. "The grown-up detective has bad guys to catch."

Daniel turned back to the outline of Raney's shield, began filling it in with gold crayon. Raney pulled out his wallet.

"Tell Junior it's on the house," Clara said.

Raney lifted the cup.

"Thanks again," he said. "I'll be in touch."

He felt her watching him go. *It should have been me,* Mavis said. Why did Clara choose to share that detail? Was she advocating for or against her friend?

Outside, his phone rang.

"We found the Mexies' truck," Bay said.

"Yeah?"

"Or at least *a* truck."

"Where?"

"Burned to shit in a ditch, a mile or so up Canyon Road. One of the plates is intact, but it's a fake. From this side of the border."

"How far is Canyon Road from the Wilkins ranch?"

"A healthy pair of legs could walk it in an hour."

"And probably did," Raney said. "Or else arranged a ride back."

"I know it," Bay said.

"Anything else?"

"I have a preliminary autopsy report. They said to stress the preliminary part."

"What did they find?"

"All three had empty stomachs. They were badly dehydrated, most likely delusional by the end. No mystery as to the cause of death, but the morgue-like conditions make it impossible to pinpoint a time. No more than ten days, no less than seven."

Raney looked over his shoulder, lowered his voice.

"Was the girl raped?"

"No, sir. Believe it or not, she died a virgin."

"I guess she was as good a Catholic as she could be under the circumstances."

Since he'd left New York, Raney's professional life consisted largely of cases that solved themselves: meth lab explosions, domestics so routine he couldn't remember which spouse went with which murderer. The past eighteen years were not the future he'd once imagined. He'd been exiled from the lives and the work he valued most, though *exile* wasn't the right word: he'd long since stopped pretending he had no choice. With time, he'd adapted to his new home, found some meaning in his job and more outside of it, but still he felt, a little less keenly as the years passed, shrouded in defeat. This morning, he allowed himself to imagine the shroud lifting, if only for as long as it took to solve this case.

A trucker flashed his brights, the universal signal that a cop sat lurking around the bend. Raney pulled up behind Junior's squad car, skimmed the bumper stickers advocating sobriety and offering rewards for solid information. The car appeared empty, or else Junior had fallen so deeply asleep as to have slumped all the way forward.

"Rise and shine," Raney called.

He came up on the driver's side of the squad car, coffee in hand. Flies darted in and out of the open window. Junior's forehead pressed against the top of the steering wheel, his arms hanging limp, his gun in his holster. Blood spatter on the windshield, the dash. Blood soaking the floor around his feet. Raney tossed the cup, took the deputy by his shoulders and tugged him slowly back, revealing the same deep and sideways cut he'd seen twice before. Raney pulled his gun from its holster, ran across the two-lane county road, through a clutch of pampas grass and onto the Wilkins property. The front door stood wide open. There was a thick trail of blood beginning at the steps and leading across the gravel to the driveway exit. A second trail led in the opposite direction. Raney scanned the house windows, the garage windows, the sedge and scrub. He raised his gun in both hands, started forward.

There had been a hard-fought battle in the living room—glass coffee table shattered, love seat overturned, portions of the far wall caved in, blood marking every surface. In the kitchen he found Mavis lying faceup on the floor, a gash across her throat, one arm reaching, as though someone had posed her in imitation of her husband. Her blood pooled on the slate tiles, spilled across the floor.

He cleared the house room by room, found it undisturbed past the kitchen: no bloody shoe prints, no closets rifled through, nothing different from the day before save two large suitcases lying open on Mavis's bed. One was crammed with women's clothing. The other was empty.

Raney holstered his gun, waited for his breathing to slow, then called Bay.

He had time before the sheriff and his team arrived. He stood out front on the stone steps, eyeballing the blood trails. The shorter trail ended a few yards shy of the road, where the assailant must have climbed into a vehicle and driven off, or been driven off. The second trail exited the driveway and continued beyond Raney's line of vision. He followed it onto the road, where the blood thinned, became more sporadic, most likely stayed by a makeshift tourniquet. It kept on around a bend, stopped abruptly in a bed of sorghum grass. Raney looked back: Junior's squad car was hidden behind a stand of Douglas fir. There were tire tracks in the grass, solid imprints that might be used for comparison. Whoever drove this car came up on the Wilkins ranch, saw Junior, kept going, and stopped here. Sometime in the dead of night, when this part of the county was pitch-black and there would be no witnesses to begin with. And then? He snuck up on Junior and slit his throat.

Raney crossed the road, slipped through a parting in the scrub, serpentined his way through a maze of juniper until he was standing a few quick strides from Junior's car. Junior would have been dozing with the window open. He never saw it coming. Raney doubled back, searching the dirt for prints that weren't his own, looking for any scrap of fabric clinging to a branch or thistle. The earth here was hard and compact, but he found, in three separate places, boot prints marked by a heavy heel and faint toe.

He walked back up to the house, heard sirens bearing down.

11

Word spread once the road was closed off. News crews came from Santa Fe and Albuquerque. Bay kept them behind the yellow tape. He was content to play hall monitor, to bark orders at people who didn't matter while Raney investigated the deaths Bay felt he had caused or at least failed to prevent. He'd sent a child to protect a woman from a killer. He hadn't taken Raney seriously—or not seriously enough. The notion of a Mexican assassin prowling a remote county road seemed too far-fetched. He hadn't been able to make the image real, had thought Junior would be grateful for the easy overtime. He should have been parked out on that road himself, a shotgun across his knees.

"Don't make me tell you again," Bay snapped.

The cameraman looked confused: Bay hadn't told him anything to begin with.

Raney walked back through the house, scrub booties on his feet, lab techs swarming, following his instructions to swab this, photograph that. There were two unfinished cups of coffee on the kitchen table, two wineglasses in the sink. He crouched over Mavis's body, tilted her head back with the eraser end of a pencil, just far enough to discern the trajectory of the blade. He had one of the techs take a Polaroid, then carried the photo out to the squad car, walking back through the pampas grass.

A lab tech was kneeling on the hood, photographing Junior through the windshield. Raney showed her the image. She climbed down, held it up beside Junior's neck.

"Do you see it?" Raney asked.

"A different angle from the others," she said.

"Different angle, different blade."

"It's too early to say for sure."

"The deputy's cut runs straight across, and deep. The head is nearly severed. Mavis's wound is superficial by comparison. It's jagged, diagonal."

"Maybe because she's a woman. Or maybe the killer was interrupted."

"Maybe. But there were two men fighting in that living room. Both of them were wounded, and neither of them stuck around. Neither of them called for help."

"What are you thinking?"

"I'm not thinking so much as wondering."

"Wondering what?"

"How two separate knifemen wound up in the Wilkins home at the same time."

Raney walked back toward the house, stopped to peer in the garage window. The Jaguar was gone. He went around to the front, found the roll-up door shut, the handle locked. He speed-dialed Bay.

"Come take a look at this, would you?" he said. "I'm by the garage."

Bay crossed the gravel, his head hung low, as though he were searching the ground for clues.

"What is it?" he said.

Raney pointed to the garage door.

"No blood on the handle, no blood on the ground. No broken panels. Someone even took the time to lock it."

"So?"

"Now look inside."

They walked around to the window. Bay pressed his face to the glass.

"It's gone."

"Uh-huh. The question is who took it and when. It had to have been gone before the fight or else the garage would look like another crime scene."

"So someone drove the Jag right past Junior while he was still alive?" Bay said.

"Looks like it."

"Someone who came back later and killed him?"

"Maybe. Or maybe that was someone else."

"Shit," Bay said. "This don't make a damn bit of sense."

"Not yet, but it will."

Bay nodded.

"This wasn't your fault," Raney said. "None of it."

"I'll tell that to Junior's folks."

12

Clara answered the door in sweatpants and a T-shirt, one hand clutching a wad of tissue. The hallway reeked of pot.

"It's all over the news," she said.

"I should have called," Raney said. "I'm sorry."

"You have more questions?"

Her affect was numb, but her eyes were welling.

"No," he said. "I just need to borrow the keys to the store."

"Christ," she said. "What the fuck am I supposed to do with that place?"

Mavis kept an office at the back of the shop, a converted storage space with no window. Her desk was overflowing with junk mail, the only bookcase in disarray. Stacks of paper teetered along the baseboards. Raney held this space up against a mental image of the Wilkins home. If he were going to hide something, he would hide it here, in the back room of an innocuous business, the disorder acting as camouflage.

He started at the desk. On one side sat a column of crisp-looking local newspapers, on the other a pile of crumpled invoices stamped PAID and UNPAID. Some dated back a decade, some were as recent as last week. The oldest and newest shared the same paper, the same watermark, the same bright ink. Raney slipped a small camera from his pocket, photographed every page.

The center of the desk was buried under a mound of unopened envelopes, crafts-related catalogs, expired coupons, dated flyers, glossy postcard advertisements. At the bottom of the heap he found what he hoped was pay dirt: a sleek laptop, recent model, plugged in and fully charged. He balanced it atop the newspapers, opened the screen, switched it on. A moment to boot, followed by a flashing demand for a password. He tried Mavis, mavis, Mavisartsandcrafts, MAVISARTSANDCRAFTS. Bay would have to call on the county techs.

He spent hours sorting through piles of paper, discovered a hoarding so random he felt certain it was a mask for something more deliberate. He found what she was concealing behind the bottom shelf of the bookcase—a single drawer built into the woodwork, blocked from view by a mismatched lineup of encyclopedias. He cleared the books away, pulled the drawer from the wall. Inside were two long, neat rows of envelopes, arranged chronologically and dating back to 1962. The address on the first was written in a child's scrawl, the address on the last in an adult-male hand. Hundreds of letters, carefully preserved, the envelopes cut open with scissors, the recipient's address always the same—Mavis Wilkins, c/o Mavis Arts and Crafts—the return address changing over the years, though usually attached to an institution: a home for children, a juvie center, a psychiatric ward, two different prisons, all in Massachusetts.

The name of the sender was likewise always the same: Kurt Adler. The oldest letter came from an orphanage in Salem, the most recent from an apartment in Jamaica Plain, Boston. The orphanage letter was written in green crayon on a piece of orange construction paper:

DEAR mommy,

Thank you for writing me. I saw where you live on a map. It is far, but I don't know why my letter can go there and I can't. Here is a drawing for you. It is a turtle ship—a space ship that looks like a turtle when it is in its shell. Some day I will learn how to build one. Ms. Fox helped me write this letter. Her name is spelled like the animal.

LOVE kurt.

The *k* came out like an *h*: *LOVE hurt*. The spaceship was more snail than turtle.

The final letter, written in May of 1996, was hardly longer than the first:

Mother,

Happy to hear you are doing well. We don't see many black bears in Boston. Maybe Jack is right—maybe you should carry a gun on your walks.

To answer your question—I've been clean for a year and plan to stay that way. My employer would not keep me on otherwise. I'm sorry to be vague about my work, but I promise I am doing very well—better than I could have hoped. You were right to push me

*to get my GED. I have a home here now and it will stay my home.
Know that I am in good hands.*

Kurt

Mavis had a son. A son who predated Jack. A son she kept
buried in a hidden drawer in a rat's nest of an office. In 1996 this
son either died or opened an e-mail account. Raney hoped for
e-mail. He sat in the wooden swivel chair behind Mavis's desk,
called Bay.

"I need a background check on a guy named Kurt Adler.
Chances are he's in Boston, if he's still alive."

"Who is he?"

"Mavis's son."

"You're big on slinging surprises, Raney? Mavis never had a
kid. It was something she always regretted."

"The regret part rings true. Adler will be about forty-five. And
he'll have a record."

"You know this how?"

"I found letters."

"Where?"

"Her office."

"We have a warrant for that?"

"An employee of the store gave me permission to search the
premises."

"Clara. All right, Raney. I'll get on it."

"There's something else."

"What?"

"We need the county computer geeks. Mavis had a laptop."

"You're after that ledger?"

"Among other things."

"I'll see if I can get one down here."

"The sooner the better."

Clara invited him up.

"You know, I used to work narcotics," he said.

"Pot isn't a narcotic."

"It isn't legal, either."

"Then arrest me. I would have thought you had more important things to do."

"I'm just returning your keys."

Her tone softened.

"If I put this out, will you stay?" she asked. "Daniel's asleep. I don't smoke in front of him, if that's what you're worried about."

Raney hesitated.

"I'll make us tea," Clara said.

"As long as it isn't herbal."

"I don't drink my herbs."

He followed her upstairs. She'd changed into jeans but wore the same faded yellow T-shirt. The back read NM ARTS FESTIVAL, 2000 above a blood-orange rendering of the Zia sun symbol.

"Did you grow up in New Mexico?" Raney asked.

"Outside Sacramento. You?"

"Brooklyn."

"Two coasts, meeting in the middle," she said. "Or somewhere near the middle."

The apartment was a converted loft: kitchenette and bathroom cubicle along one wall, gypsum-board bedrooms off a slim back corridor. Television, couch, coffee table in the living space. An easel set on a canvas tarp facing the front window. The window was open, a pedestal fan blowing fumes and smoke out above the street. The painting-in-progress looked like a New Mexico vista if the colors from different times of day all bled together and the mountains turned flat. There were a dozen more paintings lined against the wall, each part of the same series.

"They're beautiful," Raney said. "You're talented."

"Whether I am or not doesn't matter today."

"No," Raney said. "But it will again."

The TV was on. The screen showed an aerial view of the Wilkins ranch, the tagline COUPLE KILLED DAYS APART streaming across the bottom. Raney thought: What about Junior?

"They'll start calling it the murder ranch now," Clara said.

Raney caught a snippet of the commentary: "Police claim to have leads but are refusing to release any information at this time."

Bay was holding firm.

"Is it true?" Clara said. "You have leads?"

"We have a clear direction to look in."

"The side business?"

"Maybe."

"That's all you can say?"

"For now."

The kettle started to rattle. She dropped tea bags into two oversize mugs, stirred in sugar and milk.

"Oh, shit," she said. "I should have asked."

"It's fine," Raney said.

They sat at arm's length on the couch. Clara switched off the TV.

"Did you find anything in the shop?"

"I'm not sure. Let me ask you——how do you explain the difference between Mavis's office and home?"

"You mean the clutter?"

"That's a kind word."

"The house was all Jack," she said. "He wouldn't stand for a hair out of place. The office was compensatory. I think the real Mavis was somewhere in between."

They were quiet for a moment. Then Raney said:

"What do you know about Mavis's life before Jack?"

"Not much. She'd been here so long that the early years never really came up. And I had the impression she didn't want to talk about it, like she was afraid of resurrecting some trauma."

"What kind of trauma?"

"Family, I'm guessing."

"Did she give you any details?"

"No. But she invited me over every Christmas and Thanksgiving. No one else came. No one called."

And *your* family? Raney thought.

"What was it that made you so fond of her?"

"I don't know. She was a good person. She was kind. Protective."

"Of you in particular?"

"Of anyone she cared about. But yes, of me in particular. And of Daniel. She brought Mrs. Hardin out of retirement, made her salary part of my stipend. Mrs. Hardin works with Daniel every day. There's no other resource for him here. How could you call that anything but pure kindness on Mavis's part? And she's never wanted a thing from me beyond what we'd agreed to at the beginning."

"What was that?"

"She advertised a kind of fellowship or grant—I'm not even sure what to call it. She had this loft above her store in a small town in the New Mexico mountains. Whoever she chose could live there with free rent and a small allowance. In exchange, they'd give a few classes in the community and look after the store now and again. You had to submit a letter of interest and some slides. Mavis never said it, but I think I'm the only one who applied. It was supposed to be for the summer—June through August. That was three years ago."

"Sounds like fate."

"It was what I needed at the time. A clean break."

"From?"

"My own drama. And Daniel's. Really, Mavis gave me what she wanted for herself. She had fantasies of starting over—selling the store, dumping Jack, moving to Buenos Aires."

"She said that?"

"More than once."

"Why Buenos Aires?"

"It's beautiful and cheap. And she spoke enough Spanish to get by."

Raney made a mental note.

"What about the community service?"

"It was something she would have loved to do herself. She wanted to teach, work with children. But she had horrible stage fright. The thought of getting up in front of a group of people, even a group of toddlers, made her sick to her stomach. That might have been the saddest fact of her life."

Raney tried to sound casual:

"She never had children of her own?"

"No. Jack couldn't. And he refused to see a doctor."

No, Raney thought. He saw hookers instead. Mavis parsed out her secrets. She told her lover about her husband's penchant for whores, told Clara about the dreams she hadn't realized. Had she told anyone about her son?

"So she had you teaching classes at the store?"

"No—that was my idea. I did it to bring in a little extra money. *Very* little. Saturdays I teach kids up at the reservation, at the community center they built alongside the casino."

"Do you enjoy it?"

"Now I love it. At first it made me uncomfortable. I felt like a missionary, like a white girl putting a face on history. But Mavis kept saying: 'No, you're sharing a skill with fellow human beings. That's all.' She donated thousands of dollars' worth of supplies to the center."

Mavis was *compensatory* all the way around: desert a son, take in a grown daughter; make money trafficking, funnel some of it to the reservation.

"What about her mood? Any changes in the last few weeks?"

"I don't really know. She kept to herself more than usual. I hardly saw her. When she was at the store she spent most of the time in her office. And then there were those trips."

"Trips?"

"She started going away overnight. Two, sometimes three times a week. Sometimes she was gone a couple of days."

"Had that ever happened before?"

"No, never. She said she wanted to turn part of the store into a gallery. She told me she was scouting for talent."

"What did you think of the idea?"

"Not much, to be honest. For a gallery to thrive, there has to be more than one. There has to be a scene. This is a place people come to when they want to escape a scene. But if anyone could have made it work, it's Mavis. And I'm not just saying that. She had to be a good businesswoman just to keep this place going."

She found a way to subsidize, Raney thought.

A guttural scream reverberated from the back of the apartment.

"Shit," Clara said.

She ran down the hall, shut Daniel's door behind her. The sound swelled, then subsided. After a while, Raney heard Clara singing, a nursery rhyme he didn't recognize or couldn't remember. He stood, thought maybe he should leave, decided to wait. He drifted over to Clara's paintings, ran his eyes across them, felt somehow comforted by the abrupt changes in color, the way she'd reduced the desert to its most essential hues. A mahogany storage unit sat beside the easel, a single horizontal drawer atop a long vertical cabinet. The cabinet door had been removed, the interior stocked with brushes, rags, tubes of paint, palette knives, cans of linseed oil. The top drawer was partially open. Raney peered inside, found a well-used rolling tray and a dwindling bag of weed. He glanced over his shoulder, slid the drawer all the way out. Pushed to the back was a .32 H&R revolver with a Crimson Trace grip. Raney palmed the drawer shut, then, remembering, tugged it partway open again. He felt certain the gun was a present from Mavis. Why? Why would Clara need a firearm in a town that until recently had no crime to speak of?

Clara returned, bouncing Daniel in her arms. The boy rubbed his eyes, seemed confused, as though he felt the aftertremors but couldn't recall the event that caused them.

"See?" Clara said. "The man with the badge is here to keep you safe."

Daniel glanced at Raney, signed something to his mother.

"He wants you to read him a story," Clara said.

"Me?"

"He's smitten."

She handed her son over. The boy radiated warmth through his one-piece pajamas.

"I set a book on his pillow," Clara said. "Last door on the right."

She nodded at Raney's gun. Raney, supporting Daniel with one arm, unclipped his holster, set it on the coffee table.

"Thank you," Clara said.

The bedroom was small and makeshift, the partition walls coming up shy of the ceiling. Mavis, it seemed, had converted the loft specifically for Clara and Daniel. A column of awkwardly installed shelves housed action figures from movies or television shows Raney couldn't place; the glow-in-the dark constellation stickers on the ceiling were no different from the ones Raney had gazed at as a child. He tucked Daniel under a handwoven cotton blanket, remembered the loom in Mavis's study. Mavis had adopted Clara and Daniel as her own. Clara saw no ulterior motive; Raney saw nothing else. Mavis was building a surrogate family. She was distancing herself from Jack, making him disposable.

"You've got a lot of cool stuff here, buddy," Raney said.

Daniel nodded, his eyes still red around the rims. A strand of Clara's hair clung to the boy's shoulder. Raney lifted it away, sat on the edge of the bed, began reading. Another desert-themed book. This one cast an armadillo as the pariah of a sagebrush community, shunned because he was ugly and difficult to eat. Daniel fell asleep before Raney could discover the happy resolution. He shut the book, lay a hand across Daniel's forehead, felt a rush of guilt when he realized he'd been imagining Ella as his audience.

Clara was sitting on the couch, drinking a glass of white wine. There was a second glass on the coffee table.

"If you don't want it, I'm thirsty enough for us both," she said.

He sat beside her, leaving one cushion between them, and took up the glass.

"I'm sorry about that, by the way," she said.

"Does it happen often?"

"It used to. This is the first in a while. It's my fault. He saw me crying today. That probably set him back another year."

Raney stopped himself from asking what had set Daniel back in

84

the first place. What did the gun in her drawer have to do with Daniel's silence? Who was it that might return?

"I should be going, Clara," he said. "Let me know if you need anything. Anytime."

He set his glass on the table. Clara stood with him, blocked his path.

"Who?" she said. "Tell me who did this."

"We're working on it."

"That's bullshit," she said. "You know, or you have a damn good idea. Tell me."

"I don't know anything for sure. But it looks like you were right: Jack put Mavis in danger."

She let her forehead drop against his chest, grabbed his blazer in her fists. He felt her shaking against him. He started to put his arms around her, then held back, resolved to stand there until the storm passed.

13

He did a line in stalled traffic on the Verrazano, felt himself come alert, felt his body moving though the car was still. Sophia would get there before him now; her father would set the tone. Raney played out the conversation in his head:

Father: A cop can't afford this city anymore. Not an honest one.

Sophia: Who says he's honest?

Father: Don't joke. Better men have succumbed.

Sophia: Then I might as well stick with Wes. Besides, I have a career of my own.

Father: Social work? You'll burn out, Sophia. Those people will burn you out.

Sophia: Those people? It's strange how you're so full of one kind of courage but completely lack another.

Father: Meaning?

Sophia: You'd rather have a man point a gun at you than talk to you.

Father: Because I know what the guy with the gun wants. Take the gun out of his hand, and he becomes a salesman.

Sophia: Why do you say things you don't mean?

Father: You tell me. You're the shrink.

Sophia: Social worker. And admit you like Wes.

Father: I do like him. I never said I didn't. But he's not the man you need.

Sophia: I don't need a man at all.

The dialogue would run much the same with Raney sitting there. Former police captain Ed Ferguson was blunt, sometimes brutal. It was how he'd made cases—cases that led to promotions he'd never asked for but accepted, in his mind, for the sake of his daughter's future. Sophia's theory: longer hours and greater pay made parenting a question of project management. A staff swelled around the policeman's little girl—nanny, housekeeper, piano teacher, tutors—even a shrink to tease out any lingering trauma caused by her mother's death, though Sophia had been less than a year old at the time. *It takes good opportunities to prevent bad ones:* Captain Ferguson's credo.

Traffic picked up, then stalled again on the BQE. He was forty minutes late by the time he parked in front of the retired captain's house: a solid upper-middle-class home in Kew Gardens, with shutters on the windows and a grapevine out back. The home Sophia had grown up in. The home her mother had died in. *The house you'll inherit someday,* Ferguson was fond of saying. *Worth fifty times what I paid for it.*

He was greeted at the door by Sophia and Jake, the Irish setter. Of the two, Jake seemed happier to see him.

"Well, you have his attention," Sophia said. Then, catching the red in his eyes:

"Are you all right?"

"I'm fine."

She stepped out onto the small porch, pushed Jake back behind the door.

"I'm worried about you. You never call."

"This guy's got me close."

"What guy?"

"I can't say."

She glared.

She'd come straight from work. Her red dress brought out the pink in her skin—skin that held an impression at the slightest touch. She raised up on tiptoes, stood balanced with her blue-gray eyes inches from his.

"Well?" she said.

Her father's voice shot through the cracked door:

"Let the man in. Dinner isn't getting any younger, and neither am I."

Ferguson ran the place like a manor, with a cook and a maid he claimed was a physical therapist. He'd hired a contractor, installed antique ceiling fans, swapped out linoleum for bamboo, laminate for granite. The walls were thick with art from places he'd never visited: Thailand, Mexico, Nigeria. Jake had a bed in every room, all of them red, to match his coat. Ferguson sat at the head of the table, holding court, his face flushed with alcohol, his full crop of gray hair looking a little less tame in retirement.

"I've always been a meat-and-potatoes man, but now the meat has a French name and the potatoes come with parsley. Invest your money, Detective Raney. I don't care if it's ten dollars to start. You think when you're my age you'll be too old to enjoy life. Let me tell you, you're not. Your joints may not bend so easy, but that's just Mother Nature saying it's time to slow down and reap the fruits of your labor."

He talked to Raney as though Sophia weren't there, or as though she had brought Raney to him for the purpose of some obscure interrogation. Ferguson was playing nice now, gaining trust, but there would be a postprandial accusation, an authoritative lecture on the pitfalls Raney was already failing to dodge.

"I hear you're undercover," Ferguson said.

"Dad, no talking shop at dinner."

"You're marrying a policeman, but you don't want me to talk police work with him? That's mean-spirited."

Raney heard the exchange as though through a haze of distortion.

"Yes, sir," he said. "I'm undercover now."

"No wonder you look so tired."

"Dad!"

"What? I'm empathizing with the man. There's no tougher assignment."

"All the more reason to give him a night off."

Raney reached for the bottle of wine, started to fill his own glass, then, remembering where he was, made the rounds first. The bottle came back empty. Ferguson's smile went on a beat too long.

The rest of the conversation was a monologue that Raney caught in bits and pieces. Ferguson was upset with a longtime friend for cashing in his pension and moving to Idaho; he found the panic surrounding the sanitation strike amusing. Or maybe he was upset by the strike and found his friend's departure amusing. His patriarchal drone competed with the recollection of scenes from Raney's first month as Dunham's sidekick: ringside seats for a Hagler fight; strip club after strip club; blow and benzos; hours at the bar watching coked-out jazz musicians blaze through whatever tune Dunham called. In between, midnight collections, payoffs, a score of evacuations, the riot act read to the lowest earners. Meno's name never mentioned. The uneasy feeling that Dunham was grooming him for some unsanctioned side business that would get them both killed.

After dinner, Armagnac in the living room, followed by a predictable request:

"Sophia, would you mind taking Jake around the block for me?"

"I should go with you," Raney said.

"Jake's all the chaperone she needs. There hasn't been a violent crime in this zip code for a decade. Unless you count domestics."

"Before I go," Sophia said, "tell me exactly how you're going to scare him off."

"Nonsense. I just want to ply him for gossip. It would bore you."

"I won't be long," Sophia said.

She left them alone, seated a few feet apart in matching armchairs, faint classical music coming from speakers Raney couldn't locate.

Ferguson leaned in, rounded his shoulders, seemed suddenly primitive—a man who was about to fight instead of flee.

"You stupid ass," he said.

"Excuse me?"

"You heard me. My daughter is trained to spot the signs. She won't be able to fool herself much longer."

"It's not what you think."

"It's exactly what I think. What on earth possessed you? Did you believe you could cozy up to a man like Dunham without losing your soul?"

"You still have your sources."

"You're damned right I do. And I'll be keeping a close watch. When I was commander, I wouldn't let a married man go undercover, not for an afternoon. And now you're marrying my daughter. Tell me the truth: Are you hooked?"

"It's nothing I can't beat."

"I've heard that before."

"Captain, I'm close. I'm really fucking close."

"You're even picking up the cadence of a junkie."

"I'm no junkie."

Ferguson emptied his glass, poured another.

"No, that was unfair. You're young. You're ambitious. You have a hard-on for adventure, and you want to save the world. But there are little Dunhams incubating by the thousands. Stone knows this. He also knows the glory will be his. If you make the case, he runs for mayor. You get a small pay bump and a stint at Betty Ford. I'm telling you, walk away. The reward doesn't measure up to the risk. This is years of experience talking. If you want a thrill, try skydiving."

"I'm a cop."

"And an honest one, from what I hear. But there are better ways to serve and protect. Safer, more lucrative ways."

"Like what?"

"How about the mayor's detail? I could get you reassigned tomorrow."

"I want to work cases."

"The private sector, then. You'd be making more on day one than I made my first twenty years on the job."

"Maybe."

"That means no. You think you have your hooks in him, but it's the other way around. I'm going to tell you something it took me my whole career to accept. Some people are broken. They just are. They can't be saved or redeemed. They'll cause immeasurable pain for as long as they walk the earth, and they should be put down. If you see an opportunity, take it. You'll sleep better with this psychopath dead and buried. The badge will protect you. Chances are you'll get a medal for it. And Stone can find some other case to pin his candidacy on."

She walked him to his car. They held hands, took slow steps across Ferguson's lawn. Lights were on in the houses, but the street was empty, quiet: just the sound of automatic sprinklers and an occasional plane flying overhead.

Sophia nibbled at his shoulder.

"I miss you, Detective," she said. "I mean a lot."

"It won't be much longer."

He leaned back against the passenger-side door. Sophia pressed her body to his. He locked his arms around her waist, felt her hair brushing his skin as he kissed her neck. He lingered there, almost sober.

"It's like we're teenagers," she said.

"Did you kiss a lot of teenage boys out here?"

"I wanted to be ready when I met you."

"You think the old perv is watching us?"

She reached under his shirt, scratched his chest.

"What? You wouldn't keep an eye on your daughter?" she said.

"When she was seventeen, maybe."

"To him, I'm still seventeen. Let's take a spin."

"All right."

She stroked his cheek with the backs of her fingers while he drove.

"I know you can't give me details," she said. "I understand that. But are you safe, Wes? Tell me the truth."

"I am," he said. "I just have to play it right."

"And what if you don't?"

"I will."

"How can you be sure?"

"Things are going well. The guy I'm working trusts me."

"But you look so tired."

"He keeps odd hours."

"I'm worried."

"About what?"

"You. Us. I think about you every day."

"It's temporary," Raney said. "I promise."

"The case is," she said. "But not the work. You don't know what's coming next."

He wanted to reassure her. He wanted to reassure himself. He turned onto a tree-lined side street, pulled to the curb.

"Let's keep playing teenager," he said.

He spooled through the conversation with Ferguson all the way to south Brooklyn: *Some people are broken...If you see an opportunity, take it.* Is that what Ferguson had done to Bruno—*put him down?* If so, the badge had protected him. He'd been promoted straight from detective to lieutenant just a few months later. The ceremony was televised on local stations.

What bothered Raney wasn't the content of Ferguson's advice—the man had come up in a different time, was publicly and unapologetically sorry to see that time go—but rather his paternal tone, his easy confidence. *How about the mayor's detail?*

An offer he knew Raney would turn down. The 1954 Ferguson would have stuck a gun in Raney's face, told him to sober up or stay the fuck away from his daughter. People mellowed with age, but they also guarded secrets. Was it coincidence that Bruno had been young Meno's rival?

Or was Raney just spinning stories to keep the craving at bay?

14

He lay in bed, sipping Scotch, reading the letters from Mavis's son. Over the years, *Mommy* turned to *Mom, Mom* to *Mother*. The letters themselves were mechanical, written out of obligation rather than love. Still, a biography emerged. The early years included a trail of institutions and foster homes about which the less said, apparently, the better. Young Adler chose factual, detached adjectives. His foster parents were tall or short; the mothers had blond or brown or red hair; one father had muscles and another dressed in plaid suits. The homes they lived in were one or two stories tall. The yards were large or small, came with or without trees.

The adolescent letters featured a single recurring character: Miss Bailey, a social worker. Mavis must have been in touch with this woman; Kurt never explained why he'd been moved from one facility to another, one home to the next, and there was no indication that Mavis asked. Always it was Miss Bailey who picked Kurt up and dropped him off. She drove a purple car with scented strips of paper hanging from the mirror. She drove with the windows up or down. The trips were longer or shorter than an hour.

Mavis sent her son gifts, toys she'd ordered from catalogs. He thanked her in joyless phrases that never varied by more than a word: *Thank you for the spaceship; Thank you for sending me the dinosaur puzzle; Thanks for the astronaut action figures.* He shared a short burst of emotion when an older kid stole his basketball. *I ran after him but he only laughed at me and then I cried so hard I couldn't see.* In the next letter, he thanked Mavis for the new ball.

Age thirteen: Miss Bailey mysteriously absent, Kurt's first stint in juvie. The circumstances were never discussed. He described his peers by size, crime, age: the tall kid who broke into a car but couldn't get it started; the fat kid who stole from the Salvation Army; the older kid who set his neighbor's house on fire. A brief admission: *They put me to live by myself because of the fighting.* No mention of whom he fought with or why, no comment on the merits and drawbacks of solitude, only: *My new cell is the same size as my old cell even though there's no one else in it.*

Age fifteen: Kurt says outright, *If I came to live with you there would be no trouble for me to get into because you said there are only mountains there.* Next letter: *I would not mix with the boys from the reservation. I do not know why you think that I would.* Two months later, as if out of spite, the first and last confession of a crime, the first and last detailing of an arrest, the first and last flagrant recriminations: *Tommy [foster brother] smashed the camera with a baseball bat and I held a gun on the man behind the counter and didn't have to say anything — he just emptied the register. Tommy and I took a bottle of vodka each. We were careful and wore masks but we got drunk and Jack [foster father] found the bottles and gun in our room. He called the police and they came in body armor. And now I am done with you because you are just words on paper. Don't write or visit — not that you would.*

He kept his promise for twenty-one years. Twenty-one years during which Mavis must have continued to reach out. Twenty-one years during which she kept Kurt's childhood letters either out of hope or an unwillingness to let the wound heal. And then:

Today is my 36th birthday. My time is served and I'm a better person now. I have my GED. I have a job [no details] and am well protected [again no details]. I do not need your money, but I'm glad that you and Jack are doing well. If you write to me, I will write you back. I am a man now and my life is in order.

The letter was more than ten years old. Did Mavis's promise of money mark the beginning of her new partnership with Jack? Was she looking to lure her son to her, to compensate in the second half of his life for everything she'd deprived him of in the first half? Was Kurt her motivation for killing Jack? Treasure hadn't worked, so she gave him the opportunity to rescue her? *Kurt, I've gotten myself into an awful mess . . . Kurt, I need your help . . . I have nowhere else to turn.* Was it Kurt who'd cleaned out the bunker, torched the pickup?

Raney set the letters aside, took a long sip of Bay's gift, stretched out with his feet dangling from the edge of the bed.

Raney had been more absent than Mavis, but then his child had grown up in the care of a loving mother. What had Mavis hoped to achieve by merely staying in touch? Had she done anything more than keep the pain fresh?

But then, Raney thought, who am I to judge?

Of course the comparison worked both ways. In the early years, Raney asked for photos and received no response. Eventually, he stopped asking. Sophia gave him nothing more than a name to go on: Ella. In place of memories, Raney had a bank of hazy imaginings: Ella as a toddler, Ella in grade school, Ella in her prom dress. When she was first born, he would lie in bed at night picturing the color of her hair, the complexion of her skin, based on the genetic makeup of her parents. The possibilities overwhelmed him; the effort helped him stay clean.

Raney shut off the light, then switched it back on. He pushed himself out of bed as though he'd forgotten something important. He dug the dimebags from his suitcase, balanced them on one palm, carried them into the bathroom. Setting them side by side on the vanity, he took a slow visual measurement, then opened the second bag, tilted and tapped until its contents came level with the first. He felt a quiet satisfaction, like that of a penitent lighting a candle.

He drifted off thinking of his estranged daughter, but it was Luisa Gonzalez he saw in his sleep.

15

Bay's office featured large windows interrupted by thin strips of laminate paneling. There was a fern in the corner (secretary? girlfriend?), a stuffed bass from his trip to Alaska, photos of his nephew's son and daughter. Great-Uncle Bay: the kids ran riot over his ranch two weeks out of every spring. Raney found it easy to picture. It was a shame, he thought, that Bay never had children of his own.

They sat on opposite sides of a sprawling desk. Bay set his laptop between them, clicked on a microphone icon.

Operator: Nine-one-one. What's your emergency?

Silence.

Operator: Hello?
Mavis: [Calm, detached—as though reading from a prompter] Yes, this is Mavis. Mavis Wilkins.

Operator: What's your emergency, Mrs. Wilkins?

Mavis: I found my husband on our property.

Operator: Found him?

Mavis: He was shot.

Operator: Is he breathing?

Mavis: He's dead.

Operator: Okay, Mrs. Wilkins. I'll send someone right out.

Mavis: [Suddenly emotional] Hurry. Oh, dear God, please hurry.

"That's it?" Raney said.

"Uh-huh. You get anything off it?"

"It's like she took a drug to calm herself, then fought the drug in order to sound like a woman who just found her husband murdered."

"Or like someone was coaching her," Bay said. "Standing there, telling her to turn up the hysterics."

"Someone like her son," Raney said.

"Speaking of which . . ."

Bay pushed a copy of Kurt Adler's postjuvie record across the desk. Raney skimmed, paraphrased the main points out loud:

Age eighteen: Assault and battery; six-month sentence; additional two years served for nonfatal stabbing of cell mate; moved to solitary; twice denied probation because of violent cell extractions.

Age twenty-three: Possession with intent to distribute; resisting arrest; served three years of five-year sentence.

Age twenty-five: Arrested on suspicion of trafficking; mistrial; case dropped.

Age twenty-six: Arrested for the murder of William Tinti,

failed florist turned bagman for the Ricci family. Tinti was shot point-blank in Charles River Park. The lone witness recanted; no physical evidence; case dismissed.

Age twenty-eight: Arrested for putting Tyrone Max, small-time dealer, in a body cast. Tyrone refused to ID; case dismissed.

Age thirty: Arrested for fatal stabbing of a prostitute and near-fatal beating of her pimp. Case dropped because of uncooperative witnesses.

Age thirty-one: Arrested in a bar brawl on Christmas Eve; both the bar's owner and the man Kurt hospitalized declined to pursue criminal charges.

Age thirty-three: Suspected in the shooting deaths of two Boston patrolmen. A warrant served on his home and car turned up nothing. Held for forty-eight hours; released.

Age thirty-three: Arrested on drunk and disorderly. Spent two weeks at Mass General recovering from a beating administered by unidentified jailhouse assailants. Released shortly after.

"Payback," Raney said. "The drunk and disorderly was a phony. The cops probably meant to kill him. Or have him killed."

Age thirty-three to present: Nothing. Not so much as a parking ticket.

Specs: six foot three; two twenty-five; current age forty-six.

Four years older than Raney.

"Jesus," Bay said. "This is Mavis's son?"

"Biological son."

"He's been quiet for thirteen years. You think he went straight?"

"I'm guessing he was promoted. Somewhere above street level. Maybe the beating he took finished him as muscle. Or maybe he was given his own crew to run. The cop killings would have been a rite of passage. In his last letter to Mavis, he said he was *protected now*."

"Don Corleone protected?"

"Some kind of organized crime. It's not unheard of in Boston."

"Let me see if I've got this straight: Mavis locks her husband in a bunker with the Mexie twins; the three of them turn on each other; Mavis sees the mess, calls her long-lost mobster kid to come clean up; he obliges, probably enticed by the free dope, then ends up tussling with a cartel blade man; the son and the assassin come out even, and both drive off."

"That plays. But the missing Jaguar still bothers me. There had to be a third party."

"Question: Why didn't Mr. Adler get rid of the bodies altogether? There's plenty of scrubland around here. Plenty of wild mouths to feed."

"He would have needed a small crew for that. He figured he had us beat. How do you prove murder by padlock? If Mavis stuck to the script, they'd be fine. She might even collect insurance."

"As long as she didn't get her throat slit. You think Adler has the drugs now?"

"Nothing else makes sense. But if he was here, he's a ghost. There was no sign of him at the house."

"So he holed up somewhere else with the coke."

"Someplace close by," Raney said.

"The casino?"

"Maybe. We couldn't look for him there. And he could see the Wilkins ranch from his window."

"No way to confirm it."

"Not officially."

Raney tore Adler's mug shot from the top page of the file, folded it into his pocket.

"You won't get much in the way of cooperation," Bay said.

"No, but I know someone who might."

"Someone who gives art classes up at the reservation?"

"Maybe."

"Deputize the eye candy. You're a clever son of a bitch. Tell me, did you go as hard on her as you did on Mavis?"

"The killings didn't happen on her property. She wasn't married to one of the killers."

"No, but if Mavis had an inner circle, Clara was it. Her knowing nothing don't figure. I could see Mavis holding quiet about the drugs, but about her son? A woman doesn't keep that secret from another woman."

"Maybe not. I'll press harder."

"Good. What do I do in the meantime?"

"Wait. We need the troopers to turn up that Jaguar. Preferably with the son and drugs inside."

"You think he'd be that sloppy?"

Raney shrugged.

"What about the Mexican?" Bay said. "I want the bastard who killed Junior."

"We've got uniforms searching hospitals and clinics. We've got eyes on the border. It won't be long."

"A mobster and a Mexican assassin," Bay said. "Things are getting a little too lively around here. Might be time for me to cash in my forty."

"You hear Alaska calling?"

"Louder every day."

"There is something you could do for me before you go."

"What's that?"

"See if you can find anything on Kurt's father. And his mom, for that matter. What was Mavis up to before she married Jack?"

16

Clara came to the door in a turquoise bathrobe, her hair fresh off the pillow. She appeared soft in the early morning, as though the haze through which she saw the world were somehow reflected back on her. Like an actress in an old Hollywood movie, Raney thought.

"What is it?" she said. "Have you found something?"

"Maybe. I'm hoping you can help."

She stood in the doorway, one bare foot on the pavement, pulling her robe tight over her chest.

"With what?"

"The children you teach at the reservation—are you friendly with any of their parents? Specifically, parents who work for the casino's hotel? Cleaning staff? Reception?"

"I'm friendly with a few of the mothers. Or at least they seem to like me. Why?"

"Would you mind asking them some questions? Just one question, really. A question I should ask you first."

He showed her Adler's mug shot.

"Have you seen him before?"

She took a corner of the photo between her thumb and index finger, held it at eye level. Raney watched her examine Kurt's face, caught no glint of recognition, only fear, a suspicion that she was looking at Mavis's killer.

"Is he the one?"

"He's a person of interest. I think he might have been staying at the casino, but I have no authority there. I can't ask directly, or if I did, chances are slim anyone would talk to me. All I want is confirmation that he's been here sometime in the last week."

"All right," she said. "I can do that."

"Now?"

"Give me an hour. Mrs. Hardin isn't here yet. And I'd rather not prowl around the casino in my bathrobe."

Raney walked the only commercial street, an east-west thorough-fare with residential offshoots running a few houses deep. The town did what it could to maintain its pioneer charm: raised wooden platforms in place of sidewalks; bishop's-crook lamp-posts; diagonal parking, as if the vehicles were tethered to troughs. The squat brick buildings differed in size and shape, as though they'd been constructed to fit the dimensions of the town's original makeshift structures.

He turned his back to the sharp morning sun, strolled past a hair salon, a used-car lot, a mechanic's shop, the sheriff's office, a semiabandoned movie theater that still showed revivals every Saturday afternoon, a megastore that sold everything from baby formula to guns and ammo. Why, he wondered, had this town survived instead of any one of the ghost towns within a ten-mile radius? It wasn't situated off a major highway, wasn't en route to any tourist attraction. There was no local specialty, nothing to be had here that couldn't be had anywhere else.

With the exception, maybe, of the casino. Facing east, he could see its top floors buried in the foothills, a rectangular stucco peak mounted with satellite dishes and antennae, an alien structure making a halfhearted attempt to blend in.

Clara had brushed her hair, wore a draped halter top and jeans. The rings, absent when she first answered the door, were back in place. She had a habit of tugging on the pendant around her neck. The motion of her fingers drew Raney's eyes from the road.

"Are you going to tell me who this guy is?" she asked.

"A person of interest."

"You already said that. What makes him so interesting?"

"He has a record. He fits the profile."

"Do you ever just answer a question?"

"For now, it's better if I don't give you all the details."

He knew as soon as he said it that the phrasing came out wrong.

"I see," she said. "You think because I cried for my friend, I'm—"

"No, that's not it."

"How's this? Tell me who he is, or I won't help you."

Raney hesitated, remembered his promise to Bay.

"All right," he said. "I'll tell you. But first I have to make sure you aren't holding anything back."

"Like what?"

"Anything you might know about Mavis. Her past."

"Like I said, it never came up. I didn't want to ask."

"I thought the two of you were close."

"You're being mean."

"No, I'm being a cop."

"Look, Mavis didn't open up to me. We were close, but not in that way. Sometimes I felt like a child around her. Sometimes I felt she was playing parent. Letting me into her home, letting me be around Jack, was the closest she came to confiding in me."

It rang true: all signs pointed to Mavis as someone who told people what she wanted them to know and nothing more.

"Now it's your turn," Clara said. "Who is it I'm asking about?"

Raney braced himself.

"He's Mavis's son. From before Jack."

"That's insane. I saw Mavis nearly every day for three years. She may not have told me everything, but——"

"She didn't raise him. As far as I know, she never laid eyes on him before last week."

Clara turned, stared out the window.

"You think he killed her?"

"No, but I believe he was here. He may have fought with the man who did kill her."

"You said he had a record. What kind of record?"

"A long one," Raney said. "Long and violent."

"So you think Mavis told him about Jack's business? You think she enlisted him?"

"I don't think anything. I'm following a lead."

"That's just something you feel you have to say. You've made up your mind, but you're wrong. You've overlooked something. I would at least know what Mavis was capable of. She didn't have her estranged son kill her husband and make off with a drug stash. She owned a crafts store. She was sixty-two. It's fucking absurd."

"I've been doing this job a long time . . ."

He felt her eyes gloss over.

"Spare me the *things I've seen* speech. Your years as a cop don't make you clairvoyant. I knew her, and you didn't."

Raney let it pass.

He locked his gun and holster in the glove compartment, watched Clara cross the parking lot, counted to a hundred, and followed.

No Sims, no jolly-giant bartender. There was a peace about the place in the morning; the frenzy hadn't yet begun. He dug in his pockets for loose change, walked the aisles of slot machines, hoping the right one would somehow call to him. There were nickel slots, dime slots, quarter slots; cherries, spaceships, full and half moons. He settled on one with an unlikely theme: cowboys and Indians, top prize for tomahawks straight across. He dropped in a nickel, pulled the lever. Lasso, peace pipe, stirrup. Prize: the chance to play again. Two pulls later, he won five dollars, a hundred nickels to keep him entertained until Clara came back. He found the random nature of the game liberating; with poker or blackjack you could trick yourself into believing there was skill involved, a system to be conquered. Slot machines demanded a total submission to chance. Raney understood why they were so popular with the elderly.

The action of feeding the machine turned mechanical. His mind drifted. He thought of Bay's comment: *cash in my forty.* For eighteen years, Raney's expenses had been subliminal. His car was state-issued, his gas paid for. He was even given a clothing allowance. Sophia, or, more likely, Sophia's father, had refused all child support; the checks Raney sent were either returned or never deposited. No mortgage hung over his head. Little of what he liked to do required much money. If he continued to live as he had been living, he could resign tomorrow. So why didn't he? There were days, more and more of them, when he could imagine starting over, at age forty-two, as a photographer, a park ranger. But he had no doubt that ten years from now he would still be Detective Raney. Why? To continue with something implies hope.

His phone rang. The sound startled him. Bay's name lit up the caller ID.

"Sheriff?"

"Raney, this is weird. Real goddamn weird."

"What is?"

"I ran Mavis's background like you said. I used the name on her son's birth certificate: Mavis Adler. I even called up a fed buddy to make sure I had all the databases covered."

"And?"

"There is no Mavis Adler. There never was. Not our Mavis."

"What do you mean?"

"I mean there are plenty of Mavis Adlers out there, but not one comes close to Mavis Wilkins. Either they turn up deceased, or the age is all wrong."

"Huh."

"Is that the best you can offer? Where are you, anyway? Sounds like a video arcade."

"The casino. Look, you know what to do. Run her Social against the dead Adlers. And send her prints to Interpol."

"Could it be some kind of witness protection thing?"

"Maybe. There was more to her than a crafts store, that's for sure."

"Forty years in a town this small and no one knew a goddamn thing about her. How's that possible?"

"Practice," Raney said. "And luck."

"I guess her luck ran out."

"I guess it did. What does the birth certificate say about the father?"

"Unknown."

"We'll have to ID Mavis before we can track him down."

Bay clucked his tongue, hung up.

A half hour later Raney's forty dollars had dwindled to fifteen. A church congregation occupied the machines around him, adults of all ages wearing T-shirts that read IN CHRIST WE ARE WON. They called across to each other as though Raney weren't there. The day's frenzy had arrived.

Clara tapped him on the shoulder.

"I don't know if it's good news or bad," she said.

"Was he here?"

"He still is. Or at least he never checked out."

"You get a room number?"

"Seven thirteen."

"That's good," he said. "Very good."

"So what do we do now?"

Raney handed her his depleted stash of nickels.

"Your turn," he said.

"I'm not coming with you?"

"You're too pretty for the cameras."

He walked away wishing he'd said something—anything—else.

He stopped in the gift shop, bought a baseball cap featuring a Zuni sun and an oversize sweatshirt with the name of the casino painted across the front. He changed in the men's room, bent the brim of the cap and pulled it low, folded his shirt and blazer into the gift-store bag. He kept his eyes on the carpet as he walked to the bank of elevators, mugging tourist for the cameras.

A DO NOT DISTURB sign hung outside room 713. Raney knocked just in case, then jimmied the door with a credit card, slipping the hard plastic between latch and frame quickly enough to pass for lawful entry.

The room gave an immediate impression of slovenliness: bed unmade, pajamas in a heap on the floor, iron and ironing board left out, towels scattered around the bathroom, power cord on the desk plugged into nothing. A second look revealed someone who was orderly to the point of obsession. Unlike most people, Kurt used every space the hotel provided. A half dozen identical salmon-colored dress shirts hung in the closet by the door, neatly pressed, buttons facing in the same direction; perfectly creased pants lay draped over the tiers of a slacks hanger; argyle socks, black T-shirts, and patterned boxers filled the dresser drawers. None of Kurt's clothes showed the slightest sign of wear, as though he mail-ordered a new wardrobe every few weeks.

A picture began to form. Kurt had been preparing for his day, ironing his shirt, still in his pajamas, when...had Mavis called? Did she make Gonzalez's man before he reached the house? Unlikely: Mavis and Junior had been killed in the early morning, somewhere between 2:00 and 4:00 a.m. And Mavis had been murdered in the kitchen, with no sight line to the driveway. If she'd seen the man coming, she could have raced out the back, run for the bunker.

Still, Kurt had left the hotel in a hurry. He'd grabbed anything incriminating and vanished. Raney found no weapons, no ID, no dope, no ledger. Something had spooked him. What? When? His bedside alarm was set for 8:00 a.m. Raney crossed to the window, discovered a perfect bird's-eye view of the Wilkins ranch.

Only one scenario made sense: Kurt, standing at the ironing board, had spotted the sirens, the swarm of reporters. He fled, most likely in the Jaguar given to him by Mavis. He'd have traded it for something less conspicuous by now, would be on his way back to Boston with Jack's coke in the trunk.

But then who had tangled with the cartel boy?

Maybe Wilkins's buyer grew tired of the delay.

Or maybe there was a third party, as yet unknown. Whoever shared coffee and wine with Mavis the night she died.

Raney picked up the phone, called reception.

"Hi. I'm in room seven thirteen, and I need to check out. I'm running late. I was hoping you could send someone up with the bill."

"Not a problem, sir."

"I might be in the shower, so if they could just slip it under the door, that would be great."

"You bet."

Meanwhile, he continued searching: under the bed, between the mattresses, inside the air ducts. Nothing. He picked up a pack of Gauloises from the side table and flipped open the lid. The cigarettes sat high in the box. He emptied them onto the table. A clump of tinfoil tumbled out. Raney unfolded it, discovered a small rock of heroin. He worked it back into its wrapping, left the pack as he'd found it.

A sheet of paper came sliding across the carpet. Raney took it up. Adler gave a fake name, fake address. The contact number was a long shot. On impulse, Raney took out his phone and dialed. An automated message, no name given. Pique his curiosity, Raney thought.

"Hello, this is Detective Wes Raney calling for Kurt Adler. I was wondering if you have any idea who killed your mother or where her drug stash disappeared to. You can reach me at this number, day or night."

He stopped at the bathroom, changed back into his own clothes. Clara had moved on to a different machine. She sat with her face inches from the screen, pupils dilated, mouth slightly open. Someone had given her a bucket that looked like a beach pail. Raney watched her transfer the coins from pail to slot.

"Are you ahead?" he asked.

"I won eighty-five dollars," she said. "I almost can't breathe. I've never won money before in my life."

"Then it's a good time to quit."

"One last try," she said.

She slid in a nickel, pulled. Lemon, kiwi, coconut.

"Come on," Raney said.

She stood, shook her head as though breaking a trance.

"Did you find anything?" she asked.

"Maybe."

"Not good enough," she said. "I want a full report. I earned it on this one."

"I'll tell you in the car."

"All right," she said. "But I'll know if you're holding back."

The hills below the reservation were steep. Raney kept one foot hovering above the brake, saw Clara's legs lock at every bend. The blue sheen cast by the morning light was muted now; the landscape seemed duller, less alert. Storm clouds to the east, the sky overhead clear.

"Well?" Clara said.

He told her about the view from Adler's window, his penchant for order, his closet full of salmon-colored shirts.

"Makes sense," Clara said. "He was in and out of prison his whole life."

Why hadn't the thought occurred to Raney? Because understanding the psychology behind Adler's wardrobe wouldn't lead him to the missing coke? Or because fifteen years in the desert had slowed his faculties?

"And now the hunt?" Clara asked.

"Yes. Adler's probably ditched the Jaguar, so we'll have the marshals and troopers focus on junkyards and chop shops."

"While you...?"

"Wait. We've got people checking hospitals and morgues for stabbing victims. Forensics is processing DNA from the house. Mavis's computer is with the techs. Something will come back."

The country leveled off. Clara leaned against the passenger door, one elbow out the window.

"I let Mavis down," she said.

"Let her down?"

"She was there for us. I didn't even realize she needed help."

"She kept big secrets," Raney said.

They crested the summit of a hill on the outskirts of town. Main Street came into view. There was activity now: a cluster of pickup trucks in the megastore parking lot, a scattering of sun-beaten faces strolling between shops.

"Where do you eat around here?" Clara asked. "I can't imagine they feed you at that hotel."

"The diner, mostly."

"The diner? That place fries everything in lard. Why don't you let me fix you a real dinner tonight? Daniel has an open invitation with Mrs. Hardin."

Raney hesitated: Clara wasn't a suspect, was at most a material witness.

"Sounds good," he said.

"Great. Pick me up at seven."

"Pick you up?"

"You'll see."

17

An old-timer was playing solo piano on the stage at Dunham's club, tunes Raney recognized from his childhood—"Moon River," "I Can't Give You Anything but Love"—songs from albums his father used to play. How long had it been, he wondered, since he'd visited his father's grave? A year, maybe more. It seemed all the images he could conjure of the man came from photos instead of real life.

"This guy's eighty-four fucking years old," Dunham said. "He played Minton's. He sat in with Miles. Miles fucking Davis. Can you believe it? A living legend. And listen to him now. His fingers may have slowed a little, but he can still kill a ballad. I'll be happy to wipe my own ass at that age."

You won't live to that age, Raney thought.

The tables were empty; the legend played for Dunham alone. A thousand-dollar check lay in the tip jar.

"Listen," Raney said. "I shouldn't come along on this one."

"What are you talking about?"

"I told you. I fought Mora in the amateurs."

"You win?"

"Once by TKO, once by split decision."

"So what's the problem?"

"He knows who I am."

"Yeah? I bet he knows who I am, too. Don't worry, we're going to play nice."

"A payoff won't do it. Mora only cares about one thing."

"His fifteen illegitimate kids?"

"A shot at a title."

"You kicked his ass twice. Maybe it's time he moved on to a different dream."

"He won't see it that way."

"Enough, Deadly. Take a fucking benzo. And go see if Pierre is done. I had him cook us up something for the road."

They crossed the bridge and drove up 4th Avenue into Sunset Park, Dunham at the wheel, Raney holding a paper bag filled with potato gnocchi, sautéed asparagus, a double portion of tiramisu. Pierre even threw in a bottle of wine.

"How do you know Mora won't already be there?" Raney asked.

"He works the day shift at a pet-food plant in Red Hook. He's the forklift guy. Then he trains at Gleason's from five to nine. The poor bastard must be dead in his skin."

"When does he fight Malone?"

"Six weeks. Atlantic City, you and me, front row."

Six weeks. Rousting junkies was one thing; tanking Mora's career was something else. He remembered Ferguson's injunction: *If you see an opportunity, take it.* But then Meno would just send someone else. That had been Stone's point all along: Dunham was a cog. Remove him prematurely, and the machine would keep churning.

None of which would matter once Mora saw his face. Raney would have to arrest Dunham right there, call for a squad car, tell Stone to postpone his mayoral run.

They parked in front of a square brick low-rise off the avenue on 43rd Street.

"Looks like the box some other building came in," Dunham said.

An elderly Hispanic woman sat on the stoop, separating a cart of whites and colors into two baskets. It was the laundry that made him think of it. He popped the glove compartment, pulled out the ski masks—casual, as though he assumed they were part of the job.

"Nah, we don't need those," Dunham said. "They won't have cameras in a dump like this. Besides, I hate those fucking things. Sweat gets stuck in them and then your head stinks like a cunt."

"All due respect," Raney said, "but there's no way this guy doesn't make me."

Dunham slapped the steering wheel.

"Don't be such a pussy. Mora can't do shit. We've got him over a barrel. But if you want to wear the mask, then wear the fucking mask. Just wash your face after."

They started for the building. Dunham nodded to the old woman.

"Buenos días," he said.

"I speak English, asshole."

"Yeah?" Dunham said. "And I bet you've got a few cats, too."

Someone had propped open the lobby door with a Spanish-language Yellow Pages. Dunham tapped it with his foot.

"This is what the spics call a doorman building."

119

A bank of rusted mailboxes took up an entire wall. Dunham searched for Mora's name, pulled a small nail file from his wallet and picked the lock. Inside, a coupon flyer and three envelopes with plastic windows.

"He owes, he owes, so off to work he goes."

Dunham stuck the mail back in the box, shut the lid. They took the elevator up five flights. The same nail file worked on Mora's front door. Inside, an efficiency with a dorm-size fridge, a microwave, a Murphy bed folded into the wall. Frayed carpeting. Water stains on the ceiling.

"If rats were human size, this is how big the traps would be," Dunham said.

Columns of milk crates for a dresser, the top row filled with medals, trophies, an amateur belt. This fight with Malone was supposed to be Mora's break, his first spot on national TV, part of the undercard for a Hearns bout.

"He's disciplined," Dunham said. "I'll give him that. It's not easy to keep a place this size looking clean."

Dunham emptied a column of milk crates onto the floor, stacked them in the center of the room, dragged over a pair of folding chairs. Raney set Pierre's meal atop the mini fridge.

"What now?" he asked.

"We have time before he shows. Let's get comfy. Do a little blow, eat some nice food, watch some TV."

"What TV?"

Dunham scanned the room.

"Jesus," he said. "Fat cats really do feed on skinny mice."

It was the closest he'd come to naming Meno.

Take-out tins lay scattered across the carpet. Dunham's high had him jabbering, pacing Mora's three hundred square feet, dropping to pump out a set of push-ups. Raney stuck to the peephole.

Mora got off the elevator at a little after ten, dressed in a wifebeater and shorts, weighted down with a gym bag, a back-pack, a sack of groceries. Raney pulled on his mask.

"It's about fucking time," Dunham said. "I was starting to get jail-cell flashbacks. Take a seat at the table and keep quiet— you're making me nervous. Just be sure he sees your piece."

The lock turned. Dunham grabbed Mora by the ear, yanked him inside, waved his Glock. Mora dropped the groceries, un-leashed a string of expletives in Spanish.

"Yeah, that's nice," Dunham said. "Hands against the wall."

"Fuck you, *pendejo*. I know why you're here, and the answer is kiss my ass."

"You've got it all wrong. I just want to talk."

"Call me next time."

"What next time? We're going to get everything nice and set-tled."

Mora spat.

"That's your floor, dipshit."

Dunham took Mora's shoulder, spun him around. The fighter was shorter than Raney remembered, but he'd bulked up: a legit middleweight. He still wore a beard to mask the long scar run-ning above his right jawline, but the tats were new—props to accentuate the muscle. A tiny pair of silver boxing gloves hung from a chain around his neck.

"What am I going to find?" Dunham asked.

"A switchblade in my left sock."

"Nothing else?"

"Why don't you put down that gun and we'll work this out like men?"

"You know, your English is really good."

"I'm from Washington Heights, *dipshit*."

"Like I said, your English is really good."

Raney watched, wondering what he would do if Dunham turned up in his living room, threatening to kill Sophia unless he took a dive against a fighter whose prime was five bouts behind him.

Dunham tossed the switchblade across the room. Mora turned, eyeballed Raney for the first time.

"This your torture bitch?"

"Nah, nothing like that. He just has a blood condition. Why don't you sit down? I saved you a glass of wine."

"I'll stand."

"Come on," Raney said. "Have a seat."

"The piece-of-shit coward in the mask talks," Mora said.

Dunham smacked him hard across the back of the head.

"Easy, suede man. I might turn the tables real quick."

"Sit the fuck down and let's get this over with."

Mora took the chair opposite Raney. Dunham crouched between them: a parody of a prefight interview.

"I'll get straight to the point," Dunham said.

He tucked his gun in his waistband, lifted two envelopes from inside his jacket, dropped one on the makeshift table.

"There's ten grand in there. Double what we offered last time."

"Fuck you twice as hard."

"You sure? You could buy yourself a nice TV."

"Where would I put it?"

"How about a bigger pad?"

"Man, enough with the clown act. Just show me what's in envelope two."

Dunham stood, rubbing his palms together.

"I'm trying here," he said. "But I'm starting to take a personal dislike to you. You don't want that."

"Step from behind that gun. Then we'll see who wants what."

"Fine," Dunham said. "It'll be more fun this way."

He tossed the second envelope on Mora's lap.

"Open it."

Mora pulled out a thick sheaf of paper, unfolded pages of maps and itineraries: the location of his kids' schools, the routes they took home, the places where their mothers worked. Mora shrugged, folded the pages back into the envelope, handed it to Dunham.

"You think I give a shit?"

Dunham leaned inches from Mora's ear.

"I'll kill every one of those kids," he said. "I'll do it myself. And if the mama's a piece of ass, I'll fuck her first."

"Man, go for it. Please. What you got in envelope two will save me ten times what you got in envelope one. Hell, you even missed a kid. You want his address?"

"This isn't a game," Raney said. "Spare yourself a lot of pain. Take the ten grand."

"Why is the retard in the mask playing good cop? Don't you got it backwards? Yo, I'll take that glass of wine now, bitch. This shit's worth celebrating."

"You're bluffing," Dunham said. "I'm not."

"Man, I'm the same as you," Mora said. "The only life I give a fuck about is my own."

"Let's put that theory to the test."

Dunham stepped behind Raney, tore off his mask. He pushed the muzzle of his Glock hard against Raney's skull.

"You recognize your pal Dixon here?"

"Dixon?"

Mora's face went soft. He looked confused, even hurt. Raney mouthed the word *cop*. He kept mouthing it until Mora caught on.

"Yo, Dix, man. How can you fuck me like this? What's this psychopath into you for?"

"Joey," Raney said. "What the fuck are you doing?"

"Shut up."

To Mora:

"Take the ten grand or I swear to God I'll do him right here. I'll do him and be back in an hour with your oldest kid's cock."

Take it, Raney mouthed. *It's okay. Take it.*

Mora leaned back.

"Like, fuck it, man," he said. "Fuck it: I can use the cash. For real."

"Good boy," Dunham said. "Just remember—third round, no later. Say it back to me."

"I dive in the third."

"That's smart, because if the bell rings for a fourth, your life won't be worth shit."

"Yeah, I got it."

Dunham lowered the gun.

"Let's go, Deadly."

The stoop granny had company now, was part of a small crowd gathered around a parrot in a bamboo cage. People were laughing, listening to the bird fire off a pattern of staccato squeals. Dunham stopped to look.

"It's the rats," a man said. "He imitates the rats."

"Fucking hell," Dunham said.

They drove south on 3rd Avenue. At the first red light, Raney slammed the gearshift into park, pulled out his gun and shoved the barrel against Dunham's cheekbone.

"You like it?"

"Jesus, Deadly. There are cars all around us."

"I don't give a fuck. You try that shit again and you better fucking pull the trigger."

"Relax. I never would have done it. It was an act. I thought you knew."

"An act?"

"Yeah, and it worked, didn't it?"

Raney hesitated, thought: The badge will protect you.

"So what's it going to be?" Dunham said. "You going to kill me right here?" Raney felt the blow fading, felt suddenly on the verge of sleep. He pocketed his gun, stepped out into the center lane of traffic. Cars honked and swerved. Raney cranked up a middle finger.

"Come on," Dunham said. "Get in. No hard feelings."

"I'll catch the subway."

"It was an act, Deadly. I thought you understood."

"I didn't like it."

"I know. I got it. It won't happen again. Are we square now?"

Raney shrugged.

"I'll cool down," he said.

"So get in. It's Friday night. The clubs have their best girls working."

"I need some air."

"You're too serious, Deadly."

"I'm as serious as I need to be."

"But I'll see you tomorrow?"

"Like I said, I'll cool down."

He watched Dunham drive off, felt his legs quiver. Act my ass, he thought. Mora saved his life. Dunham had doubts. Maybe he'd researched Mike Dixon's amateur record, noticed Mora wasn't listed.

He walked over to 4th Avenue, scanning for Dunham's car. In the subway, he bought a token, sat on the platform, thinking, letting trains go by. His mind was muddled. He needed a fix. He wondered if it showed on him, if any narco strolling by would glom his habit.

He waited fifteen minutes, then walked back through the turnstile. Above ground, the neighborhood was still alive, or was maybe just now coming alive. Friday night in the barrio. Warm, muggy. A party on every stoop. Competing boom boxes. Cabals of old men playing cards in front of bodegas. Kids chasing each other with foam pistols. Gossip on fire escapes. Everyone seemed to know everyone else.

He felt his head nod as he walked. He stopped in a café, ordered two double espressos. Men sat at the tables lined up against one wall, drinking beer and talking. He heard a voice say *policía*: the only scenario that fit a white guy drinking espresso in a Mexican hood at a little before midnight.

Raney felt his paranoia flare. There was a question he needed answered.

"Teléfono?" he asked the bartender.

The man nodded toward the back. Patrons stared as he walked past. The telephone hung on a wall between a door marked GAUCHO and another marked VAQUERA. The space smelled faintly of vomit. Raney pulled a fistful of coins from his pocket, dialed his old lieutenant.

Hutchinson answered.

"It's Raney."

"Wes? You in trouble?"

"No."

"Then why the fuck are you calling me?"

Raney could see him at his desk, leaning back in his swivel chair, gut bulging, phone pinned between his neck and shoulder, chucking darts at a board he'd sketched himself on the back of his office door.

"I'm kidding," Hutchinson said. "What is it?"

"I need to know who put me forward for this case."

"You know that already. It wasn't a who—it was the boxing thing. It made sense."

"That wasn't all of it. It couldn't have been. I barely had a year out of uniform. Someone backed me, and I know it wasn't you."

"All right," Hutchinson said. "Fuck it, I don't think it's any big secret. You can send the thank you card to my esteemed colleague Lieutenant Kee. He pushed hard. Said he saw something in you. I figure it's capital for me down the road. Kee's up for promotion."

"I'm sure he'll get it," Raney said.

"You're welcome," Hutchinson said.

Raney hung up. Kee had been at Ferguson's side all through his captaincy. Before that, he'd been Ferguson's partner on the street. He'd been sitting in a squad car outside the Queensboro Apartments the night Ferguson killed Bruno. And he'd never so much as laid eyes on Raney.

The stoop granny was gone. Raney passed through a small crowd with his head down. No one seemed to notice him.

The elevator reeked now of onions and ammonia. The fluorescent bulb stung his eyes. He walked to the end of Mora's hallway, knocked. No answer. He heard children fighting somewhere behind him. He knocked again. An eye showed at the peephole. The door swung open. Mora pulled him inside, pressed a blade to his throat.

"Tell me why I shouldn't kill you," he said.

Raney laughed. He kept laughing. Once he'd started, he couldn't stop. Tears striped his cheeks. Mora backed away, confused.

"Yo, man. What the fuck's wrong with you?"

"Nothing. Nothing's wrong."

"You high?"

"I'm coming down."

Mora pocketed the knife, kicked the door shut. The milk crates were back in place, the Murphy bed folded out. Mora gestured for Raney to sit.

"You want some of that wine you left me?"

Raney waved it off.

"All right, let's hear how you're going to get me the fuck out of this," Mora said.

"I'm making a case. Dunham and Meno will be locked up before you step in the ring."

"It's one thing to say it. What if you can't make your case?"

"I have the DA's ear. I'll get protection for you and your family."

"Protection don't come free."

"He'll want you to testify."

Mora looked hard at Raney.

"Hell," he said. "If you can keep yourself alive long enough to arrest those cocksuckers, I'll testify day and night."

"Good."

"Will I have to give back the ten grand?"

"It's evidence."

"How about we say it was five thousand and I get half for my hardship?"

"You'll have a nice purse from the Malone fight."

"In other words, fuck you."

Raney stood to leave.

"By the way," Mora said, "that split decision was bullshit. I won every round."

"Doesn't change the knockout," Raney said.

"I could've kept going. The ref was a pussy."

"I just hope you've worked on your defense. You were easy as hell to hit."

18

Their campsite was surrounded by scrub pine. Raney got a fire going in the adobe pit. Clara set out two folding chairs, placed a cooler between them.

"Drink!" Clara said.

Raney uncorked a bottle. Clara took it from him, read the label.

"South African," she said. "Is that good? I don't know anything about wine."

"The man at the shop recommended it."

"Spirits and Live Bait? It's like this is still a mining town."

"Bay says I'm living in the former brothel."

"It's true. They've kept some of the old bedposts."

"I'm not sure they changed the mattresses, either."

"It suits you. Legend has it Wild Bill Hickok slept there. Another itinerant lawman."

Raney filled two plastic wineglasses. They toasted.

"We're a ways from New York, huh?" Clara said.

Strands of auburn hair seemed painted against her off-white sweater.

They ate long skewers of vegetables and shrimp, then sat watching the fire and talking until after the sun had set. Raney wanted to kiss her, couldn't decide if this was the right or wrong moment, didn't know how to close the distance between the chairs. Would she have brought him out here if she didn't want to be kissed? Maybe, he thought. Her friend and mentor had died. Her future was uncertain. Maybe she wanted companionship. Maybe she didn't know what she wanted.

"It's a bright night," Clara said. "If we walk away from the fire, it will be like the stars are on top of us."

"Okay."

"Bring the booze," she said.

They stood, circled the fire in opposite directions, met on the other side. Raney took her hand.

"Brave man," she said.

She bumped him with her hip.

"It's been a while."

He'd almost said eighteen years.

"It's easy to be chaste in the desert," she said. "Unless you're Mavis."

They navigated the scrub, sat with their backs against the bole of a juniper tree. The breeze was cool and dry. Raney put his arm around her shoulder, felt her lean in.

"Can you name the constellations?" she asked.

"I know some," he said. "The Big Dipper. Orion."

He pointed.

"Don't bother," Clara said. "People have been trying to teach me since I was five, and I've never been able to see them. I usually just nod. It was Mavis who put up the stickers in Daniel's room. Maybe there's something wrong with my brain, or maybe I just don't want to see them."

"Why not?"

"It's hard to be in awe of something once you've named it. It's like you're done with it. You never have to look at it again."

"For me it's the opposite. When I came here, I had to train myself to look. I had to learn the names of every tree and shrub so I'd stop feeling overwhelmed, so I could calm down and actually see them."

"That's because you're a detective. Your job is to keep identifying the parts until you have a whole. I like my world ill-defined and vaguely mystical."

"That isn't frightening?"

"Do I seem frightened?"

"No."

"Of course I do."

She leaned forward, pressed her palms to her eyes.

"There's something I have to tell you," she said. "Or at least I *feel* like I have to tell you. It's stupid. We only just met. But then that was Mavis's problem, wasn't it? Once you've let a lie live for too long, it becomes impossible to back away from it. It's too late to ask for help."

Raney let his hand rest on the small of her back.

"What is it?"

"Daniel's my brother," she said. "My half brother."

"Okay."

"No," she said. "It's not okay."

"Why not?"

She took up a juniper needle and rolled it between her palms.

"I think I know why Daniel's always reaching for your badge," she said.

"Why?"

"One of my first memories is of my father nearly beating a man to death. This was in the trailer park where I grew up. I was watching from a window. He was out of control, pounding this guy in the head when he was already unconscious. There were people gathered around, most of them cheering. The sheriff drove up. My father didn't stop. The sheriff grabbed his neck, pulled him off, put a knee in his back, and cuffed him. No baton, no pepper spray, no gun. I remember my father screaming into the dirt. The sheriff just looked annoyed. He wasn't afraid of my father. He was the only one."

"And Daniel has similar memories?"

"The man with the badge makes his father stop doing scary things. I wasn't there for the first years of Daniel's life. I didn't even know he'd been born. But I know my father."

"When did you find out?"

"That I was a big sister?"

Raney nodded.

"I was interning at a museum in Baltimore. I bumped into a woman I hadn't seen since high school. She'd just moved to DC. She asked me how my brother was. I said I didn't have a brother. I thought she must be remembering someone else. 'Holy shit,' she said. 'You don't know.'

"Two days later I was on a plane to California. I rented a car and drove straight to the trailer. Nobody was home. The door was open. It was always open. My father ripped out the doorknob. According to him, a man with a reputation doesn't need a lock. I found Daniel sitting naked in a dog pen, slapping at puddles of urine. He had bruises all over his back and thighs. He wasn't crying. He didn't seem to notice me. I took him. I just took him and left. Neighbors saw me. I don't know if my father tried to follow us. Last I heard he was back in prison. This has been the perfect hideaway. There's no reason he'd look here. And now . . ."

"And now?"

"I have to leave. I need a job. An income for two."

She slid back beside him.

"Unless you plan to arrest me for kidnapping."

Raney kissed her forehead.

"The truth is," she said, "I don't know what Daniel remembers. Maybe nothing. Maybe just an impression he can't get past. When he tries to talk, it's like there's an image in his mind blocking the words. It's more than a stutter—it's like he's choking to death. It's horrible. The sign language is supposed to take the pressure off."

"He'll be all right," Raney said. "He has you as a mother now."

She turned toward him, traced his lips with her fingers.

"I wish we'd met under different circumstances," she said. "But these will have to do."

In the dark, Raney felt years fall away.

19

It was the Mexican who turned up first. He'd driven a hundred miles, bleeding, looking for the closest doctor on the cartel payroll: a veterinarian with a back room. He landed in the right town, stumbled into the wrong clinic, soaked in sweat, muttering, half exsanguinated. The vet in charge sedated him, called nine-one-one.

"Now he's in some backwoods hospital," Bay said, "surrounded by feds. They've ID'd him as Mongo Rivera. Dumbest goddamn name I ever heard. Apparently he's a mainstay on their watch list. They're willing to let us talk to him so long as he's conscious. Let's hope the bastard doesn't check out before we get there."

Bay broke a hundred on the speedometer, ran his siren whether or not there was traffic. The country seemed to deaden a little with each passing mile, the mountains growing leaner in the rearview mirror, the colors fading, the scrubland flattening.

"It's my turn to take lead," Bay said. "Junior was my man."

"Just make sure you know what you want from him."

"I want him to confess."

"A confession won't change anything. He's in fed hands now. What we need is information. We need to know who he fought with. We need to know if he killed Mavis or if she was dead already when he got there. We need to know what kind of operation Jack was running."

Bay smacked the steering wheel with the heel of his palm.

"For a detective," he said, "you have a real tendency to leap out ahead of the facts. You can't say that because the son's room was messy someone else fucked up Rivera. It's too big a coincidence. Mavis has a mobbed-up kid whose record says he's plenty good at killing folks. There's a bloodbath in her living room. Two plus two is four. Case closed."

"Then who took the Jaguar? The DNA hasn't come back yet. Rivera hasn't ID'd Kurt. We don't have forensics on his vehicle and clothes."

"Is this you telling me to keep an open mind? That's rich. You've convinced yourself there was a third man. You want everything good and complicated so you can be the one to sort it out."

"Let's see what Rivera says."

"You tie me up in knots, Raney. Honest to God you do."

It was a small but state-of-the-art hospital, built just a year earlier with funds raised in part by the archdiocese. Three flags hung out front: American, Roman Catholic, Mexican.

"Looks like he wound up in the right place," Bay said.

A nurse directed them to a third-floor suite. Two feds in custom suits flanked the door. Two more sat in the waiting area, watching the news on a wide-screen TV.

"He must be a four-star prize," Bay said.

"They think they can squeeze him," Raney said. "By now the cartel knows he's in custody. He's damaged goods. The feds will offer him protection in exchange for information."

"You mean they'll put him up in a shiny cell with a television and a private shower."

"If they don't find him a house in Alaska."

"I'll kill him first."

Raney flashed his badge to the feds outside the door. One was tall and lean with coat-hanger shoulders and a severe widow's peak; the other was short and stocky, his scalp shaved to the bone.

"I'm Detective Wes Raney. This is Sheriff Joshua Bay. We were told we could have a few words with Rivera."

"You better hurry," the stocky one said.

"That bad?"

"It's a miracle he's talking at all," the tall one said. "Someone tore him from the floor up. Punctured this, fractured that. He left more blood in his car than he had in his body. I guess killing people for a living teaches you how to survive. The interpreter is sitting with him now, in case he mumbles something in his sleep. They've got him doped up pretty good, which should work in your favor."

"Thanks," Raney said.

"I hope he makes it," the stocky one said. "I really do. He could be a gold mine."

Bay grunted.

"We'll be gentle," Raney said.

"And brief," the tall one said. "Doctor's orders."

The interpreter was sitting at Rivera's bedside, filling in a crossword puzzle. He looked up, nodded. Rivera's eyes were shut. A morphine drip and a sack of blood hung from metal hooks on the wall behind him. His hair was long and greasy, his face a patchwork of old scars and freshly stitched gashes. Whoever he fought with had missed his right eye by a centimeter, jerked the blade straight down his cheek.

"Tough bastard," Raney said.

"I'd be more afraid of the guy who did this to him," Bay said.

The interpreter placed a hand on Rivera's shoulder, said his name. Rivera's eyes opened in slow motion. Raney and Bay stepped closer, stood hovering over the bed. Bay glowered.

"All right, gentlemen," the interpreter said. "Best make this quick. He's in and out."

Bay had three photos in his hand. He held up Adler's mug shot first.

"Ask him if this is the man he fought with. The man who put him in this bed."

Rivera tried to speak, tried to cough, found his mouth too dry. The interpreter picked up a Styrofoam cup and slid an ice chip into Rivera's mouth. Rivera moved it around with his tongue, swallowed.

"No," he said.

"He sure?" Bay asked.

"*Sí,*" Rivera said. The man he'd fought with had blue eyes and a square face. He was short and thick and bald, like the man outside the door.

"Shit," Bay said. To Raney: "You ever get tired of being right?"

"Had he ever seen his attacker before?" Raney asked.

Rivera answered no.

"How badly did Rivera hurt him?"

Translation: "He jumped me from behind. When he left, he had my knife in his thigh."

"Can't you afford a gun?" Bay said.

The interpreter smirked. Bay held up a second photo: Mavis.

"You kill her?"

Rivera shut his eyes.

"No," he said in English. "Already dead."

"But you were sent to kill her?"

"*Sí.*"

"By who?"

"You know who."

"Tell us anyway."

"Gonzalez," he said.

Bay showed him Junior's picture.

"What about him?"

"*Sí,*" Rivera said. "I did that one."

"You take over, Raney," Bay said. "I feel my objectivity slipping."

"He won't last much longer," the interpreter said.

"Just a few more questions," Raney said. "How did he get to the Wilkins ranch so fast? How did he know already that things had gone bad?"

Translation: "Someone called up Gonzalez, said the kids are dead and I got your stuff."

"Ask him if he found the drugs at the house."

No, Rivera said. There hadn't been time to look.

"Did he know where the drugs were supposed to end up? Did he know who Wilkins sold to?"

Rivera nodded off. The interpreter tapped his shoulder, asked the question. Rivera shook his head no.

"She never said."

"She?" Raney asked.

"*Sí.*"

"Who?"

Translation: "The woman in the picture."

"Bullshit," Bay said.

Rivera's eyes shut. His mouth hung open.

"I'm afraid that's it," the interpreter said.

The tall fed had been right: whatever cocktail they were serving Rivera worked like truth serum. Or maybe beneath the narcotics he was running scared, playing model snitch, looking ahead to his new government-sanctioned life. Assuming he survived.

"We got what we came for," Raney said. "Thank you for your help."

They sat in the cafeteria, eating breaded pork chops and canned green beans.

"This tastes about how I feel," Bay said.

"I know it," Raney said.

Bay snapped the tines from his plastic fork, one by one.

"It's taken me this long to realize I'm just a guy with a badge who likes to fish," he said. "Usually that's enough out here. The peace more or less keeps itself. But I got lazy. I stopped knowing the people around me. I stopped believing anything very bad could happen. That's why that piece of shit they're keeping alive up there was able to kill Junior like it was nothing. Twenty years old. That boy had family in his future."

"You're talking about things beyond your control," Raney said.

"It don't feel that way."

"I know."

"I'm not sure I want it to, either. This is it for me. The town needs fresh eyes. And my eyes need a rest."

"Then go out on top. Help me solve this one."

"You believe the Mexican when he says he didn't kill Mavis?"

"Her wound didn't match the others."

"Then how do we track this bald fucker?"

"We start with the forensics."

140

"They're slow as shit around here."

"You've got someone on Mavis's computer?"

"Yeah. I had to send it to him. He says he'll drive it back tomorrow, but it'll more likely be a few days."

"Keep on him."

"I will," Bay said. "And I'll find out who Mavis was if it takes me from here to my grave."

"It almost doesn't matter now."

"It matters to me," Bay said.

20

Raney couldn't shake the sensation of being caged, locked in his own skin. He rolled onto his side, switched on the light.

Two in the morning. He glanced around the room: Bay's Scotch on the windowsill, his suitcase on the floor beside the nightstand. Why had he swiped the coke? Impulse? Reflex? He remembered one of Stone's edicts: *We enter law enforcement to police ourselves.* Raney had gone eighteen years without an infraction. Stone would say he was due.

He sat on the edge of the bed, unlocked his suitcase. Nobody, he told himself, made it from day to day without some kind of help. Bay had his liquor; Clara had her pot. Were they addicts? Junkies? People are ill equipped for the demands placed on them, the demands they place on themselves. We're the only animal, Raney thought, who believes survival isn't enough.

Still, something held him back. A distant awareness of what he was talking himself into. A fear that the decision would be irreversible.

He slammed the suitcase shut, slid it under the bed. Tomorrow, he told himself, he would make a double offering.

He lay back down, replaying his date with Clara, angry with himself for fantasizing, already, about their future together, about the young man Daniel would become.

In the morning, everything seemed a little quieter, a little more real. He showered, shaved, dressed in a T-shirt and jeans. No blazer. The thought of eating alone depressed him. He called Clara.

"I would," she said. "But we've already had breakfast. And you know how I feel about the food in this town."

"Okay," Raney said. "How about a late-morning hike? There are some beautiful trails on the other side of the reservation."

"A hike?"

He felt her searching for a reason to say no.

"Did I call too soon?"

"No, but I have Daniel today."

"Even better."

"Shouldn't you—"

"We're waiting on forensics," Raney said. "I need some air."

A slight pause. Then:

"All right. Daniel will love it."

"I'll pick you up in an hour."

The day was mild, the sky a single, piercing shade of blue. They chose a trail a mile or so below the tree line. Raney parked in the small space allotted to hikers. Daniel jumped out, charged for the woods. Clara called him back.

"Hey, Daniel," Raney said. "I've got something for you."

"Oh, really?" Clara said. "I wonder what it could be."

Daniel sidled forward. Raney reached into his blazer pocket, drew out a blank shield.

"It's a clip-on, like mine. No pins or needles."

"His head's going to explode," Clara said.

Raney crouched down, held up the badge, pulled it back when Daniel swiped for it.

"I don't give these to just anyone," Raney said. "If you take it, you have to promise to look after your mother and do what she tells you. You have to be kind to people and animals, and you have to help anyone who needs it."

Raney caught himself speaking at half speed, as though the boy were deaf and just learning to lip read. Daniel didn't seem to notice. He nodded, crossed his heart, reached again for the badge.

"All right, then," Raney said. "I hereby name you Junior Deputy Detective Daniel Remler."

He clipped the badge to Daniel's belt. Daniel tapped Raney's chest three times.

"A friend for life," Clara said. "He made that one up himself."

The trail followed a creek for the first quarter mile. Daniel ran out ahead, brandishing a stick, ready to fend off all comers. He startled a dusky grouse, gave a small scream as it darted into the woods.

"Careful, Deputy Detective Remler," Clara called. "Stay where I can see you."

Daniel sprinted forward, waited, sprinted again. Clara took Raney's hand.

"What kind of cactus is that?" she asked.

"Fishhook."

"And that tree?"

"Mesquite."

"You know," she said, "I just realized I've made this hike before. If you climb to the summit at night, it's like you're face-to-face with the moon."

And who made the hike with you? Raney wondered.

They were resting, lingering in the shade of a large outcropping. Daniel sat a few yards distant, straddling the low-lying branch of a cottonwood. Clara tied her hair back in a ponytail, wiped a faint sheen from her skin. To the west, a vista of peaks and foothills marred by the top stories of the casino.

"What are you thinking?" Clara asked.

"That people belong in cities," he said. "They don't know what to do with a place like this."

"You're talking about the casino?"

"That's part of it."

"Mavis is another part?"

"Yes."

"I thought this was supposed to be a reprieve."

"You're right," Raney said. "I'm sorry."

They started walking again. A gentle pace, upslope into the last stretch of forest before the tree line. Daniel continued scouting, ducking behind rocks and tree stumps, then darting forward.

"So if people belong in cities," Clara said, "why are you here?"

"I guess I'm trying to prove myself wrong."

"Most of us go through life trying to prove ourselves right."

"Either way, it's a full-time job."

He felt her palm against his, the tips of her fingers pressing into his skin.

"Someday you'll tell me," she said.

"Tell you what?"

"Why you left home."

"Okay."

"Someday," she said. "But not today."

21.

So you think it was a test?" Stone said. "Dunham expected Mora to ID you?"

"That's my read. Mora saved my life."

Raney hadn't slept, hadn't gone back to the apartment in Fort Hamilton. Instead, he'd walked over the Brooklyn Bridge at 1:00 a.m., then kept walking. He cut diagonals through Central Park, thinking, waiting for the sun to rise.

"But then why call you by name before he pulled off the mask? Why risk tipping Mora?"

They sat on Stone's couch, drinking coffee, facing a long window that gave onto the pale southern skyline.

"He knows, but he doesn't want it to be true. He likes having me around. So he slipped Mora an out."

"But you're safe now. Mora put Dunham at ease."

"For the time being. I think Dunham's stalling. He'll keep testing me until he can't pretend anymore."

Stone turned sideways on the couch, gave Raney a long look.

"I should pull you," he said. "You sound paranoid. Your eyes are dilated. And you don't smell very good."

"You're not going to pull me."

"Don't be so sure."

"Just tell me what you need to finish this. What is it I haven't given you?"

"I need Meno. I need Dunham on tape saying it's been Meno all along."

"I can't walk in there wearing a wire. Not now."

"Then I'm pulling you."

"Bullshit. You'll never get anyone this close again."

"I'm not sure you are close."

"I'm close. But I'm walking on eggshells. I need to hand Dunham something big. Something he won't have to share with Meno. Something that will erase his doubt about me."

"It can't be drugs. We can't give that animal junk to put on the street."

"Maybe he doesn't put it on the street. Maybe I turn over a complete package—buyer and seller. Somewhere outside Meno's turf."

"That would require product, cash, manpower."

"You've got two out of three sitting in evidence lockers around the city."

"Look," Stone said. "Stop stringing me along. What do you have in mind?"

"It's simple. Someone I knew upstate just got out. He has a sweet operation in place but he's cash poor, and he's too hot to run it himself. He's laying low until his parole is done. All he wants is a taste, enough to keep him afloat."

"What's the operation?"

"Stuff comes to us close to pure from somewhere down south.

Baltimore or DC, anywhere Dunham has no contacts. We step on it three times over, sell it to a string of dealers up north, where addicts don't know anything better. Maine, maybe. Or New Hampshire."

"And you're bringing Dunham in on this because . . ."

"He's the money guy. My jailbird friend needs a bankroll."

"He'll know you're setting him up."

"He'll suspect, but he'll be tempted. He's looking to branch out on his own."

Stone stared into the bottom of his cup.

"And you want to stage all this just to gain the man's trust?"

"Without that, we don't get Meno. And there's a good chance I end up dead."

"All right," Stone said. "I'll see what I can pull together."

"That's not good enough. I need to give Dunham something tonight. He can't have time to think."

"Listen to you," Stone said. "I thought I was calling the shots. I tell you what: check back with me at five o'clock."

"There's something else."

"What's that?"

"Mora wins his fight. That means we wrap this up inside of six weeks. Mora can't get hurt. No one in his family can get hurt."

"He'll testify?"

"If we protect him."

"Then we'll make it work."

Raney hesitated.

"And what about Captain Ferguson?" he said.

Stone raised an eyebrow.

"You mean your future father-in-law?"

"If I'm in, I want in all the way. Someone's been giving Meno a clear path. This case starts in 1954, doesn't it?"

Stone shrugged.

"I'm ninety percent sure," he said. "I need Meno to give me the other ten percent."

"What do you know about the Bruno shooting?"

"I've read the files, talked to a few old-timers. Ferguson claimed to be acting on a tip, said there was no time to call for backup. For reasons unknown, Kee stayed with the squad car. Bruno was ducking a federal warrant, laying low in the Queensboro Apartments. Ferguson shot him in the back. The two other men he killed were just residents of the building, people Bruno paid to put him up in what he thought was the last place anyone would look. They weren't armed, but you could keep that sort of thing out of the papers back then. Especially if the men were black."

"And since then?"

"Roy Meno has led a charmed life. Raids on faulty addresses. Missing evidence. Witness suicides."

"Son of a bitch," Raney said.

"You told me you wanted in."

"One thing doesn't make sense."

"What's that?"

"If you knew about Ferguson, then why'd you take me on Kee's recommendation? Why'd you take me knowing I was engaged to Ferguson's daughter?"

"I couldn't veto Kee's pick without raising the wrong shackles. Besides, when I read your jacket it seemed to me Ferguson was making a sloppy bet. Was I wrong?"

"No," Raney said. "You weren't wrong."

He should have gone home to bed, should have slept for the few hours he had until Dunham expected him at the club, but instead he called Sophia, asked her to meet.

"What the fuck, Wes?" she said. "Why am I at a coffee shop in Jackson Heights in the middle of a weekday?"

She wore a brick-red wiggle dress, sat with her back pressed flat against the bench, looking like a person poised to say no to whatever was asked of her.

"I wanted to talk," Raney said.

"So we can talk at home."

"I need to be extra careful right now."

"Why? What's going on?"

"Nothing."

"Nothing? You sound like a teenager. You remember we're getting married, right? We should be sampling cake and making seating arrangements. We don't even have a venue."

"Six weeks," he said. "That's what I wanted to tell you. Six more weeks and I'm done. Maybe less."

"Can you last six weeks?"

"What does that mean?"

"It means you look like you're about to nod off."

"I haven't been sleeping much."

"What have you been doing instead?"

"Staying awake."

"How? I'm not blind, Wes."

"It's only once in a while. To keep my cover. It's part of the job."

"Bullshit. I spend most of my day taking children away from their junkie parents. It doesn't matter if you're pretending. The shit you're doing is real."

"What do you want from me?"

"What do I want from you? Come home. Now. Not in six weeks. Now. My father's made calls. There's an opening in Homicide. In Ozone Park, but still. Isn't that what every detective dreams of? Homicide?"

Raney stabbed at his salad.

"Your father still has a lot of pull, doesn't he?"

"He was captain for twenty years. People listen."

"He must go through Kee now. How well do you know him?"

"Wes, why are you asking about my father's partner? We have more important things——"

"Did your father ever talk about his work in front of you? Did you overhear things?"

She dug a fingernail into the back of his hand, cocked her head.

"Come home," she said. "Come home now."

"I have to finish this."

"Why?"

"Because I started it."

He ran his thumbs over the grooved edge of the table, searching for a way into the conversation he wanted to have.

"Wes," Sophia said, "look at me. You're bouncing around in your seat like a third grader."

"Am I a teenager or a third grader?"

"You're a prick."

She was crying now, or trying not to, swallowing air, turning her head away. Raney leaned across, touched her cheek.

"I'm sorry," he said. "You're right."

"I'm afraid," she said.

"Of what?"

"You're out there, doing things, putting yourself at risk, and you're not right. Your mind isn't right, Wes."

He pulled back.

"Jesus Christ," he said. "I don't need this shit right now."

"You're high. This isn't you, Wes."

"Then who the fuck is it?" he said.

"Wes, you're shouting."

"You know what? You're right, I'm high. I'm fucking high. Fuck you and your father."

He dropped a twenty on the table and walked out. Somewhere behind him he heard a woman's voice say, "Anything you want, sweetie. On the house."

22

There was no reception in the mountains. By the time they got back to town, Raney's voice mail was full. At first, Bay sounded upset, like someone struggling to suppress information he'd rather not have in the first place. By the end, he was mad, as if Raney's absence marked a deliberate betrayal.

"Goddamn it, Raney, I can't say this shit over the phone. My stomach's churning. Get to my office now."

"Everything all right?" Clara asked.

They were sitting in his car, in front of Mavis's store, Daniel asleep in the backseat.

"I don't know," he said. "Bay wants to see me. He wouldn't say why."

"Back to work, then."

"Back to work."

"Thank you," she said. "It was good to get away. Even just for a morning. Good for me and for Daniel."

* * *

"Shut the door and take a seat," Bay said.

"What has you so riled?"

"Mavis's prints came back."

"And?"

"Her name wasn't Mavis at all."

He tossed a manila folder across the desk. Raney opened it, started reading. Cheryl Wilner, born 1940. Six counts of solicitation between '56 and '59, two in Philadelphia, four in Boston. In 1960: a warrant for capital murder, still open. She and her pimp, Jonathan Flory, were wanted in the stabbing death of thirty-nine-year-old Mundell Stewart, a bachelor with a trust fund. Stewart's body was discovered by the cleaning crew in a Roxbury motel on the morning of September 18. Witnesses, including the night clerk, saw both Wilner and Flory exit the deceased's room at approximately midnight. Stewart's wallet and keys were not found at the scene, and his 1958 Jaguar was gone from the lot. Subsequent investigation revealed that Stewart's Beacon Hill loft was burglarized later that morning, though there was no sign of forced entry. Police discovered his Jaguar parked in the building's underground garage.

"Well," Raney said. "I guess we know who Jack Wilkins is. And where he got his taste for cars."

"A pimp and a prostie. Part of me still thinks there has to be a mistake."

"It's sad," Raney said.

"How do you figure?"

"She was sixteen the first time they cited her. Chances are she started younger."

"Yeah, and she died a drug-trafficking murderess."

"Some people don't recover."

"From what?"

"The hand they were dealt."

Bay pushed a quarter around the surface of his desk.

"I had no idea who she was, Raney. None whatsoever. Not even when I was sleeping with her. But you had her pegged from the get-go. How?"

"I didn't have forty years of memories standing in the way."

"I don't suppose this changes our case any."

"It explains some things. Bob Sims told me Jack had a fetish for call girls. Said he did his fishing in Nevada."

"I believe it. Jack never did care who Mavis was seen with."

"The good news is we get to help the Boston PD close a forty-two-year-old cold case."

"Shit," Bay said. "Right under my fucking nose."

An hour later, Bay called Raney back to his office.

"They found the Jaguar. And a body lying twenty yards away, with three bullets in its back."

"Adler?"

"That's what we're going to find out," Bay said.

"Where?"

"About an hour north of here."

"North?"

"Yeah, why?"

"I figured he'd be taking the dope back East."

"If it's Adler," Bay said.

It was Adler—a tight cluster of bullet holes in the center of his back, his salmon-colored shirt running with blood. The staties had taped off a wide perimeter. Camera crews from across the state gathered on every side. The area was secluded, the road

156

unpaved. Kurt must have been avoiding the highways. The front driver's side of the Jaguar was caved in. Someone had knocked the car into an arroyo, then shot Adler while he ran for cover. There was blood from a head wound on the steering wheel. Adler, disoriented, had fled without his weapon: a .38 lay under a fold of newspaper on the passenger seat.

The responding officers found 9mm shell casings among the tire tracks and skid marks. The trunk of the Jaguar was left open, nothing but a hand jack and a blanket inside. In Adler's pockets, a wallet and a hotel key card. No phone.

Raney and Bay stood on opposite sides of the body. He'd fallen forward, landed with his head turned, half his face exposed. Raney bent down, brushed away the ants.

"Pretty spot to die in," Bay said.

"He couldn't have been here long," Raney said. "The animals hadn't found him yet."

"Whoever killed him didn't do much to cover it up."

"His mind was somewhere else."

"So he has the coke now?"

"He must. If he didn't, the key card would be missing. The question is, why come so hard after *this* supply? The guy we're chasing is willing to go to war with a Mexican cartel and a Boston crime boss."

"He seems up to the job, too," Bay said.

"Someone with military training, maybe."

Technicians loaded the Jaguar onto a flatbed truck. There would be more processing, more waiting. Raney followed Bay back to the squad car. Bay turned the ignition but didn't pull out.

"You positive it's just one guy?" he asked.

"No, but this is starting to feel personal. Like some kind of vengeance specific to this package. Rivera said Mavis was already dead when he found her. He said he was jumped from behind. But if the stocky bald man had the drop on Rivera, then why not just shoot him, like he did Kurt?"

"Maybe he went there to kill a sixty-two-year-old woman. Maybe he didn't bring his gun. Or maybe Rivera's a fucking liar."

"I think he wanted the fight. He wanted to inflict pain. Maybe he wanted to feel pain. Maybe this all starts with his own sense of guilt."

"That's a lot of maybes," Bay said.

"What else do we have?"

"We have his DNA. And we have DNA tests that take two menstrual cycles to come back."

"There might be another way to ID this guy, or at least get a photo of him. Where are the lab techs with Mavis's computer?"

"Nowhere fast. We can force the issue, drive up there ourselves tomorrow. Why? What are you thinking?"

"Clara said Mavis was seeing someone online."

"You think our guy is the someone?"

"It would fit."

"If you're right, he sure had it figured from all angles."

"Yeah, and he's not done. There's still whoever Jack and Mavis sold to."

Raney sat up in bed, laptop on his knees, downloading the photos of Mavis's invoices. He found nothing: no code to crack, no trail leading back to the buyer or buyers. Just the purchase and sale of art supplies, the pages out of order, as though Mavis had spilled them across the floor and shuffled them back together.

He called up a search engine and typed in his daughter's name. He let his ring finger hover over the Return key, a ritual he'd performed almost daily since the county issued him a laptop. Always he resisted, shut the page. There was no upside to watching from afar.

He set aside his computer, lay picking small noises from the silence: a passing car, a dog barking from some distant ranch, a breeze rattling the windowpanes. For the better part of eighteen years he'd slept alone, woken alone. It was a fact of his life he rarely questioned. But now the solitude made him feel absurd, unreal—a creature cut off from every other creature. He thought that Clara, lying alone in her bed just a few short blocks away, must be feeling something similar. He checked his phone to make sure the ringer was turned on, then cursed himself for behaving like a teenager.

He sat up, reached for his suitcase. He remembered a line from *The Maltese Falcon,* a film he'd watched time and again with his father: *I won't because all of me wants to.* He dug out a single bag, flushed it whole.

23

The warehouse was brimming, bodies pressing together on every side of the ring. Dunham stood with Raney by the skirts, watching Spike redeem himself, tagging a bodybuilder's face as though he were working a speed bag.

Dunham wiped his forehead with a handkerchief.

"It's like a fucking sauna for the homeless in here," he said. "Since you KO'd Spike, every luckless shit sack thinks he can spot a ringer. Fuck my uncle—I'll retire off this place."

"Want to slip me a percentage?"

"What, I'm not paying you enough?"

"I don't know what that would be."

Dunham grinned, looked at his watch. "When's this guy gonna show?"

"Any minute."

"Remind me how you know him."

"From inside."

"Cellie?"

"Bible school."

"Bible school?"

"It helps with parole."

The bodybuilder's head took a double bounce off the canvas. The crowd jeered, stamped their feet.

"Nice one, Spike," Dunham called. "These fuckers all bet against you."

Spike stepped over his opponent, stared down at Raney.

"I'm waiting on that rematch," he said.

"Sorry," Raney said. "I retired."

"Smart," Spike said.

The emcee announced the next fighter—a scrawny teenager from Bed-Stuy.

"Jesus," Dunham said. "The stripper I fucked last night weighs more than this kid."

He stepped up on the edge of the ring, scanned the back wall, pointed.

"I swear to God, Cobra," he said, "if you don't drop this stick inside a minute you're finished."

The undercover sidled up next to Raney, tapped his shoulder. He was over six feet, between 230 and 250, his dull-brown hair streaked silver and pulled back in a ponytail. He wore a black leather jacket open in the front, his gut spilling over his jeans. Raney nodded, waited for Dunham to hop back off the canvas.

"This is Doug Farlow," Raney said. "Doug, this is Joey Dunham."

They shook hands. Farlow smiled, held Dunham's stare.

"You've got a good thing here."

"Thanks," Dunham said. "You want to go a few rounds? You look like you could handle yourself."

"Maybe if you've got a senior division."

The bell rang. Dunham looked up at Cobra.

"What the fuck is this asshole bobbing and weaving for? *Knock the kid out!* Christ, I can't watch this shit. Let's find somewhere quiet."

He led them through the crowd and into a windowless side room furnished with a minibar and a long folding table. He turned to Farlow.

"You just got out, right?"

"Yes, sir."

"Then you know the drill."

"Which one?" Farlow said. "There were a lot of drills."

"The one where you strip."

"You're shitting me."

Dunham shook his head, locked the door from the inside.

"Your boys already patted me down."

"The totem poles are mostly for show. It's not personal."

"Joey, come on," Raney said. "I vouched for the guy."

"So maybe you should join him." To Farlow: "You can say no, and we'll all just go about our evening."

Farlow kicked at the floor.

"Don't worry," Dunham said. "I won't stick my finger up your ass. Deadly's going to do that."

Raney and Farlow swapped looks.

"It's a joke, fellas. Don't be so serious."

Farlow tossed his jacket onto the table, followed by his jeans, T-shirt, boxers. Dunham made a spinning motion with his index finger. Farlow held his arms out to the side, turned in a slow circle.

"A sight to behold, I know."

"You've got nothing to be ashamed of," Dunham said. "Deadly, give his clothes the once-over."

Raney emptied Farlow's pockets, felt inside his pants legs, shook out his boots.

"Nothing," he said.

"Let me see his wallet."

Raney tossed it over. Dunham checked the billfold, flipped through the glassine windows.

"Your parole officer's a woman?" he said.

"How do you like that?"

"What's her name? I can't quite make it out on the card."

"Jesus, you're careful," Farlow said. "I call her Pamela Polack. I don't know how you say the last name. It starts with *W-R* and ends with 'zinski.'"

"Is she nice-looking, at least?"

"With a name like that?"

Dunham grinned. Farlow zipped up his fly, pulled on his T-shirt.

"No hard feelings," Dunham said.

"It's just business, right?"

"Speaking of which . . ."

Dunham and Raney sat on one side of the table, Farlow on the other. Dunham lit a cigarette, slid the pack over.

"So what are we talking about?"

"It's simple," Farlow said. "I've got a connect in DC. He'll deliver up to twenty kilos, at twelve thousand dollars per, plus a ten-percent handling fee. This stuff is as close to pure as it gets. You step on it three times over, sell it to some hillbilly dealers I know in Maine for whatever price you want. Fiends up there can't get anything better."

"How do you know these hillbillies?"

"They're blood. Two cousins and a half brother."

"And what about your connect?"

"He's sixty-four and never served a day. No flash, no conflict. Lives in a one-bedroom apartment over a dry cleaner's and steers clear of street sales. He keeps a small crew of guys he came up with."

"The senior citizen brigade."

"Watch it, son," Farlow said. "I'm not so far off myself."

"Why do you need me?"

"Funding," Farlow said. "I'm cash poor. Not to mention my front-line days are behind me. I told myself if I ever got busted again I'd tie it off right there. I don't want to die in a jumpsuit surrounded by COs calling me Pops. A one-bedroom over a dry cleaner's would suit me fine. Minimal risk, just enough reward. That's all I'm after."

Dunham rocked back in his chair. Farlow held his cigarette between his middle and ring fingers, pawed at the smoke with his free hand. He was steady, deliberate. Dunham seemed to like him. Raney wanted to ask how he'd lasted so long.

"One thing bothers me," Dunham said.

"What's that?"

"I thought hillbillies ate tree branches and bathed in mud puddles. How'd they come by this kind of cash?"

"You can make money anywhere," Farlow said, "as long as you know how to cook meth and film little girls touching themselves. It ain't pretty, but that's what it is."

"No, it ain't pretty," Dunham said. "But green is green."

"We have a deal, then?"

"Give me a day to think on it. I'll have Deadly send word."

24

Luisa Gonzalez was screaming from somewhere behind a burlap curtain when the phone woke him. The nightstand clock read 5:00 a.m.

"I'm sorry if you were asleep," Clara said. "I'm watching the news. What in the hell is going on?"

Shit, Raney thought. They would have broadcast the same mug shot she'd been passing around the casino. Why hadn't he thought to warn her?

"Are you okay?" he asked.

"No," she said. "No, I'm not okay."

"I'll be there as soon as I can."

She came to the door wearing a long nightshirt and ankle-high socks. Her hair was disheveled, her skin mottled. Raney reached out to touch her arm. She spun away, ran up the stairs. He found her sitting in front of the television, hunched forward, mechanically grinding a metal whisk through a bowl of thick batter. He sat beside her, let his hand rest on her back. Her skin felt cool through the thin cotton fabric.

"I couldn't sleep," she said. "I thought I'd get a head start on Daniel's breakfast."

The early morning news ran footage of the crime scene: forensics hoisting the Jaguar onto the flatbed, Raney and Bay crossing the arroyo, the ME and her team following with the body. A voice-over ID'd the victim as Kurt Adler, said the Jaguar belonged to Jack Wilkins. The police were as yet unaware of any link between the "Boston mobster" and the killings at the Wilkins ranch.

"What will it be tomorrow?" Clara asked. "Why stop at family? Why not kill her only employee? And her employee's 'child'?"

"Because you have no connection to the drugs."

"For God's sake, who's doing this?"

"I don't know."

She shook his hand from her back.

"Then why are you here? Why aren't you out looking for him? How was he able to find Mavis's son before you did? How did he even know she had a son?"

"He's been planning this for a long time, Clara. We're playing catch-up."

"You don't even know who you're looking for."

"I have an idea," he said. "An idea you gave me."

"What's that?"

The news switched to a commercial break; the jump in volume startled her. She turned off the TV, set the bowl and whisk on the floor.

"You told me Mavis was seeing someone online," Raney said.

"The schoolteacher. She mentioned him a few times. Why?"

"I'd like to talk to him."

"She never used his name," Clara said. "The more I think about it, the more I realize she hardly told me anything."

"She thought of you as a daughter," Raney said.

Clara dropped her head on Raney's shoulder, took his hand.

"I'm fucking hungry," she said.

"Why don't I finish making you breakfast?"

He reached for the bowl and whisk.

"I have a better idea," she said.

She took his face in her hands, brushed her cheek against his, let her lips rest on his chin.

"Before Daniel wakes up."

He left with Bay for Albuquerque at a little after 11:00 a.m.

"I told the tech we'd be there at two thirty whether he was ready for us or not. I said if he wasn't ready, we'd sit with him in his cubicle until he was. I told him you had halitosis real bad. I probably should have mentioned you were county Homicide—might have carried more weight."

"I doubt it."

"You do smell different today," Bay said. "Not bad, unless you think it's bad for a man to smell like flowers."

He'd showered at Clara's.

"Hotel shampoo," Raney said.

"You really ought to come stay at my place. I've got a nice A-frame by the creek. Wouldn't be any hassle at all."

"You lonely, Bay?"

"Ain't you?"

Raney shrugged. He still felt Clara pressing against him.

"I guess you wouldn't be," Bay said. "You're the type to get lost in your own head. But too much of that's no good for a man. Shit, you're still young, Raney. A year or two younger than I was when

I met you. Now, there's a swift kick in the pants. We both been alone more or less this whole time. You get past a certain age, it's hard to find a woman out here. At least one that's not already found."

"Are you going to run that siren all the way to Albuquerque?"

"You mean the siren or my mouth?"

Raney gave another shrug.

"All right," Bay said, "I'll switch it off. Not much traffic here anyway. But if you want to shut me up, you're going to have to talk some yourself. You're too damn quiet, Raney. You could put a man to sleep at the wheel. Try being companionable once in a while. You might find you like it. It might even stick."

"What do you want me to say?"

"I've got to choose the topic now? You were undercover in New York City. Why not start there?"

"I didn't last very long."

"Long enough to have one goddamn story worth telling."

"You're a bull in a china shop, Bay."

"Meaning you're the china? Shit, Raney, if there's a PTSD thing here then I'll shut my mouth and drive. You can nap if you want to."

"No, it's okay," Raney said. "Just give me a minute to get started."

25

He leaned against the hood of his car, watched a bivouac of homeless men congregate under the awning of an abandoned supermarket, drinking and smoking and sniffing from a tube. They'd sized him up, decided he wasn't a threat. Otherwise, the lot was empty, dark. Someone had shot out the streetlights on the north.

A middle-aged black man in a dusty Toyota pulled up beside Raney at exactly 10:00 p.m. He rolled down the driver's-side window, smiled. He was wearing a sweatshirt and jeans.

"You said no flash, right?"

"Yeah, you look the part," Raney said.

"I hear you're working a real solid case."

"Thanks."

"So where's our next stop?"

Raney handed him a piece of paper with an address scribbled on it.

"Dunham's playing it tight. We're supposed to wait here twenty minutes. Then you pull out and I follow. Once we get there, we wait another twenty."

"This is a good spot he picked. You can see who's coming and going in three directions."

"He's smart when he needs to be."

"You've got him now, though. All you got to do is outlast him. When's the drive north?"

"We step on the shipment tonight," Raney said. "It goes out to-morrow morning. He doesn't want the shit in his possession more than a day."

"Long hours for you."

"Yeah."

"Wanna head out?"

"Let's wait the full twenty."

The undercover grinned.

"Dunham ain't the only one who's careful."

"I've got a lot riding on this. What should I call you, by the way?"

"Dizzy."

"Dizzy?"

"Like Gillespie."

"You and Dunham have something in common. He's a lunatic for jazz."

"Yeah, well...I don't plan on getting cozy with the man."

"Lucky you."

"Just hang in there, son. You're almost home."

Dizzy stuck to the speed limit, slowed at yellow lights, drove like a man with dope in his trunk. Raney stuck a car's length behind, followed him down side streets from East New York to

Howard Beach. They pulled in front of a one-story warehouse with a side staircase and a bright-orange roll-up door. Dunham sat on the metal stairs, smoking. He nodded at Raney, checked his watch, went inside. Twenty minutes later, Raney gave two staccato honks, and the orange door lifted. Raney drove in, parked behind Dunham's Lincoln. Dizzy followed. The loading dock was large enough to fit two semis. Beyond the dock was a brick wall with a second roll-up door.

"They make glass here," Dunham said. "High-end stuff. One of my fighters is foreman."

He jumped down off the dock, his gun tucked in his front waistband.

"That sure was a lot of driving and waiting," Dizzy said.

"Next year I'll have you over to the house for Thanksgiving," Dunham said. "Right now, I don't know who the fuck you are."

"Hey, I ain't complaining. Cautious is good."

"I'm glad you feel that way. Deadly, give the man our standard greeting."

Dizzy held his arms out to the sides. "Just don't let your hands linger nowhere," he said.

"Normally I'd make you strip," Dunham said. "But we're short on time."

"Yeah, I heard about that. Wish you had it on film."

"He's clean," Raney said.

"Last thing," Dunham said. "You have a tape deck in that jalopy?"

"Yeah."

Dunham tossed him a cassette.

"Pop this in and crank the volume. A little Coltrane to set the mood."

"At least you got taste."

There was a long solo before the band joined in. The sax came out tinny through the car's old speakers.

"All right," Dunham said, "let's do this."

Dizzy opened the trunk. It was crammed full of brown paper bags teeming with canned and boxed food.

"You hid the coke in shopping bags?" Dunham said.

"Nah, these are honest-to-God groceries. No perishables. I don't want nothing spoiling while you got me touring the boroughs."

"So where are the bricks?"

"Underneath. You help me unload, this'll go a lot quicker."

They cleared the trunk down to a spare tire and a flathead screwdriver, then lifted out the tire and set it beside the paper bags. Dizzy peeled the carpet back, used the screwdriver to pry up the metal flooring.

"There she is," he said. "Twenty keys, pure enough for you to fuck with all you want. You could step on this shit five times over and it'll still kick."

Dunham pulled a knife from his back pocket, sprung the blade, took up a brick and poked a hole in the packaging.

"That's right," Dizzy said. "Have a taste. I hope you got a ride home, though."

Dunham drew a small mound of powder up into his nose, threw his head back, wiped water from his eyes. He stood for a beat, listening to the music.

"Was I lying?" Dizzy asked.

"No, you told the goddamn truth. Deadly, let's bag this shit."

"Hold on, now," Dizzy said. "There's a matter of payment first."

"I gave your broker friend half up front. You get the second half after I've been paid."

Dizzy waved his hands.

"You got it wrong, chief. Second half on delivery. I just delivered."

"Check with Farlow. That ain't the agreement."

"Shit, man, I knew this was too fuckin' smooth."

"You'll get the rest in forty-eight hours. What could be smoother than that?'

"Putting the goddamn cash in my hand while I'm standing here would be a fuckload smoother."

"Here's the problem," Dunham said. "You and your DC pals are only half the picture. What if I get up north and the hillbillies don't check out? What if they snatch the shit at gunpoint and disappear into the woods?"

"That shit's between you and them. We got nothin' to do with those Marlboro Men."

"Farlow's your broker, not mine. I need assurance. You'll get paid when I get paid. You have my word. If that's not enough, all you have to do is give me back what I already laid out. We'll just hang on to the product in the meantime."

Dunham grinned. Dizzy rocked back on his heels.

"Well played, motherfucker."

"So we're good?"

"Shit, man . . . in for a penny . . ."

"I thought you'd see it that way."

"It's me in a garage with two strapped crackers. How else am I gonna see it?"

26

The lab tech led them into a cramped conference room, left them alone with Mavis's computer and a fifty-page printout listing sites visited, accounts and passwords, the title of every folder and document on her hard drive.

"Not bad," Bay said.

"Not bad at all. Let's hope our guy is in here somewhere."

"Where do we start?"

Raney scanned the icons on Mavis's desktop.

"Is there a password on that printout for something called FiftyPlus?" he asked.

"FiftyPlus? Sounds like a vitamin."

Bay slid on his reading glasses, skimmed the top page.

"Goddamn," he said. "She spent her life on that site. Let's see . . . Here it is. Oh, you're going to like this one, Raney."

"What is it?"

" 'Screw Jack'—one word, all caps. And the *a* is an 'at' symbol. Mavis sure was a pistol. That much of her was real."

"Here we go," Raney said.

A small blue banner at the top of the home page read WELCOME BACK MAVISW! YOUR LAST LOG-IN WAS JULY 20.

"Hard to believe she was alive just a few days ago," Bay said.

Beneath the banner was Mavis's own profile, a large green Edit button positioned in the top right-hand corner. She described herself as *outgoing and vivacious...an artist in love with life...a successful businesswoman.* "I'm interested in people," she wrote, "which means I'm interested in anything people do." Her ideal man was "cultured and athletic...someone whose perfect day would include a hike in the morning, a museum in the afternoon, a concert in the evening, a glass of fine wine under the stars."

"That describes exactly no one for about two hundred miles," Bay said.

"I think Mavis was happy to travel."

She'd shaved a few years from her age, trimmed off a pound or two, but the photo looked current. As a kind of flourish, she wrote: "I promise not to judge you. I don't care about your flaws, as long as you promise not to cover them up." And then, the fine print: "If you do not already have a profile, please include a photo with your e-mail. E-mails with no profile link and no photo will be deleted."

"She had a gift for irony," Raney said.

"Or else she couldn't tell when the lies stopped."

Beneath her profile were two columns: on the left, links to pages she'd visited; on the right, a short list of members recommended by FiftyPlus based on her recent activity.

"Let's see if Mavis reached out to any stocky bald men," Raney said.

He started clicking. The photos were hard to read. Most of the men posted head shots that revealed little about their heft or height. The few who were bald gave specs that made them too tall or short, fat or thin.

"He could be wearing a toupee," Bay said. "If Mavis went with Bob Sims, she wouldn't have minded a bit."

Beyond their photos and occupations, there was little to distinguish one candidate from the next. They were divorced or widowed, had grown or almost-grown children, loved dogs and nature and good books. They were teachers, librarians, journalists, photographers. All vaguely literary or artistic. They were Jack's opposite: men who fit the life Mavis wished she'd had.

"Who knew there were so many of us out there?" Bay said.

"Us?"

"Single men over fifty living in the state of New Mexico."

"You getting ideas?"

"Maybe."

Raney navigated back to the home page. At the bottom right, beneath the column of recommendations, was another green icon labeled MESSAGE CENTER.

"How will we know it's him when we find him?" Bay asked.

"There were two coffee cups on the kitchen table the night Mavis was killed, two wineglasses in the sink. We know now that the second person wasn't Kurt. So it must have been our man. He wasn't hiding in the bushes. He was invited. He was lying in wait, but he was doing it in plain sight."

"And he knew what he was lying in wait for cause he was the one who called the Mexies."

"Must be."

"You think he started this whole fucking thing? You think he planted the idea to kill Jack?"

"Planted it or made it seem like a real possibility."

"Sounds like a lot of work. The guy knows how to handle himself. Why not just hijack the Mexie kids before they ever get to the bunker? Leave Jack and Mavis out of it."

"There's something personal here. Something emotional."

"Maybe it's got to do with the guy they killed in Boston."

"Maybe."

They read backwards from the morning of her death to the approximate date of Jack's entombment. She'd received more than a hundred messages from sixty different candidates. Most were easy to eliminate:

Dear Maves,

U r yourself an artwork. Let's meat.

N.D.

Dear Mavis,

You are a beautiful woman, and we have many interests in common, but before I go any further I must know: Do you accept Jesus Christ as your savior?

Ian R.

"I guess it beats sitting down with these guys," Bay said. "Hell, I might look damn good in their company."

"It's like applying for jobs," Raney said. "The CV doesn't matter if you botch the cover letter."

There were only six men Mavis corresponded with regularly in the period leading up to Jack's death. Four signed with their first names, two with their initials. Raney clicked back through the profiles Mavis had visited; of the six men on the list, one was Native American, another black. Only one taught art in an Albuquerque public school.

"We'll start with him," Raney said.

"Joseph V.?"

"Mavis told Clara she was chatting with a teacher."

"That would make for a nice cover," Bay said. "You wouldn't expect your kid's homeroom monitor to turn special ops for a summer."

"Do me a favor. Give your tech friend Joseph V.'s address and ask him to track down where his e-mails were sent from. Not just one of them, but as many as he can."

"All right. But don't get too far ahead of me."

Raney isolated the messages from Joseph V. in Mavis's in-box. There were eighty-five total, the oldest sent six weeks before her death:

Dear Mavis,

I can say with all honesty that you are the only woman on this site whom I have felt compelled to contact. If you read my profile, you'll see that we have much in common. You're an artist; I teach art (K–12). I also have a small (emphasis on small) collection of artworks gathered from the smattering of cities I've been fortunate enough to visit: Tokyo, Sydney, New York, and a few others. I'm nearing retirement, and my greatest ambition for the coming years is to travel more, preferably in the company of someone who shares my passion for beauty and culture.

*Of course, I don't mean to get ahead of myself. We should prob-
ably start with a cup of coffee. :)*

I very much hope to hear from you.

Best wishes,
Joseph V.

Mavis's response:

Dear Joseph,

*I don't see why we shouldn't get coffee! And if coffee in Albuquerque
leads to coffee in Paris, so much the better! I believe people should
say what they want right from the start, especially those of us who
are looking at fifty in the rearview mirror.*

*I'm guessing you're on summer break. Where and when would
you like to meet? I more or less make my own schedule, as long as
the girl who works for me can cover the store.*

So glad you reached out—

Mavis W.

It took a short exchange of messages to nail down a place and
time. Then, a few days later, this from Joseph:

Dear Mavis,

*I agree with you: people our age should know what they want, and
they should say it. When I think about my retirement, when I allow myself to dream about it, I know I want nothing but days like*

*the one we just spent together. Only I want each day to be a little
bit different. Maybe we drink tea instead of coffee; maybe we drink
white wine instead of red. Or maybe every day happens fifty miles
south of the day before, until we get to Buenos Aires. Maybe we land
there and never leave. It sounds like I'm spinning fantasies, but I
know this: a day with you has me wound up like a teenager.*

Until next time, which I hope will be very soon,
J. V.

Bay sat back down beside Raney.

"The kid's on it," he said. "I miss anything?"

"They met for coffee here in Albuquerque. He's working her
pretty hard."

Bay slapped Raney on the back.

"We're closing in," he said. "I feel it."

"Let's keep reading."

Over the next few weeks, Mavis and Joseph V. e-mailed one
another every few hours. They swapped love notes. He sent her
a video of a tango lesson, an advertisement for a dance school in
Buenos Aires. She sent him photos of paintings she claimed were
her own, though Raney recognized them from Clara's studio.
They made plans to spend a full weekend together. The following
Monday, Joseph wrote:

Mavis,

*I have thought about it, and while there are lies I might be able to
tolerate, this is not one of them. I'm sorry, but I stand by what I
said earlier.*

J. V.

Mavis's response:

Dearest Joseph,

I was so afraid of this. I was trying to tell you that my marriage isn't a real marriage. It never was. Yes, I go home to another man, but not to his bed. Not to his love. Not to his companionship. Please agree to see me just one more time. I'm not good with words like you are. This is more than I can manage over the computer.

Love,
Mavis

"Trouble in paradise," Bay said.
"He's turning the focus to Jack," Raney said.
"If this is our guy."
"If it is."
Mavis and Joseph met at a Mexican bar in Santa Fe. Afterward, Joseph forgave her, turned apologetic:

It was wrong of me to judge you. I had no idea what you'd been through, what you continue to endure. I'm glad Jack was there when you needed him. But that was four decades ago. Nothing excuses the man he is today.

"She told him," Bay said.
"She told him something. Maybe some version of the truth. A parallel version."

"Parallel how?"

"Maybe Stewart turned violent during sex. Maybe Jack saved her life, her dignity. They moved out here to heal. But they grew apart. Jack took to drink. He became mean."

"So she's lying to him, and he knows she's lying, but he pretends not to know, which is another lie," Bay said. "Makes you wonder if you ever heard a true word."

There was a spate of forwarded articles and jokes, more sweet nothings, a promise to let Mavis visit one of his art classes. They spent a second weekend together. Both signed their e-mails "Love."

And then, two weeks before Mavis's nine-one-one call:

Dear Cheryl,

You see, I've learned something about you. About you and Jonathan. I didn't mean to, and I wish to God I hadn't. I wish to God it weren't true. I've never been so devastated.

This isn't something I want to discuss here or over the phone. Come to my place tonight.

I know I shouldn't give you this chance. I know I should call the authorities straightaway.

J.V.

"This is him," Bay said. "It's got to be. He's on his way to blackmailing her — 'lock that bunker door or die in jail.' She half wanted to kill Jack anyway."

"Maybe," Raney said. "Let's see if the tech found any hits."

"I'll go get him," Bay said.

Raney searched "Joseph V" in the Albuquerque public school directory. Only one name came up: Joseph Vignola. He checked the White Pages, found a J. Vignola living on the outskirts of the city.

Too easy, he thought. Too easy by far.

He knew before he searched that he wouldn't find a single image of Joseph Vignola, art teacher, anywhere on the Web. The stocky bald man had grafted himself onto a faceless virtual imprint.

Bay came bounding back.

"The messages were sent from libraries all over town. Even a few in Santa Fe."

"Makes sense," Raney said. "Our man isn't dumb."

"We got him," Bay said.

"I'm not sure."

"What do you mean?"

"There's a real Joseph Vignola teaching art in Albuquerque, but he didn't send these messages."

"You positive?"

"There's only one way to find out," Raney said. "Let's go knock on his door."

27

Dunham watched Dizzy pull out and drive away before he drew down the door.

"Time to work," he said. "We're going to do this right here."

They filled four duffel bags, hooked one strap over each shoulder, climbed the steps to the loading dock. Dunham unlocked the door and flicked a switch. Inside was a seemingly endless space broken into workstations, each with its own machinery. The place smelled like it had been hosed down with bleach.

"I'd give you a tour," Dunham said. "But what the fuck do I know about glass?"

Raney followed him through a maze of furnaces and conveyor belts.

"That foreman I mentioned? He's the guy you beat the shit out of. Spike. This started as his parole gig. Now he's boss of the worker bees. I said I needed a space to get some shit done. I didn't say what shit, but unless you damaged his brain he must have more or less figured it out. Spike wouldn't set me up, though. He's the only one of my fighters who wouldn't. That's why I let him come back. Normally, one loss and they're finished. I wish you'd taken that Cobra prick. The guy's a colossal fuck-up, and he's boring as hell to watch. But rules are rules. I can't cut him loose until someone puts him down."

The drafting table sat in a workstation at the far end of the floor. Dunham had adjusted the surface so it lay flat, stocked the cubicle with Saran wrap, razor blades, baking soda, duct tape.

"The morning crew gets in at five. We've got about four hours of work here, so let's keep the bathroom breaks to a minimum. If someone shows early, they'd have to make it across the floor before they got to us. In which case we clean up fast, and I drop Spike's name."

He measured out two sheets of Saran wrap, sliced open a brick, spilled half onto his sheet and the other half onto Raney's.

"That's a pretty big cut," Raney said.

"Yeah, and the bitch of it is, Farlow's inbreeds will step on it again. The tree people of Maine are in for a very slight buzz."

They worked in quiet until the chopping and sifting and wrapping turned rhythmic and the bricks seemed to materialize on their own.

"I must have done this a thousand times," Dunham said, "but never for myself. If this goes right, it could be the start of a new era. The Dunham era. No more whipping boy. I gotta give props, Deadly: I'm glad you knocked me off that stool. I owe you. Don't think I don't know. I'm not like my douche-bag uncle. I won't hold you down so you have to keep coming back. You'll get a third of everything. And if one day you've had enough, you just walk away. I won't come after you. Not unless you talk, which I know you'd never do. I'll admit I had my doubts with the Mora situation, but then I thought about it. You and him were both fighters. That's like a brotherhood. So shaking the guy down was hard for you. You're loyal. I get it. I'm loyal, too. And I mean to people, not just money. This isn't an in-for-life thing we have here. It's time for that old-school bullshit to die a fast death. If a guy wants to move on, I say let him move on. As long as he's not fucking you over."

"So these jobs we've been doing have all been for your uncle?"

"Like you didn't know. When you showed up looking for work, I wondered about that. If you knew who I was, then you knew who he was. So why come to me and not him? Then I figured it was a parole thing. You ain't looking to do your full bit, so why not pick the guy who's already buried? Meno's got eyes on him twenty-four seven. You made the smart move."

Meno, Raney thought. It's out in the open now.

They drove in two cars, Raney carrying one duffel bag, Dunham the others. Two traffic jams, two stops for gas, one meal at a drive-through, three lines of coke. Nine hours total. They set the meet in a state park, at a campground just off the coast. Raney pulled in first. Dunham hung back, parked in a spread of beach grass. If the buyers seemed legit, Raney would wave him on. If they didn't, Dunham would have Raney's back.

There were three of them gathered around a fire and drinking from oversized aluminum cans. They'd pitched a tent, parked a rusted-out pickup on the periphery. Anyone driving by would see a clutch of good old boys kicking back on a weekend afternoon. They even looked like a brood Farlow might have sprung from:

tall and burly, with the same dull-brown hair. DA Stone was thorough, even on short notice.

He pulled straight up to the fire. The undercovers fanned out around his car, two with hunting rifles, the third with a shotgun. Raney rolled down his window. The one with the shotgun moved closer. Raney kept his hands on the wheel. For a moment he forgot he was dealing with cops, forgot he was a cop himself.

"I thought there was two of you," the man said.

"Dunham's hanging back. I'm Raney."

"You mean Dixon? We saw a picture. Step on out. Let's make this look right."

Raney put his hands on the hood, took his turn being patted down.

"What should I call you?" Raney asked.

"You don't call me shit."

"You local?"

"We work the Bronx. Different precincts. Now open the trunk."

"I've got to see the money first."

"Back of the pickup. Look but don't touch."

Raney started for the truck. The two with rifles watched him. The one who did the talking searched the dirt road beyond the campsite.

"I see him," he said. "It really just the two of you?"

"Yeah."

"The guy's got balls."

Raney gave the signal. Dunham coasted in, took a long sip from a twenty-ounce coffee, and stepped from the car. The lead undercover leveled his shotgun.

"Whoa there, boss," Dunham said. "I come in peace."

"You'll leave in pieces you don't take it nice and slow."

Raney noticed an abrupt shift in accent, from the Bronx to northern New England.

"A punster," Dunham said. "I like it. Sorry if I move too quick. Must be a city thing."

"That some kind of crack?"

"Nah—you kidding me? It's beautiful here. You can smell Canada."

"Put your hands up there on the hood."

"I'm not going to do that," Dunham said.

"Come again?"

"I don't like men with beards touching me. It's a thing. You want to know what I got on me, just ask."

"How about I save myself some money and squeeze this trigger?"

"You could do that. But then this would be a one-time deal, which you don't want. Plus you'd have the hassle of getting rid of the bodies. The cars, too. And there are people who know where I am and who I'm with. Shoot me and chances are you won't live out the week. So the Glock I'm carrying stays where it is."

"You're a cocky SOB."

"Yeah, people don't like me. So let's just swap what we have to swap and I'll get the fuck out of your ponytail."

The lead undercover spat tobacco.

"One of you boys fetch that sack."

The man nearest the pickup pulled out a green trash bag with stretch marks at the handle. He walked over, threw it at Dunham's feet.

"I don't bite," Dunham said.

"You did, I'd put you down."

Dunham grinned.

"If you plan on counting it," the lead said, "then get started. Meanwhile have your boy here fetch us what's ours."

Dunham opened the bag, peered inside.

"You heard him, boy," he said. "Fetch."

An hour later, they were sitting in Dunham's car, snorting blow and sharing a drive-through combo meal.

"This is solid," Dunham said. "This could keep us earning for a long time. The hardest part is driving the speed limit."

"I thought the hardest part was staying up forty-eight hours straight."

"Don't whine, Deadly. I know you've never seen a payday anywhere near this one. Tomorrow you can go back to sleeping in."

Raney smiled.

"How do you plan to spend yours?"

"I been thinking about that. We have to put aside enough for the next shipment. The class move would be to launder the rest in real estate. But I've got other projects I need to fund."

"What projects?"

"Just one, really. And it's more of a war than a project."

"A war?"

"Call it a hostile takeover. The kind of hostility I have in mind costs money. And then when it's done, you've gotta be able to show the soldiers left standing that you'll look after them better than the last guy. You've got to show them there was a reason for doing what you did."

"Jesus. You're talking about your uncle."

"The prick has been tops on my list ever since my aunt married him. A guy threatens to kill you enough times and you have to figure that sooner or later he'll get around to it. I've got nothing to lose and a fuckload to gain."

"Why move now?"

"Cause I've got two things I never had before: steady capital and a general."

"A general?"

"General Deadly. You ready for battle?"

28

Joseph Vignola lived in an adobe bungalow at the end of a cul-de-sac. The lights were on in the front of the house. A Subaru sedan sat in the driveway, its back window covered in pine needles.

"Looks like he's home," Bay said. "What do we do when he answers?"

"If he's six foot seven and rail thin, we ask if he's seen anyone suspicious in the neighborhood and hope he says no."

"And if he's short, bald, and stocky?"

"Then we hope he doesn't kill us."

The steps were lined with potted cacti. Plants hung in baskets on either side of the door. Bay rang the bell.

"Police, Mr. Vignola. Open up."

No answer. Bay waited, then knocked on the door with the side of his fist.

"You think he's ducking us?"

"Maybe he's in the shower. I'll go have a look in back."

"Shouldn't we stick together?"

"He's a schoolteacher, Bay. This isn't the guy."

There was no fence sectioning off the yard, just a long open space shared by the neighbors on either side. Vignola was allotted a small patio furnished with lawn chairs and a barbecue. The vertical blinds over the sliding glass door were drawn, but the door was open. Raney parted the slats, called hello. No response. He stepped inside.

An island separated a kitchen to the left from a dining area to the right. A small metal wine rack hung above the island. The counters and cabinet tops were covered with misshapen vases and imperfectly glazed bowls. More student work hung on the far wall. Some of the paintings were framed.

Raney stepped through an arched doorway and into the living area.

"Mr. Vignola," he called.

He saw the blood before he saw the body, pools and rivulets blending with the Saltillo tile. A man was bound to a plain wooden chair in the center of the room, zip ties around his hands and feet, rope holding up his torso. Raney pulled his gun, kept an eye on the staircase to his right as he walked a wide circle around the blood, then stood in front of a partially dismembered Joseph Vignola—toes severed, nose and one ear gone, penis fitted through the loops where his belt buckle should have been. His T-shirt was torn down the front, and there was a nail hammered into his chest. A small, clear Baggie filled with white powder hung from the nail.

Bay rapped on the window. Raney holstered his gun, opened the door.

"I'm not sure you want to see this," he said.

"See what? I thought we were ID'ing a schoolteacher."

"We were."

"Don't treat me with kid gloves, Raney."

"Suit yourself."

He stepped aside.

"Jesus, Mary, and . . ."

Bay stopped himself.

"Makes a slit throat look like a love tap," he said.

"He took his time with this one," Raney said. "There was no Rivera to interrupt him."

"How much of it do you figure happened while he was alive?"

"All of it, except maybe the nail. Looks like he stopped when Vignola stopped breathing. He left an ear intact, didn't touch the fingers."

"We couldn't have missed him by much."

"Hard to say. A few hours. Maybe more."

Bay bent forward, inspected the Baggie.

"Well, we found about an ounce of our missing dope."

"Yeah. Let's hope it doesn't all turn up the same way."

"I've got to call this in. We're out of jurisdiction here."

"All right," Raney said. "I'm going to take a look around."

"Shouldn't we wait for the locals?"

"He isn't waiting for us."

The second floor was carpeted. Raney slipped out of his boots, took a pair of latex gloves from his pocket. Family pictures hung in the hallway, one of a young man who could only be Vignola dressed in cap and gown and flanked by beaming parents. The young Vignola was handsome, with a cleft in his chin and long dark bangs sweeping over his forehead. He looked happy, full of promise. His mother and father each had an arm around him, his father's large hand gripping the boy's shoulder, pulling him close.

The first door on the left opened to a small bedroom so tidy and impersonal that Raney wondered if Vignola rented it out. The dresser drawers were empty, the closet stocked with linens. A print of one of Monet's water-lily paintings hung above the bed. Raney moved on. In the bathroom at the end of the hallway, he found prescription bottles of Amitiza, Klonopin, Ambien: bad stomach, bad nerves, bad sleep. He ran a gloved finger over the labels, left the bottles in the cabinet.

Vignola had done most of his living in the master bedroom. A cluttered desk with an ancient-looking computer took up one corner. The bed was unmade, the floor littered with laundry. On the nightstand, framed photos of Vignola with another man stood arranged in a progression that looked to span more than twenty years. The oldest showed them holding hands at the Grand Canyon; the most recent showed them kissing on the steps of Notre Dame. Physically, the boyfriend was Vignola's opposite: short, blond, overweight. A single white candle and a plain silver ring sat among the photos. A final portrait hung on the wall above the shrine. It was taken in black-and-white and showed Vignola's lover sitting up in his hospital bed, a bandanna wrapped around his forehead, tubes running from his veins. The man did not appear afraid or angry or in pain. Instead, his expression was loving, tender. He was looking somewhere to the left of the camera. At Joseph. Somehow there could be no doubt.

Raney turned to the dresser, uncovered a small bag of weed tucked into a pile of sweaters, a bong stashed beneath a column of neatly folded boxer shorts. Klonopin, Ambien, marijuana. Had the anxiety started before or after his partner died?

In the walk-in closet, Raney found a long shelf dedicated exclusively to high school yearbooks. He took one up, memorized the name and address of the school, read through the inscriptions:

Mr. V., Thank you for all your support and kindness over the last four years. You're the only one of them who's one of us.

Mr. V., This place would suck without you. It sucks with you, but a lot less.

Mr. V., I never knew my art was any good until you told me. Thank you again for everything. I won't forget.

Raney heard the sirens arriving out front. He peered from behind the window shade: squad cars, an ambulance, a fire truck. Why did they always send a fire truck? He hurried downstairs, slipped back into his boots.

"Here's the cavalry," Bay said.

"You think you can handle them without me?"

"Where are you going?"

"Vignola's school."

"It's summer."

"I'm looking for the after-school crowd."

"All right," Bay said. "I'll show them in."

"I hope he fought," Raney said. "I hope he at least took a swipe at the bastard."

He walked back through the sliding doors, sprinted until he reached the main avenue.

The school looked urban, institutional—not unlike the high school Raney attended. A chain-link fence marked the periphery of a concrete yard comprising basketball courts on one side, handball courts on the other. Raney tucked his tie into his jacket pocket, undid the top buttons of his shirt. There were groups of teenage boys scattered across the lot, some playing Hacky Sack, some on skateboards, some mixing with adults in a game of pickup basketball. He saw only one girl. She sat alone on a bench, wearing a pair of old-fashioned Rollerblades. Raney walked over to her, smiled, held out his badge. She'd been watching the boys on skateboards take turns jumping over a grocery cart. Raney startled her. She stood, tried to speed off, but instead fell face-forward, scraping her hands. She rose to a crouch and glanced around, hoping Raney was the sole witness. He helped her up, set her back on the bench.

"Are you all right?" he asked.

"I'm fine," she said.

She was plump, heavily freckled, wore long sleeves and leggings in late July. Public school had not been kind.

"I really am a cop," Raney said. "All I want is to ask a few questions about one of your teachers."

She seemed suddenly more alert.

"Which one?"

"Mr. Vignola."

"The art teacher?"

"Yes. Have you taken any of his classes?"

"Not yet. Freshmen are only allowed to take one elective, and I chose band."

"So you're going to be a sophomore?"

"Yes. Is Mr. V. in trouble?"

"He hasn't done anything wrong," Raney said. "What can you tell me about him?"

"He's the most popular teacher here. You have to submit a portfolio just to get into his classes, and even then there's a waiting list."

"You don't seem surprised that I'm asking about him."

She rolled her eyes.

"What is it I'm missing?"

"Mr. V. is a mellow guy," she said. "A *really* mellow guy."

"I see. And everyone knows how he got to be so mellow?"

"It's practically the first thing you hear about freshman year."

"What do you hear, exactly?"

"That he grows the weed himself and shares it with seniors at graduation. Not every senior—just his favorites. He has a party for them at his house."

She remembered who Raney was, changed her tone:

"But it's just a rumor," she said. "No one with any brains believes it. I mean, they'd fire him, and he's been here, like, since before I was born."

"Don't worry," Raney said. "I'm not that kind of police."

"Then what kind are you?"

"Just an ordinary detective."

He saw her suspicion come rushing back.

"It's almost dinner," she said. "I've got to go."

"Thank you for your help."

He watched her skate awkwardly away, found himself calculating the difference in age between her and Luisa Gonzalez: three, maybe four years. He made a silent wish for his own daughter.

It was nine o'clock before they cleared Santa Fe.

"On the way up here," Bay said, "you were telling me about a guy named Dunham."

"It's been a long day," Raney said. "I don't think I can——"

"I've just got one thing to say."

"What's that?"

"Some situations can't be helped. Not past the first step you take. And you always think that first step is the right one. At least you do when you're young."

"Meaning?"

"I enlisted in Vietnam. Uncle Sam didn't have to come chasing me down. I was eighteen and stupid and hadn't traveled more than a hundred square miles in my life. Six months later I'm in the jungle with a group of guys I don't much care for, least of all the one in charge. We were tracking some VC who'd shot at us while we were passing through what we thought was a deserted village. After a while, we come across this cave. It was tall and wide and you could see it was deep, but you couldn't see very far inside. The sergeant waved me and another private over and ordered us to take aim and empty our magazines. We had a damn good idea there were people from that village holed up in there. Women and kids and civilians. But this was what we'd signed on for. We just didn't know it at the time."

He looked over at Raney.

"You see what I'm saying? You think you're choosing one thing, and you think you have a clear notion of what that thing will be. But you're a kid and you don't have a goddamn clue. You make that first choice, and then the rest are made for you. The only thing you could have done different was not be there in the first place."

"Does that make you feel better?" Raney said.

"Sometimes," Bay said.

"The cave might have been empty."

"Funny: that's what Mavis said."

"Mavis?"

"She was the only one who'd listen. It embarrasses the hell out of me now. It's so damn clear. I was a mark. The whole thing was probably Jack's idea. Keep someone from the sheriff's office close. All it took was one corny-ass line: 'Deputy Bay, why is it you look so sad all the time?' And then I'm telling her about parachuting into a mud pit and getting ambushed at the latrine. My mouth wouldn't stop running. She was the only one who wanted to hear it. Or pretended to.

"I was their lookout, and I had no idea. If a wire came from

Boston, she knew I'd tell her. But then the wire never came, and she must have gotten bored with me. I threatened to kill Jack when she broke it off. She just looked at me and said, 'You're not going to kill anyone.' That was the end of it."

"Must have stung," Raney said.

"Like hell."

Raney stared out the window, squinted a distant light into focus.

"There's something I never told you," he said.

"What's that?"

"I have a daughter."

Bay smiled. "You're shitting me."

"I think that's what she would say if I introduced myself. I've never laid eyes on her. Never heard her voice. Her mother and grandfather didn't want me near her. I guess I thought they were right."

"So you came out here?"

"That's the condensed version."

"So she's . . ."

"Eighteen. Give or take a few months."

Raney expected silence, recrimination.

"I'm sorry," Bay said. "That's tough. Damn tough. I hope you meet her someday. I hope she gets to meet you. I really do. It's too late for some things, but there's plenty that hasn't started yet."

"Less every day," Raney said.

29

He sat with Dunham in a windowless room off the kitchen, a bottle of white wine and a bowl of mussels on the table between them, a recorder strapped to his chest. He felt out of sync with his surroundings—found himself shivering though the room was warm, squinting though the light was soft. He couldn't tell if he needed more or had taken too much.

"The joint's jumping," Dunham said.

There was a sextet onstage. Their playing filtered through the kitchen, muted but clear. Dunham's right leg kept pace with the drummer. The house knew when to applaud.

Dunham used the shell of one mussel to pluck out another.

"Pierre says this is what French kings used to eat when they sat down with their ministers. I think he's full of shit, but I'm not complaining."

"So now I'm a minister?"

"There can only be one king, Deadly. That's why we're here."

Raney filled their glasses.

"You said you have a plan."

"I think you're going to like it. We use our hillbilly money to pull together a crew. I'm thinking twenty guys, five groups of four. We hit my uncle five different places on the same night at the same time. We make it a bloodbath. Gut his operation inside of an hour. Then we watch whatever rats are left jump ship."

"Why not just take him out?"

"I thought about that. It's no good if we leave his army in play. They might have different ideas about who steps up. They'd come after me for sure. We've got to wipe the whole slate clean."

Raney thought: So you and Stone want the same thing.

"Where do we get this crew?" Raney asked.

"We need ghosts," Dunham said. "Out-of-towners. Hired guns who'll be here and gone. Minimize the locals, and you minimize the chance of a tip-off."

"Twenty is a big number. You have anyone in mind?"

"We'd have to pull from all over. Twenty guys who know each other could be just as bad as leaving Meno's boys intact. Maybe we start with the hillbillies. You think they'd be up for some big-city hunting? They looked sad they didn't get to kill us."

"Wouldn't that be shitting where we eat?" Raney said. "Anything goes sideways, and we lose our funding."

"You have a better idea?"

"We could reach out to gangs from around the country. Detroit, Chicago, Cleveland, Houston, LA. Tell them we want their best and brightest for a night."

"We'd get a bunch of fuck-up street kids."

"Not if we stick with one percenters."

"Bikers?"

"They're disciplined. They know to keep their mouths shut. And they're used to consequences if they don't get results."

"You have a way in?"

"I'm thinking Farlow could make a few introductions."

"Outside of New York?"

"They have chapters around the country. Every year they pick some small town for their get-together and turn the citizens' lives to shit for a week. They all know each other. They share business. That's how the feds hit the Hells Angels with RICO violations."

"Those charges didn't hold up."

"Because no one broke rank."

"All right," Dunham said. "It's an option. Talk to Farlow. See what he gives you. I'll ask around on my end. I want this to go quick. Fucking Meno's got spies everywhere."

"I'll get with Farlow tomorrow."

"Good," Dunham said. "Now let's adjourn with a little blow."

Raney saw it: five groups of undercovers sweeping up Meno's organization in a single night. Stone would see it, too. For Dunham's plan to work, he'd have to give Raney every detail: locations, activities, people involved. Raney would have Dunham dishing up Meno on tape. Let Dunham think they were plotting a massacre while really they were planning the largest sweep in city history.

He spent that night listening to the recording, memorizing it, making one duplicate after another. Dunham's voice echoed through his barely furnished apartment while Raney did jumping jacks and ran in place, convinced that if he sat still his body would shut down, that he would become, like Dunham, nothing more than sound in an empty room.

He called the DA from a pay phone in Brooklyn, hung up on the machine, tried again. He left a message telling Stone to expect another early morning visit.

"It's blown open," he said.

He swallowed four benzos, slept in his clothes, fought his way conscious when the alarm sounded. Driving up the West Side Highway, he imagined Stone's reaction as he listened to the tape: disbelief giving way to quiet exhilaration, a stern effort to keep himself in check. Dunham had laid it all out so clearly that there would be little to add. Stone might fret about manpower and logistics, but he would come around quickly: play it right, and they'd have Meno and the bulk of his organization in lockup by the end of the month.

He parked three blocks shy of Stone's apartment, stopped to pick up an assortment of bagels and two extra-large coffees. He crested a hill, saw the avenue below blocked off with sawhorses and squad cars. An ambulance sat on the sidewalk in front of Stone's building, its back doors propped open. Reporters and camera crews lined up behind yellow tape. The chief of police stood by the entrance, waving in a platoon of detectives. Raney backed away, dropped the coffees and bagels in a trash can, sprinted for the nearest phone booth.

The desk sergeant at his old precinct confirmed what he already knew: Stone was dead. He'd been executed, shot in the forehead at point-blank range in the lobby of his building, dressed for his morning run. The doorman, the only witness, had also been killed. The sergeant couldn't say anything more.

Raney ripped the handset from its cord, beat the receiver against the cradle until the plastic shattered. Passersby slowed to watch.

He drove south, then north again, thinking, or failing to move past a single thought: Stone's active cases would stall. They'd find an underling to tread water until a new DA was appointed.

Raney would be pulled back into rotation, maybe busted down to patrol. If Stone kept detailed notes, they might cut him loose altogether, save the department the embarrassment of a trial. The immediate priority would be to find the killer, but without a living witness the field was wide open: Stone had filing cabinets' worth of enemies.

He felt a sudden need to hear Sophia's voice. He called from a bodega in midtown. An automated message said the number had been disconnected. He dialed again, listened to the same message a second time.

He drove to her apartment in Brooklyn Heights, the apartment she'd bought with her father's money, the apartment they'd lived in together for more than a year. He jogged up three flights, found that his key no longer fit the lock. He rang the bell, beat on the door. No answer. He shouted her name. An elderly neighbor eyeballed him from across the hall.

"Oh, it's you," she said. "I thought you were long gone."

"What does that mean?" Raney said.

She stared at him without blinking.

"Tell me what that means."

He started toward her. She retreated inside, clicked a series of bolts into place.

Raney did a line on the staircase, then got back on the BQE, headed for Queens.

Ferguson answered the door himself, a cigar in his mouth, Jake running circles at his side.

"Where's Sophia?" Raney said.

"Where she always is at this hour: work. If you really wanted to see her, that's where you'd be."

"I called. They said she was in the field."

"Then she's in the field."

"Why did she change the locks? Why is the phone dead?"

"I think that's obvious. Come in. I'll get you a cup of coffee. You look like you need it."

"I don't want coffee. Just tell me what's going on."

"Not here. I can't have hysterical young men standing on my stoop in the middle of the day. Come inside."

Raney fended Jake off with one arm, shut the door behind him. "Tell me why Sophia . . ."

"You aren't here about my daughter," Ferguson said. "I'm not a fool. Stone is dead. You don't know where to turn. Now keep my dog entertained while I brew a pot."

Raney sat cross-legged on the floor, holding one end of a frayed rope toy while the ex-captain's Irish setter tugged at the other. A public radio station echoed through the living room. A cross section of pundits debated whether or not it was too early to consider Stone's legacy. They were all talking at once. Raney couldn't tell if they were angry at each other or at Stone. Ferguson came back carrying a small tray.

"Looks like Jake is winning," he said.

He seemed smug, satisfied. Stone was one more person he'd outlived. He set the tray on the coffee table, silenced the radio with a remote control. They sat opposite one another in the same overstuffed armchairs they'd occupied the last time Raney was there. Jake tried to climb on Raney's lap. Ferguson clapped his hands.

"Go lie down," he said.

The dog obeyed. Raney wiped slobber from his jeans.

"Jake's a good judge of character," Ferguson said. "So is my daughter. That's why you're sitting here. But this conversation is the end of your involvement with my family. You've backed yourself into a situation, Detective, and I don't want my daughter anywhere near it."

"She can decide for herself," Raney said.

"If I were a plumber, that might be true. But I can make things happen. I can stop things from happening. I worked my entire life for that privilege, and I intend to use it liberally in whatever time I have left."

"We love each other," Raney said.

"Nonsense," Ferguson said. "Love is just biology making fools of us."

Raney pushed himself up.

"I shouldn't have come here," he said.

"But you did," Ferguson said. "So sit. I'll do the talking. I'll make it short."

Raney sat.

"Good boy," Ferguson said. "Now let me tell you about the bind you're in. You're looking for a way to save yourself and still bring Meno and Dunham to trial. You've invested a lot, and you want to come out the hero."

"I want to do my job. I want to finish what I started."

"Fair enough. But how many laws have you broken along the way? Stone had your back. He told himself he put justice above the law. Really, he put his own ambition above everything and everyone. If you brought Meno and Dunham in now, you'd have no protection. Either they'd walk, or you'd end up sharing the same cell block."

"Who will protect me if I don't bring them in?"

"Why do you think I had Sophia change the locks? I plan to sell that apartment and move her to a different borough. We live in a city where the DA is fair game. They'll come after you without a second thought. If they can't get you, they'll get whoever you care about. As far as I know, that's one person in the world: my daughter."

"You keep saying *they*. There's Dunham. That's it."

"And if something happens to Dunham now, you don't think Meno will play the good uncle? In private, he'll be grateful, but he'll have to keep up appearances, if only to make his wife happy. You didn't realize how much you had riding on one man. Without Stone, you're at sea in two worlds. You have no one to exfiltrate you from one, no one to welcome you home in the other."

"So what are my options?"

"There's always Canada."

"You know I wouldn't."

"I know," Ferguson said. "I almost pity you. You feel the walls closing in. How do you relieve that pressure?"

"What would you do?"

"What would *they* do? I mean Meno or Dunham or any of their ilk. I told you before: if you see an opportunity, take it. Now you have to make an opportunity. Get them in the same room. Finish this."

"Is that what you did to Bruno?"

"Bruno killed a cop. I did what any officer who ever wore the uniform would have done."

"What would you do to the man who killed a DA?"

"Exactly the same. But I'd need proof. And Stone leaves behind a long list of enemies."

"Including Meno."

"And everyone he prosecuted in the last decade, or was planning to prosecute in the next."

"But Meno's the one *you* want dead."

"Exercise discretion, Detective Raney. I doubt either of us wishes to cause my daughter further pain."

30

Bay pulled up in front of Hotel on Main at a little before midnight.

"We're fucked on this, ain't we?" he said. "The psychopath beat us all the way around."

"We're not done yet."

"Even so, he's had a good run on our watch."

"He has. Get some rest, Bay."

"I plan to. If you need me, I'll be bunking at the station tonight. I'm about to nod off at the wheel."

Raney started for the lobby, then thought better of it. He walked to Clara's apartment, rang the bell, waved when she looked out her window. A light came on in the hallway; her bare feet appeared on the stairs. Her shirt and jeans were spattered in earth tones. A quarter-size gob of brown stuck to her cheek. Raney rubbed it away with his thumb.

"You're painting again," he said.

"Slowly," she said. "Methodically. I don't know how else to pass the time."

"I hope I didn't wake Daniel."

"He's unwakeable."

He waited while she rinsed out her brushes in the kitchen sink, then took a fresh set of clothes into the bathroom. He walked over to the canvas she'd been working on: pockets of color he imagined would coalesce into a landscape.

"Nothing much to see yet," she said. "I'm not sure where that one's going, or if it's going anywhere."

"I know the feeling," Raney said.

She crossed to the small drafting table she used as a desk, pressed a button on her laptop. Django Reinhardt strummed from wall-mounted speakers.

"Is that all right?" she asked.

"It's lovely."

"*Lovely?* That doesn't sound like a Brooklyn word."

"Sorry," Raney said. "I meant fucking lovely."

She smiled, flicked his ear.

"I'll open a few windows," Clara said. "I don't usually smoke so much, but I spent the day planning Mavis's funeral. There's no one else to do it. I have no idea how I'll come up with the money. She died intestate."

"Bob Sims might help," Raney said. "He considers himself charitable."

"Cavalier and charitable aren't the same thing. Besides, he has financial troubles of his own."

"There have to be people willing to pitch in. She lived here forty years."

"But she wasn't the person they thought she was. Word is out. She's a pariah now. I'm not sure there's any point in even having a funeral."

"I don't know. People have a way of rallying round."

"They have a way of showing up," she said. "That's not the same thing."

"Maybe not."

"You want a drink? There's a bottle of white in the fridge. South African."

"Actually," Raney said, "I wouldn't mind smoking a little."

"Are you serious?"

"I met a man today who made me curious."

"This isn't some kind of sting?"

"SWAT's waiting outside the door."

She leaned over the coffee table, rolled a fresh joint, lit it with a candle flame. Raney took a drag, passed it back.

"You didn't cough," she said. "That's impressive."

"Thanks."

"So what do you think?"

"Fucking lovely."

"It doesn't kick in right away, you know."

Raney tried again, held the smoke deep in his lungs before exhaling.

"Who was this man?" Clara asked. "The one who made you curious."

"A schoolteacher."

"Mavis's schoolteacher?"

"I thought so, but I was wrong."

"And he's a pothead?"

"He said he smokes to calm his nerves. Is that why you smoke?"

"Sort of," she said. "I find it slows everything down. Everything seems a little less urgent, a little farther away. I'm less afraid."

"Of?"

"Most days, of losing Daniel."

"I think Daniel is yours for keeps."

"You promise?"

He realized he couldn't. The evidence was overwhelming. Mavis had lost a child. He had lost a child. Clara's father, for better or worse, had lost his children. He felt the pot taking hold. Something blurry came into focus.

"That's what this is about," he said.

"What?"

"A lost child."

"I don't follow."

"Can I borrow your laptop?"

"What's going on?"

"I need to search the Albuquerque obituaries."

He stayed up into the early morning, working at her small kitchen table, adding and deleting bookmarks from a file he labeled BEGINNING. Clara stayed awake with him, painting, taking occasional small drags. Now and again Raney would look up, watch her arm trace an arabesque as she drew the brush back and forth across the canvas. The smell of turpentine kept him alert; the smoke calmed him. He sensed Daniel sleeping quietly nearby. He scrolled through an archive of drug-related headlines, allowed himself to imagine an end to this case, a future beyond it.

31

He drove a half mile from the ex-captain's house, parked, snorted a line off the back of his hand, sat thinking. Ferguson was right about one thing: Stone's death left Raney dangling, exposed. There would be no one now to sign off on Dunham's twenty gang members. Dunham's suspicion would redouble, and when Raney disappeared, Dunham would figure out who he was and hunt him down. He'd take a blowtorch to Mora, choke out the name Wes Raney, then search Mora's amateur records to make sure. He'd kill Sophia just to let Raney know he was coming.

He called Stone's office from a pay phone in Forest Hills, dialed five times before Stone's secretary answered.

"Wes," she said. "I was hoping you'd call."

"How are you holding up, Anat?" Raney asked.

"Right now, I don't have time to think," she said.

"What's it like there?"

"A feeding frenzy. I have a thousand voices shouting in each ear, and not one of them sounds human to me."

"Any chance you can slip away for a minute?"

"I'd like to sprout wings and jump right out the window, but that isn't going to happen."

"It's important. And I can't be seen near the courthouse. There are cameras everywhere."

"Does it have to do with who shot him?"

"I think so."

"You have a lead?"

"It could be nothing," he said. "But I think it's something."

"Tell me what you need."

"A file."

"Hold on a second," Anat said.

Raney heard her talking to a male voice in the background, heard the male voice say something apologetic.

"I'm here," Anat said. "Sometimes interns feel more like un-trained pets than free labor. You said you need a file?"

"Yes."

"Whose?"

"Roy Meno's. I don't need all of it. Just the last month or so. Enough to see how Stone was tracking him."

"Meno's, huh?" Anat said. "I can do that. Where do you want to meet? It has to be close. I can't get away for long."

"There's a loading zone on Park Place, in back of the Wool-worth Building. I'll be there with my hazards on."

"When?"

"Forty minutes?"

"Okay," she said. "Try not to be late."

She was waiting for him when he pulled up, standing at the edge of the sidewalk and smoking an herbal cigarette. It was raining. She wore a slicker and carried an outsized umbrella. Her makeup was running. Her face looked blurred. Raney rolled down his passenger-side window. Anat shut her umbrella, leaned in.

"You can sit," Raney said.

"I have to get back," she said. "Not that I'm doing any good up there. How many times can a person say, 'We have no information beyond what's been reported?'"

"It will get better," he said.

"When?"

"When we have whoever did this in custody."

Anat looked at him as though he'd missed the point. The rumor was true, he thought: she'd been in love with Stone. She took a cluster of manila envelopes from her purse, set them on the passenger seat.

"Meno was his big obsession," she said. "I hope you'll see this through."

"You might be the only one who does."

"I know. You'd better hurry."

"What have you heard?"

"They're going to put a cease-fire on all Stone's cases until they can establish new oversight. That's the phrase they used."

"So I won't answer my phone for a while," Raney said. "I'm in the field. It happens."

"Be careful," she said.

"I will."

Raney watched her walk away, her heels disappearing into pools of water. She didn't bother to open her umbrella.

32

He knocked on Bay's office door, kept knocking until he heard movement inside.

"Who the hell is it?" Bay said.

"Raney. You decent?"

"Depends on your definition. Why didn't you call?"

"I did."

"Then I need a louder goddamn phone. Give me a minute. In fact, why don't you make yourself useful and put on a pot of coffee?"

"I brought you a cup," Raney said.

"Not that diner shit."

"No, sir. Brewed it myself."

The door opened. Bay stood there buttoning his pants with one hand, reaching for the cup with the other. The shades were drawn, the foldout bed unmade. Raney switched on the overhead light. Bay shielded his eyes, cursed.

"So you and Clara are a thing now?" he said.

"What gave it away?"

215

"Hotel soap my ass. Now you're bringing me homemade cof-fee."

"Not much of a morning person, are you?" Raney said.

"This better be good."

"It is."

"So tell me."

"We're headed back to Albuquerque."

"Goddamn it, Raney. When you come waking a man up at five in the morning you'd better give him all the information he needs to fully grasp the situation."

"I found him. He's a widower. His son went to Mesa Heritage High. The son died. By overdose. It has to be him."

"Found him how?" Bay said.

"Take a look."

Raney pulled a printout from his blazer pocket, unfolded it and handed it to Bay. Bay sat at his desk, slid on his glasses.

"It's an op-ed from the Albuquerque *Gazette*," Raney said. "Al-most exactly a year old. There are other articles, but this one spells it out."

Bay read:

HOW MANY TEENS HAVE TO DIE?

There is a sad fact we can no longer afford to deny: the state of New Mexico is in the throes of a major drug epidemic, and the majority of those afflicted are under the age of twenty.

According to state police sergeant Peter Break-stone, more than three hundred teenagers in the Santa Fe–Albuquerque corridor die from drug over-doses every year, and that number is rising.

"Drugs like heroin and cocaine are more accessible to our youth than ever before," says Breakstone. "Dealers are lowering prices in order to compete with designer drugs like Ecstasy. Lowering prices means diluting the product, often with some toxic substance. At the same time, dealers are branching out, targeting affluent neighborhoods. In short, the problem is getting worse, not better."

Jonathan Grant, a seventeen-year-old Albuquerque resident who would have been headed to Carnegie Mellon University in the fall, is the most recent and perhaps the most highly publicized victim. An honor student from a solid middle-class background, Grant, who died after attending a Mesa Heritage High School precollege party in June, had ingested enough cocaine and diazepam to kill a 240-pound man, according to the state autopsy report.

Three of Grant's classmates were also rushed to Presbyterian Hospital. All three survived. Grant, who bought the drugs on the boys' behalf, kept the lion's share for himself.

Grant's father, former Navy SEAL Oscar Grant, has refused all interviews, instead issuing this statement through his lawyer:

Jonathan was a model student, model son, and model citizen. He went to the wrong party with the wrong people. If Jonathan fell victim to the rise of drugs in our community, then so, too, can your child. While I do not want my son to be remembered as the face of a cause, I beg all parents to

*be vigilant, and I beg law enforcement to bear down swiftly
and unequivocally on the criminals who kill our children
for profit.*

Yet Grant, who served in both the invasion of Gre-
nada and the invasion of Panama, has had his own
public battle with substance abuse, and many will
wonder if Jonathan's relationship to narcotics was
hereditary and thus isolated. Oscar Grant was arrested multiple times on drunk and disorderly
charges in the late eighties and early nineties. Most
infamously, he was arrested in 1993 following a bar
brawl that resulted in the hospitalization of local
television anchorman James Pass. Pass, in what
Grant later called a "ratings stunt slash personal
vendetta," petitioned to get Grant treatment for psy-
chological trauma suffered in the line of duty. Grant
spent six months in a facility outside of Denver,
Colorado—six months he later called "a complete
waste of time."

Personal vendetta or not, waste of time or not,
Grant's record has remained clean since his release
nearly twenty years ago, three years before his
son was born. According to Warden Peterson of
the New Mexico Federal Penitentiary, where Grant
served as a sniper until taking early retirement last
fall, Grant was a model employee, doting father,
and loyal friend. "You can look at Jonathan's home
life all you want," Peterson said. "You won't find
anything to explain this away. Oscar kept his son
on the straight and narrow, especially after Lydia

died." Lydia Hoffman Grant, Oscar's wife, died of ovarian cancer just five years after Jonathan was born.

Warden Peterson's comments serve to bolster the essence of Oscar Grant's statement: no one's son or daughter is insulated from the drug infestation ravaging our community. To paraphrase Grant, it is up to us to be vigilant and act swiftly.

"Goddamn it, that fits," Bay said. "SEAL. Sniper. It fits all the way around. Except maybe for the teacher. Why kill him? Why torture him first?"

"We found a bag of weed at Vignola's house. There's a rumor he shared with his students."

"The gateway drug? That's a little thin."

"I'm thinking it went beyond that."

"You mean sex," Bay said. "That would explain the belt buckle. You think Grant was acting on fact or paranoia?"

"Does it matter?"

"No," Bay said. "It's funny: I remember when Grant was arrested. I remember feeling sorry for him. He saw some real shit overseas, and then that douche-bag reporter made a sideshow out of him."

Raney slid a second sheet of paper from his pocket.

"I found a photo," he said. "Of Grant."

Bay held it under his desk lamp, leaned close.

"I'd call that stocky and bald," he said.

"He's our guy," Raney said. "He has to be."

"So what's next?"

"We show Rivera a lineup. An ID will give us enough for a warrant."

"About that," Bay said. "I got some news I probably should've shared straight off. Like you said, I'm not myself at this hour."

"What news is that?"

Bay pressed a button on his office phone. A dull male voice informed Raney that Rivera had passed away at ten the night before.

"Goddamn it," Raney said.

He stood, paced the perimeter of Bay's bed, grinding his palms together.

"This fucks us," he said.

"By the time I heard it, I figured it was too late to call," Bay said.

"Rivera would have been dead whether you called or not."

"I'm thinking there's another way," Bay said.

Raney didn't seem to hear.

"The prints at the Wilkinses' house were all accounted for?" he said.

"They were."

"And they wouldn't have collected his DNA twenty years ago."

"No, they wouldn't have."

"Then everything we've got is circumstantial."

"I'm not so sure," Bay said.

"What do you mean?"

"Maybe I'm not the only one who's groggy this morning."

Bay thumbed through a file on his desk, found the page he was looking for, laid it out beside Grant's photo.

"I had my tech friend print out Mr. Vignola's FiftyPlus profile. You don't have to look very hard to see a resemblance."

Raney moved to Bay's side of the desk, stared over his shoulder.

"Even the moles match," he said.

"Every one of them."

"You think that will be enough for a judge?"

"We'll type it up real pretty. Plus I know the right guy. He's retired down to half duty. Mornings are for golf now, so if we get moving we can be there waiting for him."

Raney squeezed Bay's shoulders.

"You're invaluable, darling," he said.

"What's that, now?"

"A line from a movie I used to watch with my father."

"Raney," Bay said, "if you're calling me a father figure, I'll kick your ass."

33

According to the surveillance reports, Meno spent Friday af-
ternoons in the back room of a café on Steinway Street in
Astoria. A door at the end of a wood-paneled hallway separated
the room from the café proper. Sometimes the door was open,
sometimes closed. Open meant the room was occupied by seniors playing cards or watching soap operas pumped in via
satellite from the old country; closed meant Meno was holding
court. Meno came and went through a rear entrance. The small
lot off the alley was crowded with limousines and hidden by a
seven-foot fence. No one who lived on the block had ever seen
Meno, though everyone knew he was there. Older residents were
grateful because he kept the Egyptians on the other side of 30th
Avenue. Younger residents hoped he might one day do something
to liven up the neighborhood.

Raney passed through the alleyway behind the café, found unmarked cars at either end. There was a third car on Steinway
across from the entrance, sitting in front of a fire hydrant, the

windows rolled down, an elbow in a suit jacket resting on the driver's-side door. Stone's troops continued in his absence, at least for the moment. If they were there, then so was Meno. He must have thought it best not to break routine.

Raney parked on a side street, strolled past the undercovers. There was no one he recognized in any of the vehicles. He bought a can of ginger ale at a corner bodega, walked back to his car, snapped open the lid and dropped in two benzos. He sat behind the wheel, drinking and listening to his conversation with Dunham one more time.

He couldn't bring the tape to Meno as Mike Dixon. Even if he hand-delivered Dunham's head, there would be no reason to keep around a small-time thug with a history of betrayal. But if he approached Meno as a crooked narco—the first cop to reach out now that Stone was dead—he'd have something real to offer. Killing Dunham would be Raney's initiation, proof that he was capable, hands-on. And the badge would be his armor. Meno wouldn't risk offing a cop the day Stone was murdered.

There was a third possibility: hand the tape to the woman behind the counter, tell her to pass it to Meno, then leave before she'd reached the back room. Lay low for a while and watch the bodies fall. But that would put the entire play outside his control. One or the other would be left standing, most likely Meno, though Dunham was resourceful and not nearly as reckless as Raney had been led to believe.

He waited for the benzos to slow his pulse, then secured his gun in the glove compartment, slipped on a pair of sunglasses, and pulled an umbrella from the trunk though the rain had long since stopped. He took a deep breath, dug his badge and handcuffs from a compartment beneath the spare tire, dropped them in his blazer pockets and headed back to the café, umbrella angled toward the cameras.

The front room was shabby, uninviting—poorly laid white tiles on the floor, dropped ceiling, holes in the plaster showing between posters of Italian soccer teams. The tables were empty, the back door closed. Raney shut his umbrella, took off his glasses, wiped his shoes on a cork mat. The old woman behind the counter looked up from her paper, seemed to doubt that serving Raney would alleviate her boredom. Raney held out his badge. She squinted at it through bifocals. The shield felt new again in his palm, awkward: He was Mike Dixon impersonating an officer.

"Free," she said. "Espresso, cappuccino—however you want. On the house."

"*Grazie,*" he said. "I'll have a cappuccino, please."

The tables and chairs were plastic, like patio furniture. Raney sat while she worked the machine. He tugged a napkin from a dispenser, jotted down a quick message:

Listen to this, then let me know if you want to talk. One voice is your nephew's. The other is mine. I'm a cop. I'm sitting out front, and I'm not armed.

He folded the recorder into the napkin, twisted the ends as though wrapping a Champagne bottle. The old woman peered up from behind the machines.

"I have it ready for you," she said.

Raney stepped to the counter, blew into the foam, took a long sip.

"Best in the city," he said.

She bowed her head.

"You come here anytime. I take care of you."

"Thank you," Raney said. "Can I ask for one small favor?"

"*Sì.*"

"Would you give this to Mr. Meno?"

He handed over the recorder in its makeshift packaging. The old woman lost her smile, the creases in her forehead arching toward her scalp. Raney noticed for the first time that she wore a wig.

"*Chi?*" she said.

Raney pointed to the back door.

"Meno," he said.

"*Chi?*" she repeated. "I don't understand."

"I didn't come here to cause trouble," Raney said. "He'll want what's in this napkin."

She shook her head. Raney thrust out his badge so that the metal nearly scraped her glasses.

"Tell him you had no choice," he said.

She ambled down the back hallway, recorder and napkin in hand, tapped on the door. No answer. She summoned her courage, knocked harder. The door opened wide enough for Raney to watch an elephantine man mutter a few disgruntled words before palming the recorder.

The old lady returned to her post, gestured for Raney to wait. She took up her paper but didn't seem to be reading it. Raney sipped his cappuccino. He felt her counting the breaths until he was either sent for or sent away. He wanted to ask who she was, what she had seen. A relative of Meno's? His wife's? Another of Dunham's aunts? Raney imagined her hailing from some stone-and-mortar village where people still baked their own bread. A simpler place left over from a simpler time. The kind of place Raney suddenly longed for but knew didn't exist: this woman was here, working for Meno; her life had never been simple.

The door reopened. The man he'd seen earlier walked out, motioned for Raney to follow. The old woman watched them disappear down the hallway. Raney thought she might cross herself.

Meno sat at the far end of a long table, the rear exit a few steps behind him. He was tall, fine-boned, almost frail. Somewhere in his early sixties. He wore an ascot and silver cuff links. Like a man on his way to the symphony, Raney thought. A second bodyguard, identical in stature to the first, stood beside him with his arms neatly folded, his gut arched forward. There were empty cups and full ashtrays scattered across the table. The air was all smoke. Raney had either interrupted a meeting or arrived at the tail end of one. Stone's death seemed the only possible topic.

The first bodyguard gave him a thorough search, tossed his badge, handcuffs, wallet, and keys on the table in front of Meno.

"The handcuffs are for me," Raney said.

"A fetish?" Meno asked.

"I want us to talk alone. I thought they might make you more comfortable."

Meno drummed on the table with manicured nails, twisted in his chair, pulled a derringer from inside his suit jacket and aimed the barrel at Raney's head.

"Cuff the detective's hands behind his back," he said. "And give the cuffs a good tug."

To the second bodyguard he said:

"Take his shield and call our friend downtown. If Detective Raney isn't Detective Raney, then drive him out to the Pine Barrens and leave him in as many locations as possible. I've had enough headaches for one day."

Bodyguard 2 palmed Raney's badge and stepped from the room. The bodyguard who'd escorted Raney in attached the cuffs, pulled until Raney felt skin tear from his wrists.

"They're solid," he said.

"Then go," Meno said. "But don't stray far."

Meno set the gun on the table in front of him, waited until he heard the door click shut.

"Talk," he said.

"Can I sit?" Raney asked.

"No. Move from the spot where you're standing and I'll teach you a hard lesson. Say what you have to say."

"You've listened to the tape?"

"Obviously."

"Then you know your nephew is planning a move against you."

"Just a moment," Meno said.

He pulled a second handheld recorder from his blazer pocket, set it on the table beside Raney's and pressed a button.

"I almost forgot: I want to make a little album of my own," he said. "This will give me some insurance. As I see it, there are two possibilities: either you really have gone rogue or this is some kind of double-edged entrapment meant to bring conspiracy charges against me and my nephew both. Or maybe my nephew is cooperating, and this is one big ruse."

"You think he'd leave you alive in prison?"

"Depends on how much trouble he's in and who he's in it with. My question is: Why haven't you arrested him? You clearly have enough. And it wouldn't take much to turn the boy: I can't remember ever saying a kind word to him. I know your coming here must have something to do with Stone's death, but I can't quite make all the pieces fit. It must be the headaches. Why don't you help me out?"

"Stone was building a case against you. I reported directly to him. My job was to cozy up to Dunham, get him to talk. Everyone knows there's bad blood between you. But it took Dunham a long time to make up his mind about me. We cleared houses, threatened bookies, made collections, and he never said who we were doing any of it for. Stone wouldn't make a move until we had Dunham on tape saying your name. When he finally did, it came too late."

"Not by much. That must be very frustrating for you."

"I'm not sure it's sunk in yet," Raney said.

Meno ran the tip of his tongue over a cracked bottom lip. His skin was withered, peeling—a devotee of sunlamps.

"It seems to me it hasn't," he said. "Aren't you showing your hand prematurely? There will be other district attorneys."

"The case is messy. I doubt anyone but Stone would touch it. If his replacement wants to go after you, he'll start fresh. And it'll take him a long while to get up and running. In the meantime, Dunham will start to figure things out."

"What kind of mess did you make?"

"Your nephew goes too far. There are things I did, things I allowed him to do in order to keep my cover. Stone saw smaller crimes as part of a bigger picture. My sense is the new DA will burn the file and either bury me in archival work or shit-can me altogether."

"So you have my nephew's trust?" Meno said. "Because of these things you did?"

Raney nodded. "For now," he said.

"He's never had a friend before. I take no small pleasure in seeing him deceived in this way. Still, I don't understand what you want from me."

"I want your permission to kill him."

Meno leaned back, crossed his legs.

"I understand the impulse," he said. "But why kill him when you have the power to make his life so miserable? Dunham's been to jail before. It didn't go well. He didn't like people touching his things, or maybe his thing. Isolation nearly killed him. He took to playing with his own excrement. He'd line his turds up in a row and sing to them. If you want to hurt the boy, arrest him."

"I can't risk bringing him in. Not now. Chances are I'd end up in the cell next to him."

"And why do you need my permission?"

"From what I understand, your wife raised him. I don't want to put a bullet in his head and then find out you're coming for me."

"All you want is permission? You weren't hoping to sweeten the pot a little?"

"We can talk about that, too."

Meno pulled a thin cigar from a pack on the table, held it in his mouth, lit it without inhaling.

"No," he said. "We can't talk about that."

"Why not?"

"Because you don't have my permission."

"I thought you listened to the tape."

"I did. But the irony is that it's *you* who's given *me* permission. I've always had the desire, but never the ironclad reason. He's a relation. Not a blood relation, but, as you said, my wife raised him. She did her best, but he came to her flawed. Now, thanks to you, I can claim self-defense. The imbecile has made a real threat against me."

"So you're saying . . ."

"I'll kill him myself. Break etiquette on a thing like this and everyone falls out of line."

"Then I'm out?"

"You were never in. But you do seem to have my nephew's ear. I'd be willing to pay you a finder's fee for delivering him. He knows I despise him. I've gone to great lengths to keep from ever seeing him in person. If I call for him out of the blue, he'll know what it means—or at least he'll suspect. He's a caged animal on his best days. Having his little Judas buddy in tow might put him at ease."

"What about your three-car detail?"

"I know how to keep my federal chaperones entertained while I go about my business."

"Where do you want to do it?"

"Somewhere quiet. I want to take my time. Where would you suggest? You seem to be a man with ideas."

"My first thought would be the club. Tell him you need it for a private event. But he'd see through that. So why not tell him you need another building cleared? He'll want to go in at night. You get there first."

"That might work," Meno said. "Give me a day to consider it. If Dunham gets a call, you'll know what it means."

"All right," Raney said. "And you can keep the tape. I've got plenty of copies."

"I thought you might. Don't forget I have a tape of my own."

The bodyguard who'd taken Raney's badge opened the door and stuck his head in.

"He's legit, boss."

"Very good," Meno said. "Come and uncuff the detective. Give him his wallet and keys and then show him out."

"I need my shield," Raney said.

"And you'll have it," Meno said. "Just as soon as our business is concluded."

He tapped the recorder.

"You can't have too much insurance," he said.

"I suppose that's true," Raney said.

He stopped short of invoking Ferguson's name.

*   *   *

Outside, he felt the benzos, the blow, the caffeine swirling in his head and turning in his gut. He vomited into a trash can, made it back to his car, sat waiting for his blood to settle. By the time he reached the Triborough Bridge his clothes were soaked through. He flipped the air conditioner to high, mopped his forehead with each sleeve. He promised himself, promised Sophia, that he'd get clean once Meno and Dunham were gone.

Sophia. How much did she know? How much would he have to tell her?

34

Bay's judge came through. By late afternoon they were standing outside Grant's home, watching SWAT surround the house, then take the door. Men and women dressed in combat helmets and body armor filed inside. A volley of shouting jumped from room to room. Then quiet.

"He's alive if they got him," Bay said.

"He wouldn't come alive," Raney said.

The street was nondescript, not unlike the one Vignola had lived on: semidetached bungalows, the upkeep varying from yard to yard—manicured beds of cactuses beside mounds of used car parts. No people on the porches, no faces in the windows.

SWAT came back out, guns at their sides, chin straps unbuttoned. The major addressed Raney and Bay.

"The house is empty," he said.

"Any sign of him?" Bay asked.

"When I say empty, I mean empty. Everything's gone. Furniture, appliances. There's nothing. You want to go in and take a look?"

"I guess we better," Bay said. "We should have forensics do their thing, too."

"Thanks for your help," Raney said.

"Want us to stick around?"

"No," Raney said. "He won't be back."

The rooms were barren, but the home appeared lived in. There were holes in the walls where pictures had hung. The linoleum was peeling back in the kitchen, the concrete cracking in the basement. Anything that grew had been ripped out of the backyard and replaced with gravel and a chin-up bar. Bay found a dead mouse in the attic.

They were sitting on the curb, Bay smoking, Raney drinking the remains of a coffee he'd bought that morning, when the forensics van pulled up. Bay stepped forward to greet them, spoke with a thin, gray-haired man in a blue jumpsuit.

"There ain't much in there," Bay said. "But give it all you got. This guy is a special kind of dangerous."

Raney watched them lug their supplies inside.

"They look like a cleaning crew," he said.

"I could use a goddamn nap," Bay said.

"We should talk to the neighbors. Find out how long it's been since they've seen him."

"If we can find any neighbors. No one's come or gone all day."

"They're here," Raney said. "They're laying low."

"Why, if they know Grant's gone?"

"Doesn't mean they stopped being afraid of him."

"They can relax. He's gone for good. Cleaning out the house was a final 'fuck you.'"

"Nothing's final until we find that supply," Raney said.

"Seems less and less likely, don't it?"

They canvassed the opposite side of the street first, targeting houses with empty mailboxes and cars parked in the driveway. The few people who responded claimed not to know Grant.

"Maybe he kept a low profile," Bay said.

"Maybe," Raney said. "But this isn't a neighborhood built for privacy."

They crossed back to Grant's side of the street, started with the house to the east of his, a small bungalow with a second-floor add-on, an A-frame loft that made Raney think of his cabin. A flowerless trellis hung over the walkway. The house had sight lines into Grant's kitchen and master bedroom.

"Seventh time's the charm," Bay said.

An elderly man in a walker came to the door, looked hard at Bay's uniform, then Raney's badge.

"This'd be about Grant?" he said.

"Yes, sir," Bay said. "We'd like to ask you a few questions, if you have a moment."

"You might have asked before you sent in the Delta Force. Grant cleared out weeks ago."

The man was ninety, maybe older, voice clear but dim, spine badly curved, eyes alert behind thick glasses. He wore hearing aids that looked like tiny megaphones.

"Want us to come in?" Bay asked. "Might be easier to talk sitting down."

"We can talk here. I'm supposed to stand ten minutes out of every hour. That's my exercise. I used to climb the fourteeners in Colorado. Now I wouldn't make it from the car to the trailhead. My two-year-old great-granddaughter falls less than I do."

"This will work fine," Raney said. "What can you tell us about Grant?"

"I can tell you what you already know—he had the whole block shitting their pants. I've been watching you knock on doors. You didn't get more than two or three people who answered, and my guess is they didn't say a thing worth hearing."

"Good guess," Bay said. "What'd he do to frighten everyone?"

"The man's a scowl come to life. You couldn't squeeze a drop of friendliness out of him. He used to sit out on his stoop cleaning his guns. There'd be kids playing stickball in the street. If the ball got loose and rolled over to him he wouldn't toss it back. He'd just sit there, daring them to come get it. There was always something with him. Once someone blocked his driveway and Grant slashed the guy's tires. Now that don't make sense to me, cause how is the guy who's in his way supposed to move after his tires are slashed?"

"Did you have any personal dealings with him?" Raney asked.

"With Oscar? No, never. Molly did, though. Get her in the right frame of mind and she ain't afraid of no one."

"Molly?"

"My live-in nurse. Caretaker, I think she calls herself. I'm not just old, I'm riddled with cancer. That's how my doctor put it: 'riddled with cancer.' Hell of a bedside manner. So my daughter dumped that triangle on top of my house and hired Molly to live in it. She's a godsend, really. Feeds me, gives me my meds, runs me through my physical therapy. Sometimes she sits and watches TV with me. It'll be her who finds me. I hate knowing that."

"You say she talked to Grant?" Raney asked.

"A few times. She was close with his boy."

"Jonathan?"

"Yeah. That's one apple landed miles from the tree. Real sweet kid. Life keeps making less sense the older you get. Me living to my age, him dying at his."

"I know the feeling," Bay said.

"Molly wouldn't happen to be home now, would she?" Raney asked.

"She's up in her triangle, taking a nap. If I want her this time of day I'm supposed to ring a buzzer."

"Would you mind if we talked to her?" Bay asked.

"No, sir. My ten minutes are about up anyway. And I feel it, too. You know what they say: getting old ain't for the faint of heart. And I've been old for a long time."

They followed him into a well-lit and sparsely furnished living room—armchair and couch against one wall, television against the other, no sharp edges, ample room for a walker to pass through. The old man stood at the bottom of the stairs, pressed a button on an intercom, shouted into the receiver.

"Lund to angel of death," he said. "You have gentlemen callers."

He took his finger off the button.

"She'll think I'm hallucinating. Sometimes if I skip my meds I see little robots chewing on the baseboards."

Molly came hustling down the stairs, stopped short when she saw Raney and Bay standing there.

"Told you," Lund said.

He turned, started off, then turned back.

"I don't know what he did, but I hope you get him."

"Thank you for your help," Bay said.

They watched him navigate a doorway leading to the back of the house, heard the legs of his walker clicking against linoleum.

"What can I do for you?" Molly asked.

She was flushed, not from running down the stairs, Raney

thought, but because her hair appeared slept on and she was dressed in sweatpants and a flannel shirt.

"Would you like some tea?"

"No, thank you," Raney said. "We won't need much of your time."

"At least have a seat," she said.

Raney and Bay took the sofa. Molly pulled the armchair to the center of the room.

"What is this about?" she asked.

"We're looking for Oscar Grant," Bay said.

"No surprise there. The man ran off in the dead of night. I watched him load up the rental truck. Seeing him carry away Jonathan's things broke my heart all over again."

"Mr. Lund told us you were close with Grant's son," Bay said.

"I loved that boy. He was gentle, kind. The opposite of his father in every way. He used to come and sit with Tommy . . . Mr. Lund. He'd play checkers with him when Tommy's mind was still up for it. No one asked him to—he just did it. That was when I first started working here. Jonathan was fourteen. How many fourteen-year-olds would give up their time like that?"

"Not many I know," Bay said.

"Is it possible he came here to get away from his father?" Raney asked.

"There were other places he could have gone, but maybe that was part of it. Jonathan was sensitive. Oscar tried to beat it out of him."

"Literally?"

"Literally and figuratively. Jonathan was always turning up here with scrapes and bruises he tried to explain away. One day he came over with a huge lump on his forehead. I told him enough was enough, I was going to talk to his father, but Jonathan threw himself in front of the door. He was right, of course. I'd only have made matters worse. A woman coming to fight his battles—Oscar would never have let up."

"What about figuratively?" Raney asked.

"Oscar tried to make Jonathan into someone he wasn't. He'd drag him on these weekend-long hunting trips. If Jonathan failed to kill something, Oscar would spend the week inventing ways to punish him. Once he made him get up at two in the morning and wax the car. Another time, he pulled Jonathan out of bed at four a.m., drove him up to Carlsbad, and made him run five miles with a sack of rocks on his back. He had Jonathan out on that chin-up bar every night. He'd blow his idiotic whistle and count down at the top of his lungs. He'd call Jonathan names when his arms gave out. It was horrible to watch, because that just wasn't Jonathan. No matter how hard Oscar pushed, that was never going to be Jonathan. And when Oscar finally did realize it, he cut his son off altogether, treated him like he was already dead."

"You mean when he learned that Jonathan was gay?" Raney said.

She nodded.

"And how did Oscar react when Jonathan died?" Raney asked.

"Like he'd lost the world. I'd hear him wailing at all hours. He put himself through every kind of self-flagellation imaginable, treated himself worse than he'd ever treated Jonathan. I came down before sunup one morning to check on Tommy because I thought I'd heard him moaning. But it wasn't Tommy—it was Oscar running up and down the street, barefoot, carrying an enormous rifle across his back. It scared me senseless. I almost called the police."

"What about the drugs?" Raney asked. "Did you ever know Jonathan to have a problem?"

"No, never. That was so out of character."

"Can you say more about his character? What kind of things did Jonathan like to do? Who did he want to be?"

"He was an artist. A brilliant artist, I think. He loved cameras the way his father loves guns. He knew how to take them apart and put them back together. He knew what lens to use when. He wanted to be a photojournalist. Possibly a filmmaker. And it's not just me saying he was talented. More than one school offered him a full ride."

"Do you have any of his photos here?" Raney asked.

The question seemed to startle her.

"I do," she said. "He took a whole series of me and Tommy."

"Would you mind showing them to us?"

"It would be easier if you came upstairs. They're hanging on a wall in my room. Just don't mind the mess."

The loft, a hundred years younger than the rest of the house, featured glowing bamboo floors and double-insulated windows. There was a large, unmade bed facing the stairs, a drafting table littered with magazines in one corner, an ornate harp in another. Bay seemed taken with the harp.

"You play?" he asked.

"Ever since I was little. It's an heirloom from my great-grand-mother. I play as a hobby, but it's also more than that."

"Are these Jonathan's photos here?" Raney asked, pointing to the wall beside the stairs.

"Yes. Jonathan made a little installation for me. That included painting the wall. He thought the black and white showed up nicely against blue-gray."

"He was thorough," Bay said.

"He cared about his work," she said.

The photos were candid, visceral. Raney wondered if Lund

had seen them. There was one of the old man in a bathtub, eyes shut, lather covering his torso. He looked very much like a man at peace with his age and fate, as though he enjoyed this sensual pleasure *because* he knew death was coming. Other photos featured Molly as caretaker: giving Mr. Lund a massage, wiping drool from his chin with a napkin, combing his slim ring of hair. Collectively, the photos revealed her heroism. It was as though Molly absorbed Lund's fear so that the old man could live his final moments more fully. There was a sense, too, that something of Lund would live on in her after he had died. Almost every photo seemed to foreshadow her grief. Raney had no doubt: this was the same photographer who took the portrait hanging in Vignola's bedroom.

"Do you see now what I mean?" Molly asked. "He was seventeen when he shot those. How many seventeen-year-olds see the world with that kind of maturity?"

"None," Raney said. "And not many adults."

"He was extraordinary."

Extraordinary enough, Raney thought, to have captured the affection of a fifty-year-old art teacher. Oscar knew. The relationship was part of the boy's revelation. Molly seemed to read Raney's mind.

"Oscar killed Mr. Vignola, didn't he?"

Bay stepped closer to her, made slow and deliberate eye contact.

"Jonathan was damn lucky to find you," he said. "Mr. Lund, too."

She nodded, pressed her palms to her eyes. It was what she needed to hear—the kind of thing Raney would never have thought to say.

* * *

They were cutting across Grant's lawn when Raney's phone rang, a number he didn't recognize.

"Is this Detective Wes Raney?"

"Yes. Who's this?"

"Oscar Grant."

Raney broke stride, grabbed Bay's arm, switched the phone to speaker.

"Mr. Grant," he said. "We're standing in front of your house right now."

"Jesus Christ," Bay whispered.

"You can stop looking for me," Grant said. "There's no more point. I'm done now."

Bay climbed onto the hood of a car, searched the street.

"Is that why you're calling? To tell us to stop?"

"I wanted to answer the questions you left for Mr. Adler. I killed Mavis, but then you know that by now. You also know her name wasn't Mavis, and you know she did things in her life to deserve a slower death than the one I gave her. As for what happened to her supply, be sure to watch the news this evening."

"Why not give me a hint?"

"People will take notice. They won't be able to walk around blind any longer."

"So you're a hero?"

"Call me what you like. There's no need for you to waste any more effort, Detective. You're too late. Everything you wanted to stop from happening has already happened. The world sided with me."

"But not with your son."

"Unlike most people, his death had a purpose. I made sure of that."

"What have you done? Tell me what you did."

Oscar hung up.

"The son of a bitch drove right past us," Bay said.

"I know it," Raney said.

"What now?"

"Let's go find a television."

35

They were in the alley behind the club, drinking pilsners and playing horseshoes, betting five dollars a throw. Pierre stuck his head out the back door, shouted for Dunham to come to the phone.

"I'm unavailable," Dunham said.

"It's your uncle."

Raney took a long pull from his bottle.

"Son of a bitch," Dunham said.

To Raney: "Don't touch anything while I'm gone. I know where it all goes."

Raney waited until Dunham was inside, then slipped two benzos from his pocket and washed them down with the last of his beer. Dunham came back out, cursing, knocking the heels of his palms together.

"We've got one more job for Uncle Meno," Dunham said. "The dickhead says it has to be tonight. I've got a topflight vocalist coming in. Took me three months to book her. Has a voice and tits like a young Lena Horne."

"What's the job?" Raney asked.

"Another house sweep."

Raney looked at his watch.

"Does it have to be tonight?"

"Maybe if I ask him nice . . ."

"I mean, why not do it now? We could be there and back before the first set."

"There's this thing called broad daylight," Dunham said.

"Skels aren't on a clock. And that isn't a neighborhood where people witness shit."

"You have plans or something?"

"I'm just saying. If you want to see your singer with the nice tits . . ."

He could feel Dunham giving in. Meno had done Raney a favor by calling early. There'd be time to set up a play.

"In and out," Dunham said. "No shots fired unless things go sideways."

An hour later they were in Jersey, hunting down the address Meno had given.

"It's amazing how these alleys all look exactly the fucking same," Dunham said.

"You said three sixty-six, right?"

Dunham pointed.

"Yeah. That's it right there," he said.

"The yard is empty."

"The shopping-cart brigade must be out trawling. I told you we should have waited."

"Are you sure we've got the right place? The windows are still boarded up, but when's the last time you saw a crack house with a security door?"

"This day is really starting to irritate the fuck out of me," Dunham said. "Let's go borrow a phone from the corner boys."

He let the car roll forward.

"Wait," Raney said.

He couldn't tip his hand, but he couldn't let the moment pass, either.

"What now?"

"There's another possibility," Raney said.

"What possibility?"

"It's the right address."

"Meaning?"

"Meaning maybe we got here first."

Dunham punched the brakes.

"So now this is a fucking hit?"

"I'm saying it's a possibility."

"It's a fucking possibility every minute of my life, but why today? I'm earning. I'm doing every goddamn thing he asks."

"Maybe he heard you were branching out."

"Heard from who?" Dunham said. "We were careful. Maine's a thousand miles from here. There's no way he caught wind."

"There's always a way."

"Name one."

"Spike left the warehouse cameras on."

"Bullshit," Dunham said. "Spike's too smart to pull that on me. Besides, I checked."

"Maybe he guessed. How much would Meno pay to know you were earning behind his back? Enough to turn a guy who works a factory job?"

"Even if Meno knows, that don't mean it was Spike. There's

that fat fuck Farlow with his room-over-a-dry-cleaner bullshit. He was too fucking smooth. I should have made him straight off."

"It wasn't Farlow," Raney said.

"How do you know?"

"Because he's sick. He isn't looking to make waves."

"Sick how?"

"Cancer."

"What brand?"

Raney grabbed his crotch.

"Fuck," Dunham said. "You sure he's not bullshitting you? I thought guys with cancer looked like skels."

"He's not there yet. But when he says he doesn't want to die in a prison cell, he's talking short term."

"Whoever the fuck it was," Dunham said, "the question is what do we do right now?"

"Let's go in and have a look. Maybe the skels snuck back through a window."

"And if they didn't?"

"We could drive away. Regroup."

Dunham locked his arms against the steering wheel.

"No," he said. "If I don't show, he'll know that I know."

"Then it's good we came early," Raney said.

"Yeah, but they'll have numbers."

"How many?"

"Four, maybe five guys. However many he can fit in one car. He won't want to draw attention."

"What about the driver?"

"He'll keep the motor running."

"Do you know who he'll use?"

"There's a time it would have been me. Now he's got these

twin apes that never leave his side. It'll take a clip each to bring them down. I don't know who does his driving. That used to be me, too."

"And you're sure Meno will come himself?"

"He has to. We're family. Blood or not, it doesn't matter. It has to be him who pulls the trigger. It's his own fucking rule."

"You'll be leaving his army intact."

"We got no choice now. It's either a quick ambush or a long war. The apes are the heart of his muscle, so if we take them out the rest of the crew should fall in line. You up for it, Deadly? I've seen you beat the shit out of guys, but I've never seen you point a gun at a man and squeeze the trigger."

"I'm up for it."

"There can't be any hesitation. We do it right, and we'll be the only ones shooting. We do it wrong, and we start something we won't finish."

"Then we'll do it right," Raney said.

"Like you said, let's have a look first. If the skels are already gone, then we'll hide the car and wait for my uncle to show."

He backed up to the house, reached under his seat, pulled out a box of latex gloves and handed a pair to Raney.

"Might be a future crime scene," he said.

They waded through the backyard weeds, tried the door just in case.

"Broad fucking daylight," Dunham said.

"Good thing no one has a window to look through."

Raney hoisted Dunham piggyback. Dunham used a switchblade to dig out the staples around a sheet of plywood, then pulled the sheet free and tossed it to the ground. Raney boosted him inside. A few minutes later the security door opened, and Dunham stood on the back steps.

"They've started rehabbing," he said. "They've got sanders and tarps laid out in the living room."

"What are you thinking?"

"I'm thinking those tarps aren't so much for construction."

"So how do you want to play it?" Raney asked.

"Let's get that board back up. Then you hide the car. No more than a block or two away. And be careful walking back. You can get stopped around here just for being white."

36

They drove to the closest precinct house, started up the steps, found themselves walking against a rush of uniforms and plainclothesmen. They made their way to the desk sergeant, waited for him to finish barking orders into his headset.

"What's happening?" Bay asked.

"Looks like we got some bad coke to go with our habitually bad meth," the sergeant replied.

"How bad?" Raney asked.

"Cut with rat poison."

"Shit," Bay said.

"Fatalities?" Raney asked.

"All over the city. It's like this shit hit every street in Albuquerque all at the same time."

"Who's in charge?" Bay asked.

"Depends on the precinct. We've got at least a dozen different primaries."

"But who has oversight?" Raney asked. "This might be related to a case we're working."

"That'd be Captain Redmond."

"Where can we find him?"

"He headed over to the Courtside projects. Didn't want to be seen favoring the fair-skinned."

"Courtside projects?"

"About as north as you can go and still be in the city."

The Courtside Apartments looked like a thousand other projects across the country: a maze of squat, two-story brick buildings lined with closely spaced doors. Their badges got them past the front line of uniforms. There were locals watching from every window, breezeway, rooftop. The drug crews had scattered. Detectives canvassed the apartments; medical examiners and their assistants loaded bodies into white vans while relatives begged to see their sons, daughters, sisters, brothers. Frantic cops tried to clear a path through the news vans and squad cars. Captain Redmond—a short man with an uneven mustache and medals dangling from his lapels—stood addressing the media, saying nothing, affirming his right to "protect the integrity of the investigation." He moved away from the microphones, turned his back on the reporters. Raney held out his shield, squeezed his way through a chain of uniformed officers. Bay followed.

"Captain Redmond," Raney called.

The captain huddled with his lieutenants, pretended not to hear.

"I'm county Homicide," Raney said. "I know who did this."

Redmond spun around.

"Then we better talk," he said.

* * *

They sat in an unmarked SUV with tinted windows, the captain in the passenger seat, Raney and Bay in back. Redmond stank of garlic and continued to sweat despite the air-conditioning.

"How did the bastard get the poison out that fast to that many people?"

"We don't know," Raney said. "We just know where it came from and who he killed to get it."

"Is this some kind of drug war takeover?"

"More like vengeance," Bay said.

"Vengeance? On the entire fucking city?"

"His son OD'd," Raney said. "About a year ago. He thinks the city's sitting on its hands, ignoring an epidemic."

"So he staged scenes like this one all over Albuquerque just to give the department a black eye?"

"In his mind, he's bringing the drug crisis to a head, making the problem so visible someone has to do something about it."

"Sounds like you're on his side."

"No, sir."

"Here's what I want. I want every goddamn scrap of paper you've got on Oscar Grant. I want them yesterday. If you'd caught him when you had the chance, my clerk wouldn't be requisitioning more body bags. And my head wouldn't be on the chopping block because of a psychopath I knew nothing about an hour ago."

"He's been all over the news," Bay said.

Redmond glared.

"Spoken like a man who's about to retire," he said. "I don't want to see or hear from either of you again until I have this guy in custody. If you want any kind of future in law enforcement, you damn well better make it happen quick. I'll release his photo to the media tonight."

"Are you sure, sir?" Raney said. "He's dangerous."

"I'll stress that. We want information, not vigilantes. If some paramilitary moron wants to pounce, then there's nothing we can do about it. Now get moving."

There were women comforting one another all along the yellow tape, men standing back, gawking, mugging tough. Raney and Bay passed through them, walked the long road to the main avenue where they'd parked.

"He'll be up all night plotting our crucifixion," Bay said.

"He has no jurisdiction over either one of us, and he knows it. He's the biggest fish they can fry. He's just lighting a fire."

"To burn the evidence?"

"What do you mean?"

"Grant won," Bay said. "He got every damn thing he wanted. If we arrest him now, even if we put a bullet through his head, it won't mean a thing."

"Grant agrees with you. He said as much on the phone. Maybe it's true. Or maybe he'd find a new cause a year from now."

"Where to?" Bay asked.

"Your office. Let's get the captain his report."

That night, Raney sat with Clara in front of the television, drinking a glass of wine and watching her roll a fresh joint. Oscar Grant's face was a fixture on the top right-hand corner of the screen. The number to a tip line scrolled across the bottom. A talking head said the death toll had risen above a hundred. Dozens more were hospitalized. A long-legged reporter walked the viewers through Grant's empty home. With no commentary to offer, she sounded like a real-estate agent counting off rooms. Details of Grant's earlier crimes were rehashed, from Jack and the twins to his son's art teacher. A candlelight vigil would be held for Vignola in the parking lot outside Mesa Heritage High.

Raney thought of attending, then thought he had only one memory to offer.

"This is horrific," Clara said. "It just keeps spiraling."

"It's over now."

"It should never have started. I can't think about Mavis without hating her. What does that say about me?"

"That you're human."

"And you? How do you manage it?" she said.

"Manage what?"

"All of it. You're so fucking calm."

"I just look like I am."

"You've seen this before, haven't you? Or something like it. Something on this scale."

"Only once. And that was a long time ago."

"Have you killed people?"

The question winded him.

"Clara . . ."

"What brought you out here?"

"Why are you asking?"

"Because Daniel can't stop talking about you. And because you're too damn detached. You don't want to be, but you are."

Raney set his glass on the table.

"I'm tired," he said. "I have to be up early."

"No," Clara said. "You stay here and tell me. Walk me through every detail."

37

"How will they set up?" Raney asked.

"Meno's the real-estate king. He owns this shit hole. So he'll waltz in the front, smiling, pointing at windows and drainpipes, playing it like his goons are contractors or buyers. He'll think he has the drop on us. Everybody knows I'm a night owl."

"That makes things easier."

"Just don't jump out too early. Meno's always the last one through the door. And I don't want any poetry. Step out and start blasting. End of story."

"Got it."

"Man, I wish to God I had some more blow on me," Dunham said.

He was peering through a gimlet hole in the plank covering the front window.

"I can't believe this," he said. "I can't fucking believe it. I woke up this morning thinking the day would happen one way. I had some coffee. Took a shit. Headed over to the club. And now . . ."

"What?"

"I don't know. This feels rushed. You plan something like this. You scout the area. You rehearse. But fuck it. It's not like I can ask Meno for a rain check."

"You've wanted this for a long time," Raney said. "I guess you have to take it how it comes."

"I guess. You still all right? You're almost too fucking quiet."

"Yeah, I'm okay," Raney said.

He was cold, his palms sweating. They'd been standing in the dark for an hour, Dunham describing whatever he glimpsed on the street: a group of boys gathering around a drunk on the opposite stoop, two kids from the corner racing dirt bikes, a cop car rolling past, a stray dog pissing on someone's tire. Raney sat with his back against the wall, half listening. Part of him wanted to shepherd Dunham away. It was a phenomenon Stone had talked about: *Spend enough time with anyone, and you run the risk of liking him.* Dunham enjoyed being alive. That part of him was contagious. But Ferguson was right: Dunham would cause immeasurable pain for as long as he walked the earth. Raney thought of the skel Dunham shot point-blank, the woman he made watch. He saw Dunham high from it afterward, howling in his car at a Turnpike truck stop.

He traced it back one more time, sifting through the paranoia, the exhaustion, trying to disprove what he believed to be fact just to make sure he couldn't. Why did Dunham have to die? Meno? Whatever his motives, Ferguson's reasoning had been sound. Stone's death left Raney in the crosshairs. If he brought Dunham and Meno in now, he'd have no protection. He'd gone too far. At best, he'd compromised the case and, with it, his career; at worst, he'd be the one prosecuted. Leave Dunham and Meno on the street, and it was only a matter of time before they came at him.

That much made sense. What Raney couldn't get past was the suspicion that Stone had been executed because he, Raney, took too long. Ferguson lost patience, tipped Meno. If he couldn't manipulate his would-be son-in-law into killing Meno, then he'd neutralize Stone. The private schools, the Bentley in the garage: a police captain didn't break six figures. Ferguson had been in Meno's pocket from the start. Meno would use a corrupt figurehead to shave years off his sentence. In Ferguson's mind, either Meno or Stone had to die. Why not have one kill the other?

Or maybe Raney was thinking too hard. Maybe Stone's killer had nothing to do with Meno.

"Here we go," Dunham said. "I was starting to doubt he'd show."

"How many?"

"Four. Plus the driver. Christ, Meno likes 'em big. All right, places everyone."

Raney crouched behind the wall separating the living room and hallway. Dunham shut himself in the foyer closet. There were voices coming up the walk, saying the kinds of things Dunham had predicted. They sounded like stage actors running lines.

"How much does a place like this go for once you fix it up?"

"You can't just renovate the house, you have to renovate the neighborhood."

"Okay, so how much, then?"

"Maybe a half mil."

"After you put how much into it?"

"Twenty thousand, give or take."

"Jesus, not bad."

"Let me show you around."

Raney heard a key in the lock, then Meno's voice from inside:

"He'll come through the back. You two stand watch."

The door shut, the hallway light came on. A three count, and Dunham was out and firing. Raney held his crouch. Plaster exploded above his head. One of Meno's giants stumbled into the living room, dropped at Raney's feet. Dunham's Glock spat rounds. A .38 answered. Someone fell hard. Then a struggle: a body slammed against a wall, Dunham screaming. Raney took up the dead man's revolver, stepped into the hallway. The floor was slick with blood.

One of the twin apes had Dunham by the throat, held him pinned to the front door so that his feet dangled. Dunham kicked, clawed. A second corpse lay sprawled facedown across the foyer. Meno stood watching. Raney shot Dunham's assailant in the calf. The man lost his hold, buckled. Dunham drove a stiletto into his skull. Raney leveled the revolver at Meno.

"Drop it," he said.

"Are you serious?"

"Don't make me say it twice."

Meno let a silver-plated Luger slide from his grip.

"What the fuck is this, Deadly?" Dunham said. "How long were you planning to leave me out here?"

Dunham took up the Luger, turned to Meno and grinned, his teeth shining against the blood spatter.

"I'm gonna do you with your own fucking gun."

Meno to Raney: "This isn't what we agreed on."

"Shut your mouth," Raney said.

"You're forgetting there's a tape of our conversation. There are copies in safety deposit boxes all over the city. I've got your badge. If I should happen to die by violent means—"

"I'll say it was all part of the sting. It all went bad."

"Stone might have believed you."

"What the fuck is this, Deadly?" Dunham said.

"This is you being mentally deficient," Meno said. "Your Mike Dixon is Detective Wes Raney. He's a fucking narco from the district attorney's office. You were so desperate to have a friend that you handed him every detail of our business."

Dunham pressed the muzzle of the Luger to Meno's temple.

"Fuck you," he said. "That divide-and-conquer bullshit won't work, you prick."

"Tell him," Meno said.

"You, too, Dunham," Raney said. "Put the gun down."

Dunham shook his head.

"Maybe it started like that," he said. "But things changed. Show me they changed. Kill this cocksucker right now."

"I can't do that."

"This is your last fucking chance."

"Put the gun down."

"Fuck you."

Dunham swung his arm. Raney dropped him with twin shots to the chest. Meno fumbled at the door. Raney buzzed his ear.

"Turn the fuck around."

Meno raised his hands, did as he was told.

"We both know you can't bring me in now," he said. "So let's be done with it."

"Who killed Stone?"

Meno smirked.

"I'm not the type to make confession."

"It was Ferguson who turned you on to Stone, wasn't it?"

"Ferguson?" Meno said. "You mean the former police captain? I never met the man. I make it a practice to avoid law enforcement. You've turned out to be a very sorry exception."

"Bullshit. Ferguson told you Stone was making a case. You had Stone killed."

"Does it matter if I say you're right or wrong? Once you've executed me, you can make up any story you like."

"Answer me."

"Go fuck yourself, Detective."

"You had Ferguson kill Bruno, didn't you? That's how it started."

"Do you want me to reach for that gun on the floor? Would that make it easier for you? My guess is you've never shot an unarmed man."

"Ferguson wants you dead. Why?"

"Because I've done bad things."

"That surveillance detail was local. Those were Stone's men, not feds. Ferguson told you."

"The more you talk, the more convinced I am that you won't kill me. You orchestrated all this. You're a man of intellect. You need to think things through. A man of action would have pulled the trigger by now. But as a thinker you realize that killing me makes no sense. Either you'll end up in jail or what's left of my crew will hunt you down. Work with me, and what happened here becomes a mutually beneficial turn of events."

"Work with you how?"

"You're everything Dunham wasn't, plus you can take care of yourself. You'll stay on the force. We'll find you a new assignment."

"I'm guessing you have something in mind."

"There are options."

Raney glanced at the blood pooling around Meno's feet.

"And all this is forgiven?"

"I don't see what there is to forgive. You saved my life. And you rid me of a very costly albatross. I'll send a cleaner over. He's the best at what he does. We'll move on. We'll make a lot of money. Give it a few days, then come see me."

He turned back around, set a hand on the doorknob. Raney fired above his head. Meno had one foot outside. There was a car waiting at the curb.

"You're wrong," Raney said.

Meno paused.

"About what?"

"A man of intellect would realize he had to pull the trigger. He'd have no option."

"I've just given you an option."

"You gave me a story. We both know what your next move would be."

Meno pivoted, leveled his derringer. Raney fired twice more. Meno fell backwards onto the street. His driver sped off.

38

He made some alterations, but he couldn't disguise, or wouldn't allow himself to disguise, the part he'd played in orchestrating the deaths of five men. Clara let go of his hand. Raney couldn't tell if she was judging him or if she'd hoped for something different, some vulnerability—a chance to be tender, to comfort herself by comforting him.

"You want me to leave?" he asked.

She looked everywhere but at him.

"Is that what you want?" she said.

"No," he said. "But I don't want to keep talking if you've made up your mind."

"It's like you're asking me for a verdict."

"Isn't that what it amounts to?"

"For you, maybe. Not for me."

"What, then?"

"I don't know," she said. "It's all too much. I have Daniel to think about."

The evidence would come down against him. The events of the last week had outpaced her imagination, left her with new scars to bear. Raney had come to her from a world she didn't understand and wanted no part of. She would do what she'd promised that night at the campsite: move on, find a job, raise Daniel. Raney couldn't help but think he'd like to join them.

Alone in his room, he turned on the lights and stood looking out the window, watching a gaggle of teenagers sprawled atop the hoods of their parents' cars, drinking from paper bags. He thought about arresting them, making them his company for the night, but that would only lead to more consequences with no purpose. Raney was in for the evening, cornered by the fact that he had nowhere else to go. He let the curtain fall shut, a single phrase repeating in his head: *I have Daniel to think about.* Clara would join the people who punished him by their absence.

But punish was too strong—too self-indulgent—a word. Clara *did* have her son to think about. Whatever feelings he had for her would pass, and he'd be left with a suspicion that the hikes, the photos, the nights by the creek were nothing but puffed-up distractions, pieces in an elaborate game of pretend.

He pulled the suitcase from under his bed, rooted through his belongings, brought out the dimebag and clutched it in his fist. He sat for a moment on the edge of the bed, waiting for his breath to settle, unable to shake the feeling that others were watching— Sophia, Ella, Clara—the people he thought about, for better or worse, every day. As if to outrun any impulse that might pull him back, he sprinted into the bathroom and flushed the last of his supply.

He stripped, filled the tub with lukewarm water, then sank beneath the surface, eyes open. He held himself there until the pressure became too great, waited a beat longer before shooting back up.

He lay soaking for a long while, trying to let his mind go blank, but the stillness only chafed—he'd felt more at ease on the cusp of drowning.

Bay found Raney pacing the handicap ramp outside the sheriff's office, taking long swallows from a paper cup imprinted with the diner's logo.

"Back on the cheap stuff?" Bay said.

"Only place open this early."

"The gals must've made it extra strong. You look ready to launch."

"This isn't my first."

Bay leaned his bulk against the side of the building, pulled out a pouch of tobacco and a leaf of rolling paper.

"You up for a hunting trip?" Raney asked.

"Thought you just took pictures."

"I'm talking about a manhunt."

"That's the marshals' gig. Our part's done, Raney."

"That how it feels to you?"

Bay finished rolling his cigarette, fumbled with a lighter until the paper caught flame. He stood smoking, watching Raney climb and descend the ramp.

"You sure it's Grant you can't let go of?" he asked.

"What do you mean?"

"Clara dumped you, didn't she?"

Raney broke stride, stared.

"I'm not sure."

"I bet she is."

"Fuck you, Bay."

"You've known the woman a week. Chasing down an ex-SEAL sniper seems extreme."

"So stay home."

Bay sniggered.

"Going after Grant is pure stupid, and you know it. You need someone along who's a little less stupid than you are. Someone who'll grab you by the ear and make you wait for the cavalry."

Raney crushed the cup in his hand, watched a magpie pick a gum wrapper off the sidewalk.

"That mean you're coming?" he said.

Bay nodded.

"Where do we start?"

"I called Molly. She remembered the logo on the side of the van Grant rented."

They drove without stopping, pulled up to a tin shack at the center of a sprawling parking lot dotted with white trucks. A placard chained to the roof read ADOBE RENTALS. A man stood at the door with his back to them, beating on a padlock with a hammer. Bay flashed the siren. The man tossed the hammer, raised his hands.

"It's the small pleasures," Bay said.

The man was in his midthirties—stick arms and legs, bloated gut, long gaps between rotting teeth. The name tag sewn into his breast pocket read LEWIS.

"Funny," Raney said. "This might be the only non-adobe building for a mile in any direction."

"What is it we're interrupting?" Bay asked.

"Locked my keys inside."

Bay patted him down, found a sharpened screwdriver and a crack pipe.

"Any chance you're on parole?" Bay asked.

"What's this about?"

"Relax," Raney said. "All we want is information."

"What kind of information?"

"You've seen the news, right? You know what happened yesterday."

Lewis nodded, pressed his back against the wall as though trying to slip through one of its corrugated grooves.

"I ain't mixed up in that," he said.

"What *are* you mixed up in?" Raney asked. "Let's begin there."

"I got a habit," the man said. "You seen it right off. But I don't
make the shit, and I don't sell it. Just tell me what you want. If I
can help, I'll help. Why wouldn't I?"

"Fair enough," Raney said.

He held out Grant's photo.

"Did you rent a truck to him?"

"We rent a lot of trucks."

"Look closely."

Lewis held the picture by its edges, leaned in, then bolted
back, eyes lost in his skull.

"Stan sent you to fuck with me," he said. "This ain't the guy
you're looking for. No way. Can't be."

He dropped the photo, let it lie on the asphalt. Raney picked it
up.

"Why don't we go inside?" he said. "Since you took the trouble
to break the lock."

Bay opened the door, caught a hot blast of stale smoke and
sweat.

"Jesus. Someone ought to buy you a goddamn window."

"We leave the door open, mostly."

Bay took Lewis by the shoulders, spun him around, steered

him inside. There were papers strewn across every surface, empty bottles of hard liquor serving as paperweights. Every drawer busted, every filing cabinet spilling over. Cigarette ash lay like sawdust across the floor. Bay walked Lewis behind his desk, tilted his chair so that a binder and a stack of invoices slid off, then shoved him down.

"How do you find anything in here?" Bay asked.

"He doesn't," Raney said. "Who's Stan?"

"Stan?" Lewis said.

Raney clapped his hands hard beside Lewis's ear.

"No stalling. We're not going to rough you up, and we're not going to offer you a drink to calm your nerves. Answer my questions or we'll drop you in a holding cell and forget to tell anyone you're there."

Lewis wiped his face with an oil-soaked rag, stared down at his feet.

"Stan's my brother."

"And he owns this place?"

"Yeah."

"And you're—what? The mechanic?"

"More like the janitor," Lewis said. "I clean the trucks, change the oil, sweep the lot. I do the grunt work, stay clear of the customers."

"Except when Stan's away?"

"Yeah, except when Stan's away."

Raney held up Oscar's picture a second time.

"Stan was away the day this man came in?"

"Yeah. Stan's semiretired. Works half the week. Usually has a girl who covers, but she's out pregnant. I swore up and down I could handle it. I swore to him. I said it would help get me turned around."

Raney scanned the room.

"This isn't the normal state of things, is it?"

"No, it ain't."

"You were looking for something? Something to do with Oscar Grant?"

"Who?"

"The man in the picture."

"He had a different name. Had IDs to back it up."

"But you're sure it was him?" Bay asked.

"Yeah, I'm sure."

"Why don't you start from the beginning?" Raney said. "Tell us everything."

"It's him poisoned the dope?"

"Might be," Bay said.

Lewis clawed the arms of his chair.

"Sweet fucking Jesus," he said. "The man paid me in meth. I'm gonna die, ain't I?"

"How long ago?" Raney asked.

"Maybe two weeks."

"You'd be dead already. Now tell us."

Raney waited for Lewis to catch his breath, watched the red fade from his cheeks.

"Go on, now," he said.

"The guy showed up late. Just before closing. Said he wanted to borrow a truck from then until morning. He'd have it back in ten hours. I said we only charged in twenty-four-hour cycles. That's when he said we had friends in common. Said he knew what I was about. He laid the Baggies on the desk here. 'Ten hours,' he said. 'No paperwork.'"

"Let me guess," Bay said. "You never saw the truck again."

"I know what happened to it, though."

"What's that?"

"A cop called Sunday morning. Wanted to know if we were missing any inventory. Said they found what could be one of ours burned to a skeleton up in the foothills. I told him our trucks were all accounted for, but I knew damn well what happened and who'd done it. I figured it had something to do with the meth. He'd been transporting it or using the trailer as a lab. But the cop said the truck was packed with normal shit. Furniture, clothes, electronics. All of it up in flames."

"So what were you searching for today?"

"I wasn't searching for nothing. Stan don't know yet. I was tryin' to make it look like we was robbed. Like they'd come for the cash and taken off in one of the trucks. I was gonna call it in from a pay phone."

"Why today?" Raney asked.

"I figured the cops would be too busy to care. Maybe they'd send some rookie to take a report, and that'd be it."

"We did you a favor, then, by showing up," Raney said. "If I were you, I'd put this place back in order and then come clean with your brother."

"No, I don't think you would," Lewis said. "Not if you was me. And not if he was your brother."

They sat in a café across the freeway from Adobe Rentals, drinking from outsized mugs, Bay clicking the mouse on his laptop, entering information, clicking again.

"Here it is," he said. "Just like the meth head described it. Arson on a county road. A hundred miles from Albuquerque."

"Keep looking and you'll find a dealer turned up dead a little over two weeks ago."

"But why? Why not just burn his house down? And why burn

the truck, too? Why not unload it and make a nice big barn fire?"

"Some kind of ritual? A break with the past? The real question is, how did he get back to Albuquerque? Or to wherever he was going? Someone had to give him a lift."

"You think he's got a friend in all this?"

"Or in some of it. Maybe a friend who goes way back."

"A SEAL?"

"Or a warden. Grant's boss was the go-to character witness when Jonathan OD'd."

"I guess I know where we're headed next."

Grant's former workplace sat in the flattest part of the state — no trees, no hills, just sun bleaching the scrub, casting fake ponds on the asphalt.

"This place is butt-ugly," Bay said. "The cons oughta be glad someone bricked up the windows."

They parked in the visitors' lot, checked their guns into small lockers, were escorted down a long corridor by a tired-looking CO. Warden Peterson sat at his desk, hunched over a memo. Behind him, a window overlooked the yard, gave a clear view of the sniper tower where Grant holed up forty hours a week for eighteen years. The office walls were covered with animal heads and hides: antelope, bear, cougar, wolverine. Jack Wilkins would have approved.

The warden pushed aside his memo, stood to greet them. His left leg was set in a thigh-high plaster cast. A pair of crutches lay on the floor beside his desk.

"Don't get up on our account," Bay said.

"I should know better than to ride a mountain bike at my age. Detective Raney and Sheriff Bay, right? Please have a seat. What can I do for you?"

He was larger and a little younger than Bay, with broad shoulders and hands that must have required custom-made gloves. Wire-rimmed bifocals hung from a lanyard around his neck. He had a habit of putting them on and taking them off again. His double-breasted suit made it hard to tell if his bulk was natural or something he worked for. Raney pictured him quashing fights in the cafeteria, lecturing inmates through the bars of their cell. He had the kind of presence that commanded attention.

"I think you know why we're here, Warden," Raney said.

"You've come to ask about Oscar. I'm surprised nobody came sooner."

"We read the articles," Raney said. "It sounds like you were more than his employer."

"Until recently, yes."

"How recently?"

"Jonathan had been dead a few months. I was a pallbearer at his funeral."

"What changed between you?" Bay said.

"I don't really know. I guess he needed to leave this place behind. And me with it."

"He resigned?" Raney said.

"Two years shy of a full pension."

"Any idea why?"

"There'd been an incident in the yard. A man was stabbed to death by members of a rival gang. Oscar didn't so much as fire a warning shot. When I asked him about it, he said whatever they had going on between them was none of his business. Then he handed me his weapon and left. Apart from a formal letter, I haven't seen or heard from him since. Still, I find it damn hard to believe he—"

"He did," Raney said.

"All right," the warden said. "So keep asking your questions."

"There's only one question that matters: Where do you think he is right now?"

"I couldn't say."

"You've known the man for eighteen years. You saw him every day. You were friends. You came to his defense when you didn't have to."

"So?"

"I'm sure you have an idea or two worth sharing."

The warden leaned forward.

"I understand you're doing your job," he said. "How well you're doing it is another question. If I knew Oscar was plotting mass homicide, don't you think I would have stopped him?"

"That's not what I asked."

"Since I had no idea what he was doing, how can I predict where he might be?"

"Give us your best guess."

"My best guess? He killed himself. Someplace where the animals would find him before the marshals. He did what he felt he had to do. I doubt he wanted to outlive his son by one more day."

"Why do you think he did it?" Raney asked.

"People will have to act now. He made his son a martyr. Himself, too."

"Okay, but why *Oscar?* The drug trade mass-produces bereft parents."

The warden pushed back in his chair, wiped his glasses with a handkerchief.

"I doubt what he saw in Panama helped him any," he said, "but a man who joins an elite branch of the military and then makes his living as a sniper is a man who likes to kill, and all that stands between him and killing is a cause. If he can find the right cause, then he isn't a killer, he's a vehicle. That's what the military gives a man like Grant. Jonathan became his ultimate cause."

"You make him sound pathological," Raney said. "But you were friends. You had him around your children."

"Oscar had other qualities. Qualities most people lack. Loyalty. Bravery. A work ethic. And I believed in his ability to keep himself in check. Jonathan's death was the tipping point. It would have been for anyone. This is just how it played out for Oscar."

"And for the people who died yesterday," Raney said.

"Yes," the warden said. "I'm aware."

Raney stood, set his card on the desk. Bay stood with him.

"It goes without saying that if Oscar—"

"Of course."

"I hope that leg heals quick," Bay said.

"It's too late for that," the warden said. "I just hope it heals."

Raney took a sweeping look at the mounted wildlife.

"Impressive," he said. "Who was the better shot, you or Oscar?"

The warden looked out at the sniper tower.

"No one was a better shot than Oscar."

They sat in the squad car, Bay smoking, Raney staring at nothing in particular.

"I don't like it," he said.

"Like what?"

"Him telling us Oscar is dead. The stuffed animals. The cast on his leg."

"I caught a whiff of it, too," Bay said. "Something staged."

"Plausible deniability. 'I hadn't been up there. My leg was broken. I didn't know.'"

"Hadn't been up where?"

"The man's poured a small fortune into taxidermy. I'm guessing he has a cabin in the woods someplace. A weekend getaway."

"Where Grant and his son did their hunting?"

"Uh-huh."

"And you think Grant's there now?"

"I think there's a good chance."

"If the place exists."

"Should be easy enough to check," Raney said. "Property's a matter of public record."

"Let's pay the bureau a visit."

Bay started the car.

"If he does have a place," Raney said, "I doubt it's far from where Grant burned that truck."

39

Raney inched out onto the street, dug through Meno's pockets until he recovered his shield. The words and emblems were filled in with blood. He peeled off a latex glove, slipped the badge inside.

He drove Dunham's car back to the club, stopping to dump his spattered shirt and shoes in a sewer on the Jersey side of the bridge. On Staten Island, he parked and walked barefoot through the back alley, let himself in the basement delivery door. He felt his way through the dark. At the foot of the kitchen steps, he heard Pierre shouting orders to his assistant, heard the young Lena Horne belting out a chorus of "Alone Together."

There was an industrial sink on the wall opposite the walk-in freezer. Raney scrubbed his hands with Ajax, washed his face and hair with bar soap, then emptied his pockets. He left his jeans and T-shirt soaking in bleach.

Dunham kept spare clothes and a cot in a room that had once

been the root cellar. The khakis were tight at the waist, long at the heel. The wing-tip shoes were two sizes too big. The only shirt was violet and spotted with small white circles.

He couldn't think of where to go or what to do next. He collapsed on the cot, shut his eyes, lay there feeling Dunham's clothes turn damp with sweat. He jerked upright when the nausea hit, fought it back, felt his skin turn cold.

Dunham kept his personal stash in a lockbox under the cot. Raney busted the lock open with a hammer, found the interior brimming with prescription painkillers, packets of coke, tabs of acid. He swallowed a Percocet dry, snorted a long line, then lay back down. He heard the young Lena scatting above him. Little by little, he felt his strength return, his system settle. He pock- eted his gloved shield, took up the lockbox, and carried it with him.

He drove his own car, tossed Dunham's keys into a vacant lot.

The live-in super was smoking weed. The odor rose through a basement vent, filled the street outside Sophia's building. All but a few of the windows were dark. Raney let himself into the lobby, swallowed another Percocet on the stairs. He rang Sophia's bell and waited. He stepped clear of the peephole, rang again. A suc- cession of bolts clicked free. The door opened as far as the chain would allow.

"I suppose if I don't let you in, you'll make a scene," Sophia said.

"That's not why I'm here," Raney said.

"It's one in the morning, Wes. This is already a scene."

"I want to come home."

She seemed more tired than sad, her skin flushed, her eyes ad- justing to the light.

"We can talk," she said. "But I'm not sure this is your home anymore."

She slid the chain from its plate, left the door ajar. Raney followed her into the living room. She sat on the love seat, legs crossed, terry-cloth robe wrapped tight around her chest. Raney sat leaning against one arm of the couch.

"Look at you, Wes," she said. "You're dressed like a clown. Your eyes are bloodshot. Your pupils are so dilated I can barely see them. You're sweating, and it's sixty degrees in here."

"I need help," he said. "I didn't see it before, but now I do."

"And I want to help you," she said. "But you've become too big a job for me. For any one person."

He looked at her, saw love and concern but no fear, no anger. She'd prepared herself, plotted a course of action. He volunteered.

"I'll check myself in," he said. "I'll go right now if you want."

"It's a little late," she said.

"In the morning, then."

"You can't just say that because I want to hear it."

"I'm not."

"It will be the hardest thing you've ever done, Wes."

"I know," he said. "I don't want this to be me. I never thought it could be."

She moved beside him on the couch, set a hand across the back of his neck, kissed his temple. It was what he thought he'd come here for—affection, comfort—but he felt himself recoiling, shrinking inward, not for his sake but for hers, as though his skin made her touch grotesque.

"I know people," she said. "People I went to school with. We'll find you the right facility. We'll get through this. We're going to be fine. I promise."

They sat for a while, her head on his shoulder, before she took his hand and led him into the bedroom. Raney followed, thinking he would let her believe for one more night. When she woke, he'd be gone. He'd walk into Lieutenant Hutchinson's office, hand over his badge and gun, confess to every detail. He'd refuse bail, refuse all visitors. People would know where to find him, but he'd be beyond their reach, like a ghost or a dead man. The idea gave him some relief.

Sophia sat him on the edge of the bed and undressed him, pulling off Dunham's shoes, peeling back his socks. When she was done, Raney rolled onto his side, already asleep. Sophia's voice brought him back.

"Jesus Christ, Wes," she said. "What the fuck is this?"

She was staring down at the floor, at his shield coated with blood and wrapped in latex.

"It fell out of your pocket. Whose blood is that?"

He managed to sit up, his head drooping forward, his eyes half shut. Sophia shook him conscious.

"Tell me whose blood that is. Tell me whose clothes you're wearing."

He looked up at her as though she were a remnant of the dream he'd been having.

"Not now," he said.

"Yes, now. Why are you here, dressed in someone else's clothes? Why is someone else's blood on your badge? We can fix this, but you have to tell me what happened."

"Fix this?"

He came more fully awake, found himself picturing her as a little girl, crouched at the top of the stairs, eavesdropping while Ferguson plotted cover-ups and counted money. He had no more doubt.

"Fix it how?" he asked.

She hesitated.

"I'll call my father."

Raney stood, pushed her away with one hand.

"Your father?"

"He can help. You just have to tell me what happened."

Raney slipped into Dunham's shirt, fumbled with the buttons.

"What are you doing?" Sophia asked.

"I should have known. You're too smart not to have figured it out."

"Figured out what?"

"Where the money came from. The private schools, the summers abroad. No cop can afford that. Not at any rank."

"Wes, you're slurring your words. Sit down."

"He used me, Sophia. He manipulated me into doing things. He used you to get to me. It all came back on him. He had to protect himself."

"What are you talking about?"

"DA Stone."

"Is that Stone's blood on your badge?"

"If I said it was, would you still call your father? Have him fix things?"

"Are you saying you killed Stone for my father?"

"No. He had Meno do that. Then he set me up to kill Meno. My guess is I'm next."

Sophia backed away.

"You're scaring me," she said.

He was dressed now, bending to tie Dunham's shoes.

"You should be scared."

"You're delusional, Wes. You're going to sweat this out of your system. When people are coming down, they see things. They believe things that aren't true. You just need sleep. Lie down now. Please."

He stood, stepped toward her.

"I want to hear you say it."

"Say what?"

"That you know."

"What do I know? Stop talking in code."

"That your father's a killer."

"You want me to say that my father killed the district attorney of New York City? Do you hear yourself?"

"Your father shot Bruno in the back. He murdered two innocent men. He's been taking money from Meno ever since."

"Money to do what?"

"Divert resources. Tamper with evidence. Meno paid him to let certain things happen, or to cover them up afterward. Stone knew. So did you. You were born into it, but don't pretend you're better than me."

"You're sick, Wes."

He started for the door.

"Where are you going?"

"Your father's house."

"Wes, don't."

She grabbed his arm. He spun, caught her hard with the back of his hand. She lay on the floor staring up at him.

"You fucking asshole," she said. "If you——"

"If I what?"

He moved toward her. She tore her robe open over her stomach.

"Look!" she said.

He leaned forward, lost his balance, fell against the dresser, righted himself.

"Look!"

He saw. Her belly curved, smooth. Five, maybe six months. The mother of his child, her right eye turning colors. He saw what he'd done, but not as though he'd done it. He knelt beside her.

"Get away from me," she said. "Get the fuck out or I swear to God it won't be my father I call."

"I'm sorry," he said. "I'm sorry."

He couldn't think of anything more. He stood there, watching her, seeing himself years in the future, still stuck in this moment, unable to change or move past it.

"I'm sorry, too," she said. "Sorry the father of my child is a junkie. I hope to God it isn't a boy. I don't want to see you in my son. There's no hope for you, Wes. Get out. Get the fuck out."

Raney backed from the room, shut the apartment door behind him. He heard her sobbing from the hallway. Outside, he vomited a long stream of bile onto the sidewalk, then sat on the steps waiting for his skin to dry.

40

The warden owned twenty-five acres of forested mountain land just ten miles from where Grant torched the truck. They passed the remains of the scene—charred earth, a line of police tape strung between two blackened trees—and stopped to take a look. They found a singed mirror in the understory, a small scattering of cigarette butts left behind by an idle trooper or lab tech.

"Careless," Raney said.

"Still, they kept the fire in check," Bay said. "The woods around here could've burned for days."

"Grant probably called them himself. Maybe before he tossed the match."

"Guess he wouldn't risk his buddy's land."

"Not if he's hiding on it."

According to the county map, an access road ascended a half mile to a hunting cabin perched on the summit of a small mountain.

The road was blocked now by a heavy log gate, the gate chained to a post with an industrial-looking padlock. There were a half dozen NO TRESPASSING signs nailed to the top rung. Bay rolled past the entrance, pulled over.

"You really think he's up there?"

"If he'd burned the truck two counties over, I'd have put the odds at fifty-fifty. But this close?"

"So let's call the marshals."

"They're not going to set foot on the warden's property without an ironclad reason."

"Then we'll give 'em one. Hell, I'll phone in an anonymous tip."

"Just let me lay eyes on the man. You wait here. If I catch sight of him, we'll call every agency in the state."

"Fuck you, Raney. You ain't doing this alone."

"He'll spot two people quicker than one."

"So your plan is to climb uphill toward a professional sniper? Where do you put those odds? What's this about, Raney? What'd that woman touch off in you?"

"Nothing. Just keep the motor running."

Bay laid a hand on Raney's chest, held him back.

"You know," he said, "on a good day I look at you and I don't see a shred of happiness. Not one shred. You can handle yourself, I'll give you that. But I'm thinking maybe Grant raises up and you hesitate just a second. I'm thinking maybe Clara was some kind of last straw."

"Don't think so hard, Sheriff."

Bay looked him over. Raney didn't look back.

"Sorry," Bay said. "I can't let you do it."

He palmed the clutch, shifted into gear, but Raney was already outside.

"Fuck you, then," Bay called. "I won't stand in your goddamn way."

The sky was clear, the sun sharp where it broke through the canopy. He skirted a meadow teeming with wild rose and yellow cinquefoil, walked swiftly, heel to toe, half crouching, one hand cradling his gun. He saw himself as if from someplace distant—a bowed figure cutting through a wilderness that had kept him sober and steady for eighteen years, on his way, he believed, to either kill a man or be killed. What was in him—the self-loathing, the desire to harm and be harmed—had finally spilled over: he was reverting back to himself, just as Jack and Mavis had done. Our minds have evolved in the wrong direction, he thought. Nature can only contain us for so long.

A quarter mile up he spotted a small red light buried in a cluster of needles. Then another, and another. Surveillance video, Grant watching him from a monitor somewhere nearby. Raney drew his gun, cut over to the access road, ran full speed. He reached the summit in time to catch a motorbike speeding down the opposite slope, a blur appearing and disappearing between stands of lodgepole pine, a large knapsack strapped to the driver's back. Raney continued running, fired a shot though Grant was well out of range. He fired again, stumbled over a granite outcropping, fell backwards, landed in the warden's fire pit, his spine striking black stone. He stood, braced his lower back with a flat palm, watched the bike turn west onto a paved road and vanish completely.

He dialed Bay's number, heard only static.

The cabin looked to be the last remaining structure of a long-dismantled mining camp, an adobe rehabbed with mud plaster and a recently installed red tile roof. A mesh cage with a tarp lying across the top housed a gasoline-powered generator. Grant had been kind enough to leave the front door open. Inside, more animals on the walls, a bear hide covering most of the exposed floor. A hot plate and a kiva fireplace for cooking, a dorm-size fridge for perishables. Minimal furnishing: a neatly made cot, a futon, a plywood table, and a few folding chairs. Whatever Grant had brought with him was gone. Any forensic evidence could be explained away: Grant had been coming here for eighteen years. The warden was free and clear.

Raney sat for a moment, recuperating, then took out his camera and photographed every inch of the cabin. He started downhill, cursing himself. Grant wouldn't surface again without a damn good reason. Bay had been right: Raney wasn't searching; he was hiding. As he approached the county road, he saw a chasm opening in front of him, an empty space he could think of only one way to fill.

41

When he woke the next morning he found himself facing the Narrows, the Verrazano Bridge to his left, traffic speeding down the Belt Parkway behind him. He had no memory of arriving there, no memory of switching off the engine, shutting his eyes.

He drove the short distance to his apartment in Fort Hamilton. Then nothing. The nausea was gone, but his skull ached, and his skin was sore to the touch.

He shut the door behind him, started undressing, noticed a strong odor of cigar smoke. He reached for his revolver. It wasn't there. He couldn't think of where he'd left it. He heard metal slide against metal, a bolt click into place. Ferguson stepped from the bedroom with his shotgun raised.

"Put your weapon on the ground and kick it toward me," he said.

"I'm not armed."

"Bullshit."

"I can strip if you want. Are you here to kill me?"

"You think I'm a killer?"

"I know you are."

"Even if that were true, I'm not sure you're worth killing," Ferguson said. "We're going to talk, and then I'll make up my mind what to do with you."

They sat on opposite sides of a small Formica table, Ferguson holding the twin barrels of his gun inches from Raney's chest.

"You've forgotten, haven't you?"

"Forgotten what?"

"Beating my daughter," Ferguson said. "Her right eye is swollen shut. I sat up with her for hours. She claims you were hallucinating. Ranting. I think she still wants to rescue you, but I won't let that happen. I won't let you anywhere near my grandchild."

It came back now, not little by little, but all at once, as though he were living it again, or maybe for the first time: Sophia falling, her belly exposed.

"Did she say what I was ranting about?" Raney asked.

"That's the question you want to ask me?"

"She must have. That's why you're here—to find out if there's any way Meno's death can blow back on you."

"You have some goddamned nerve pointing your finger at me. I'm here because of my daughter. Because of what you did to her. The woman who's pregnant with your child."

"I'll answer for that, but not to you. Stone was careful down to the smallest detail. Meno didn't know there was a case until you told him."

"Why on earth would I do that?"

"Because it was just a matter of time before Meno found himself in a room with Stone. A dirty police captain would have given him a card to play. It wouldn't have earned him much with Stone, but it would have been worth something."

"My daughter was right. You're spouting drug-addled nonsense. You need help. A place to go and clear your mind."

"Was Meno spouting nonsense?"

"I don't know what you're talking about."

"The man had a lot to say before he died."

"So you *were* there last night."

"You know I was. You put me there."

"What did he say?"

"It doesn't matter," Raney said. "The fact that you're asking is all the proof I need."

Ferguson leaned back in his chair, brought the shotgun level with Raney's skull.

"It's time for you to be careful now," he said.

"Don't worry: any hope of prosecuting you died last night. That's what you wanted all along, isn't it? It was some stroke of luck, having your future son-in-law working the case that would have put you in jail. But then you made your own luck. Or had your lackey Kee make it for you."

"This story gets more absurd by the minute. Soon you'll have monsters rising from the deep. And somehow that will be my fault, too."

"It's just you and me in this room, Captain, and you know what I'm saying is real. You pushed me to kill Meno from the beginning, but I wouldn't listen. That's why Stone is dead, isn't it? It had to be one or the other, and I was too damn slow. Or maybe Stone turned out to be the better choice. He would have kept on you even after Meno died. Now they're both dead, and all you had to do was whisper in the right ears."

"If this gun went off," Ferguson said, "there would be a hundred ways to explain it."

"The kickback would send you through the window. Besides, I just said I won't be coming after you. I have no proof. And now there's a child to think about."

"Proof or not, I look at you and see a problem."

"So you're going to kill me," Raney said. "You sure you want to pull the trigger yourself? You might be able to get your daughter to do it."

"I'm not as ugly as you think. And no, I'm not going to kill you. You're a manageable problem. Manageable because your problems are at least as big as mine, and I'm the only person you know who can make them go away."

"I'll get by without your help."

"Don't be stubborn just for the sake of it. Hear me out. Believe it or not, I came to make you an offer. A generous offer."

"You're going to turn yourself in?"

"I had something else in mind. I own a cabin in New Mexico. It's small, but there isn't a more beautiful spot in this country. It's been in my family a long time. I love the idea of the place, but somehow I never get there. Sophia doesn't even know it exists. I'll sign over the deed. You go out there and get yourself clean, start fresh. I can help. I know people there, too."

"You mean you're banishing me?"

"I'm giving you an opportunity."

"I'll get clean here. I'll be here for my wife and child."

"On the contrary, you'll never lay eyes on my daughter again. And you won't know your child."

"It's your turn to be careful. Maybe last night whet my appetite."

"I've outlived so many threats that I almost don't hear them anymore. Yours is particularly meaningless. You're the fool, not the hero. A righteous fool, which is the worst kind. You need to consider who has the upper hand. At the end of the day, you have nothing on me. You said so yourself. Only your word, and we both know you've done things to make that worthless. But how long do you think it will be before Homicide discovers you're connected to a quintuple murder? What do you think they'll say when my daughter tells them you showed up at her place in the middle of the night dressed in another man's clothes? And then there's the blood on your badge, which seems almost too pathetic, too contrived to be true. Do you understand what I'm saying? I can steer the investigation in a different direction. Because of your righteousness, your foolishness, you need my help. I can give it or withhold it. I can do anything to you I like."

"Then why are you here, talking to me?"

"For Sophia. For my grandchild."

"And if I'm willing to crash and burn as long as there's the smallest chance of bringing you with me?"

"Then consider this: What would you rather be to your child? A convict? Or a mystery?"

42

"Shit," Bay said. "I hate for it to end this way."

"It's up to the marshals now. You were right—I should have left it in their hands to begin with."

"Still, your instincts were dead-on, Raney. I never seen anything like it."

"Meanwhile, Grant's in the wind."

"So what's next for you? Back to the cabin?"

"Until they send me out again."

"And Clara?"

"Won't return my calls."

"Wish I had some wisdom to offer there."

"What about you?" Raney said. "On to Alaska?"

"I've got a month yet."

"Hope it's a quiet month."

"I figure the lightning struck all at once."

"You're a good man, Bay," Raney said. "I wouldn't want to be the one to fill your shoes."

Bay raised his coffee cup.

"Here's to new adventures."

"And old friends," Raney said.

Bay smiled. "I have trouble seeing you as the sentimental type," he said. "But it's damn nice of you to fake it."

The cabin was a forest-green Cape Cod set back from a creek bed and sequestered in a stand of Douglas fir. The sky was bright, the moon nearly full when Raney pulled up at just past midnight. He fished around in the small metal cabinet under the barbecue until he came up with the house key. Inside, he switched on the lights, kicked off his shoes. The neighbors' daughter had kept the bird feeder full, taken in his mail, watered his only plant. Everything was as he'd left it: the living space tidy, the loft bed made up with the same linen, the air holding the same scent of pine.

When he first arrived, and after he was sober, he'd done everything he could to erase Ferguson's presence. He'd removed the deer head from above the small fireplace, replaced the bearskin with a burlap-colored area rug. He refurnished the place with a mismatched couch and love seat, a queen-size bed with no frame, a small glass table, and a pair of discarded chairs he'd found on someone's lawn. The books he'd acquired—most of them guides to the regional flora and fauna—sat in piles against the walls. He'd bought an antique radio and hooked it up to modern speakers, stuck a floor lamp next to the couch. Now it was only when he left and came back that he remembered the place had ever belonged to Sophia's father.

He was more hungry than tired. He switched on the deck light, took a salmon steak and a half dozen asparagus stalks from the freezer, and started the barbecue. While the food was grilling, he changed into jeans, sneakers, a sweater. He poured himself a glass of white wine, sat in a wooden armchair by the creek, eating and drinking, listening to the sound of the water, feeling his body ache as though he'd returned from a week of hiking through the back country. He drifted off, woke to a coyote howling somewhere on the opposite bank. He left his empty plate and glass balanced on the arms of the chair, walked along the creek, beyond the reach of the deck light.

The smell of piñon, the sound of the water, the sharp mountain air: he caught himself wishing Clara were there to share it. He didn't resent her so much as he resented the wish.

He started the next morning with a short hike, came across a fox hunting meadow-jumping mice, spotted a pair of sandhill cranes gliding overhead. Afterward, breakfast on the deck, coffee by the creek.

The supermarket carried papers from Albuquerque and Santa Fe. Raney resisted the temptation to pick one up. At this time of the morning, he had the store to himself. He set aside his list, walked every aisle, reading labels, trying, for reasons he couldn't name, to fill his cart with products he'd never thought to buy before: farina instead of oatmeal, flavored seltzer instead of bottled water, French roast instead of Colombian, soy instead of skim. He walked back down the produce aisle, topped his cart off with gingerroot, mangoes, pearl onions.

On the way out, he glanced down at the Albuquerque *Gazette*. The front-page headline read MANHUNT CONTINUES. The date was August 1, 2002. Raney hadn't realized that July was over.

It was the date that stayed with him as he drove home, then unpacked his groceries and folded the bags. He had a vague feeling that August meant something, that there was something he was supposed to do, an event he was supposed to celebrate or at least observe. Ella's birthday? Daniel's? Sophia's? The anniversary of his father's death? The feeling nagged at him while he pumped air into the tires of his bike, did a load of laundry, grilled his dinner. His mind cycled through snapshots of the people who'd once been central in his life and now were gone from it. He felt the old craving switch on—a sudden absence in his blood. It remained with him into the early evening, when he drove above the tree line to watch a herd of bighorn sheep graze. The marvel of standing alone with these creatures in a landscape resembling tundra was tainted by the fact that he had nowhere else to be.

It wasn't until he'd climbed into bed and turned off the lights that he remembered. He hurried down the loft steps, switched on his laptop, skimmed through the bookmarks labeled GRANT. He found it: an obituary giving Jonathan Grant's date of birth as August 3, 1983.

43

Raney arrived at the Albuquerque National Cemetery at 11:00 p.m. on August 2. He wore a navy-blue jumpsuit and a matching baseball cap. The night watchman took his badge, held it under a flashlight.

"Care to tell me what you're looking for?" he asked.

"I work gangs. A baby banger in the Mexican Mafia says he hid a gun in the bushes near one of the mausoleums."

"Didn't happen to say which mausoleum?"

"No, sir."

"Then you're in for a long night."

"I guess I am."

"I was on the job," the watchman said. "Second Precinct, Robbery Division. Thirty years. What you're saying doesn't make a whole lot of sense, if you ask me."

"Which part?"

"Sending a single detective in the middle of the night to canvass an area this long and wide."

"I'm on my own time. No wife waiting at home. Nothing on TV."

"Can I ask why you're dressed like a janitor?"

"I'm undercover in the Courtside projects."

"Now, that holds water. You're the wrong color for that part of town, but no one looks twice at a maintenance man."

"That's the idea."

"Let me see your badge one more time."

Raney handed it back. "This seems like a good gig," he said. "Quiet. Not much hassle."

"There are worse," the watchman said. "I'll let you pass even though your story smells like bullshit. You didn't come here alone at this hour to look for any gun. I'm going to assume you've got your reasons and leave it at that. Just watch yourself. It's pitch-dark in there, and we got no shortage of snakes and such."

"Thank you," Raney said. "I'll keep an eye out."

The cemetery spanned three hundred heavily manicured acres, including an exotic rose garden and an arboretum imported from Japan—quiet settings where ashes could be scattered and plaques installed. Raney had downloaded a map, memorized the layout, highlighted Jonathan Grant's headstone in red marker. Still, the night watchman was right: the overhang from the trees cut the moonlight; he had trouble holding his bearings in the dark. He worked his way forward using a compass and a high-voltage flash-light. With each step he felt, or imagined he felt, small insects biting his ankles. He tripped over a memorial stone, scraped his cheek on a low-hanging branch. He kept heading north. He heard a low-pitched scream, reached for his gun before he realized the sound belonged to an owl.

Jonathan was buried at the rear of the cemetery, near the cen-

ter of a row of tombstones bookended by Civil War mausoleums.
Raney went stone by stone until he found Jonathan's plot. The
epitaph read:

I might have been so much more,
but I did not die in vain.

Oscar Grant was now the bogeyman of the urban desert, his
face branded into the imagination of every citizen in the Albuquerque–Santa Fe corridor. State and federal authorities were
offering substantial rewards for information leading to his cap-
ture. Street gangs were hunting him both for the bounty and
because of what he'd done to their sales. If Oscar was planning to
honor his son's birth, he'd likely do it at an hour when the city was
asleep; if he was brazen enough to come by daylight, then Raney
was prepared to wait. Of course, it was possible that he wouldn't
show at all, that he'd fled the state and country: a loner with fake
documents who might be standing anywhere on the globe. If that
was the case, then the marshals would be searching until Grant
died of natural causes.

Raney switched off the flashlight, lay on his stomach in the narrow space between the bushes and a wall of the mausoleum on
the western side of the cemetery. If Oscar spotted him, he'd see a
groundskeeper sleeping one off.

Hours passed. Raney kept his eyes fixed on Jonathan's tomb-
stone even as his mind began to drift. He saw Clara looking out
a window in some distant city, the early morning sun highlighting
her hair; he saw Bay dressed in waders, wrestling a salmon out of
an Alaskan river. Nobody, Raney thought, lives just one life anymore. A Boston prostitute somehow comes to own a crafts store

in southern New Mexico; a one-time Navy SEAL finds himself in the role of single dad, then fugitive. Some people, like Clara, volunteered for their second or third lives; most just fell into them. It was the burden or blessing of an increased life span.

The sky began to lighten, turn colors. Raney sipped from a small Thermos of coffee, felt like a child under the covers, fighting sleep, playing make-believe. He pretended he was a nature photographer waiting to snap a picture of some rare bird, a World War II sniper lying in wait for the Desert Fox, Billy the Kid watching a posse ride past. His legs started to cramp. The arm he'd been lying on went numb, began to tingle. He found himself doubting Oscar would come, laughed out loud at the image of a forty-two-year-old man hiding in the bushes of a cemetery, telling himself stories while he waited for a bad guy who was sleeping comfortably in a motel several thousand miles away, maybe in Buenos Aires. Maybe, as a final irony, Oscar decided to live out Mavis's dream. Maybe, Raney thought, I should book a flight to Argentina.

The cemetery would open to the public soon. Raney would have to come out of hiding, pretend to be trimming hedges or polishing marble. The need to urinate became overwhelming. He stood, shook out his legs, walked around to the back of the mausoleum. He wondered why the zipper running down the front of his jumpsuit didn't extend to the crotch. He was forced to take his arms out of the sleeves, push the suit to his ankles, lean awkwardly forward—an absurd creature, pissing among the dead. He wondered if this stakeout was anything more than Detective Wes Raney clinging to what would likely be the last substantial case of his career.

He worked the zipper back up to his neck, started toward his post, stopped cold when he turned the corner. Oscar was there, kneeling at his son's grave. He wore a shoulder-length black wig, held a bouquet of yellow tulips in one hand and a small American flag in the other. Raney crouched down, watched him screw the flag into the earth, rest the flowers against the stone. Oscar's lips were moving, but not in prayer. He was singing, whispering "Happy Birthday" to his son.

Raney lifted his gun, crept forward. He was a few yards shy when Oscar, still kneeling, turned to face him.

"Hands on top of your head," Raney said. "Now."

Oscar reached up, pulled off his wig. Bits of glue stuck to his scalp, glistened.

"I'm not armed," he said.

"Hands," Raney said.

"You're too late."

"Put your goddamn hands on your head."

Raney was on top of him now. Oscar held out his left arm, rolled up his sleeve. His veins were yellow and swollen. He sucked at the air in short, harsh breaths.

"I've already surrendered," he said. "Just not to you, Detective."

"Son of a bitch," Raney said.

He held his gun level, walked a half circle around Oscar, pushed him to the ground and planted a foot in the small of his back. He dug his phone out of his pocket, dialed nine-one-one.

"This is Detective Wes Raney, county Homicide. I'm at the Albuquerque National Cemetery. There's a man overdosing. It's Oscar Grant. I need an ambulance and additional units."

He hung up before she could ask questions.

"You're too late," Oscar repeated. "You've been too late from the beginning."

"No talking," Raney said. "Just lie still. They'll be here soon."

Oscar began wheezing, grabbing at his throat. The spasms were intermittent, then continuous. Raney dropped to his knees, flipped Oscar onto his back. Oscar's torso was bucking, his arms and legs thrashing. Raney slipped a hand under his head, pressed down on his chest. Oscar vomited into the air. Blood ran from his nose and ears.

Raney heard a brigade of sirens. Oscar calmed, quieted, and went still.

44

He drove without rest, had emptied Dunham's lockbox by the time he reached the New Mexico border. For days, he lay naked on the cabin's bathroom floor, drying his skin with a towel, rising now and again to eat peaches from pull-top cans, fighting the urge to slit his wrists with the metal edges. When he drifted off, his dreams jolted him awake: pseudomythical creatures chasing him through a stainless steel maze; a lifeless, gray mass falling from Sophia's womb. Later, after he'd graduated to the loft, he would wake to find evidence of his own sleepwalking: a puddle of urine at the center of the kitchen floor; the TV tuned to static; the doors and windows open throughout the cabin.

He stopped sleeping altogether, stayed up waiting for Meno's associates to light the place on fire and murder him as he ran out the door. He searched the cabin, found a dusty .22 rifle and a box of shells in the foyer closet. He would lie for hours on his belly in the loft, rifle cocked, listening. Now and then he'd creep down the stairs, peer through each window in turn.

When he did sleep again, it was for a very long while. Afterward, he took his first shower at the cabin, used dish soap for shampoo. His hair was long and matted. His clothes hung from his body like drapery. He had no razor to shave with.

He stared at himself in the bathroom mirror, tried to calculate how much time had passed. Sophia would have given birth by now. He saw Ferguson standing over her hospital bed, cradling the baby, promising, in Raney's absence, to be more than a grandfather.

In time, Raney left the cabin, walked barefoot to the creek, sunk his toes in the water. The physical pain was gone. Now there was only hunger and a dull withdrawal he knew he could manage.

On the strength of Ferguson's recommendation, and after a battery of interviews and field tests, the county hired him straight into Homicide. There was a two-month probation period during which he worked a suicide and a shooting in a bar full of witnesses anxious to cooperate. The job was his for as long as he wanted it.

He drove a hundred miles to the nearest library, searched the archives until he found a detailed account of the Mora-Malone fight. Mora was ahead on points when he knocked Malone out in the eleventh. He was now the mandatory challenger for the middleweight belt. *The Ring* magazine ranked him fifth in the division. Raney tried to imagine what might have been his own pro career, but he couldn't sustain the effort: he'd never seen himself as anything other than a cop.

He wrote to Sophia, received no reply. He wrote to her again and again. The letters came back marked RETURN TO SENDER. He kept them in a bundle on the shelf above his Polaroids.

*　*　*

He'd been at the cabin two years when he decided to call her. He had something to offer their daughter now: a window into another landscape, another way of living. The desert would seem exotic to a child from the city. He wouldn't be asking for custody, or even partial custody, but rather a visit in the summer, maybe another in the spring. He would take her with him on his hikes, introduce her to a hundred kinds of wildflowers, teach her to track deer, buy her a camera of her own. Ella the environmentalist, the scientist. Maybe all Raney wanted was to see the desert fresh again through his child's eyes.

He prepared for the call as though he'd be meeting Sophia face-to-face. He bought Ella a picture-book tour of the New Mexico desert featuring a chapter on cacti of every shape and size followed by a two-page spread of a coyote howling at the moon. He bought her a stuffed roadrunner that made sounds when you squeezed its stomach. He set her presents on the couch beside a manila envelope filled with the cash equivalent of all the checks Sophia had rejected. He reminded himself that his aim was not to win Sophia back or to reclaim his old life: he wanted to know his daughter; he wanted his daughter to know him.

Sophia's number remained unlisted. Raney called her office. The receptionist said she had been promoted, moved to a more potent branch of the same department. She transferred his call. This time a man answered:

"Special Services, Sophia Ferguson's office."

"I'd like to speak to Ms. Ferguson," Raney said.

"She's busy at the moment. Can I take a message?"

"I'm calling about her daughter, Ella."

"Please hold," the man said. "I'll see if she can step out of her meeting."

The line filled with Muzak. Now and again an automated voice affirmed that his call was important to the office of Special Services for Children. Was Sophia really in a meeting, or was this a routine meant to weed out unmotivated callers? The longer he waited, the more motivated Raney became.

"Special Services, this is Sophia Ferguson speaking. How may I help you?"

"It's Wes," he said. "Please don't hang up."

She was quiet for a while. Then:

"You shouldn't be calling me here."

"I know. Your home number isn't listed."

"You shouldn't be calling me at all."

"That used to be true," he said. "Things have changed. I've changed."

"Nothing has changed for me," she said. "Who you were at the end erased everything that came before."

"I'm clean. I have been since the day I got here."

"Should I applaud? Let me say this in the clearest possible terms: I won't have you anywhere near my daughter. Ever. Under any circumstances."

He heard traces of her father. Ferguson, alone to spin any tale he wanted, had cast himself as savior. For two years now he'd whispered in her ear about the man she'd almost married, the life he'd spared her. Raney had become a testament to her father's good counsel.

"The person you're talking about doesn't exist, Sophia. Not anymore."

"You mean the addict who knocked me on my ass when I was six months pregnant? It's not him I'm worried about."

"Who, then?"

"My father told me where the blood came from that night. The blood on your badge."

"What did he tell you?"

"You know what he told me."

"And you believe him?"

"If it's a clean shooting, you stand by the body. You call it in. Isn't that what you're all taught? But you left. You showed up at my place wearing another man's clothes. And then you ran."

"Your father said I ran?"

"He told me you went to him the next morning. He said you were lost, hysterical. You begged him to help you."

"That's not right. That isn't what happened."

"Of course it is. You're living in his cabin, aren't you? You're living a life he handed you. I asked him why. He said he didn't want his granddaughter to grow up a murderer's child. He wanted to spare her that stigma. I wish he'd stayed out of it."

Raney got up from the table, stood at the back door facing the creek.

"Sophia," he said, "everything I told you that night was true. I'm saying this now with a clear head."

"You mean my father had Stone killed? He manipulated you into killing the people who could hurt him? That's all been disproved a hundred times over. You're clinging to a delusion because you can't face what you did. You're a coward on top of everything else."

"Listen to me, Sophia. All I want is a chance. See me. See me in person and then judge. I'll get on the next plane. You always believed in second chances."

"You've had yours. You're living it now. You should be calling my father to thank him."

"Sophia, he's not who you think he is. He's dangerous. He . . ."

"I don't want to hear it, Wes. Anyway, there's someone else now."

"Someone else?"

"Someone Ella knows as her father. And it's going to stay that way. He's good to her. He loves her."

She was lying, spinning a story to keep him in the desert. He could tell by the change in pitch, the slight quickening of her breath.

"Who is he?"

"I'm not going to answer that."

"Did your father pick him out for you?"

"He works with me in Special Services. I've known him for a long time. Since long before you left."

"What's his name?"

"Stop it, Wes. He's real. And he's a big part of Ella's life."

He'd pressed as hard as he could. There was no point in continuing.

"At least let me send her something," he said. "You wouldn't have to tell her it's from me."

"I'd rather you didn't."

"But if I did?"

"Send it to me here at work."

"Thank you," Raney said.

She hung up.

He drove to the post office, bought a box large enough to fit a picture book and a stuffed animal. He felt his first real craving in a long while—a desire for the world to go dull. He called his county supervisor.

"My vacation plans fell through," he said. "Put me on a case. Any case at all."

45

He lay on the futon in his cabin, fully clothed, watching an eighties sitcom about an English butler running an American family. The cravings had turned frequent and immediate, as though he'd copped that morning and needed a new fix to keep the old one alive. He was done tricking himself—he wanted to get high.

He muted the television, pulled his laptop from the side table. He called up a search engine, typed in *Ella Ferguson,* hit Return.

There were hundreds, maybe thousands of Ella Fergusons out there. He added the words *Brooklyn,* then *New York City,* then *granddaughter of police captain.* His Ella began to emerge from the rest. Page by page, he pieced together a bio. She was an accomplished eighteen-year-old. She'd finished top of her class at Stuyvesant High School, spoke French, played the piano well enough to have placed in a national competition. During her first year at Columbia, she'd cofounded the Just-Us Club, a group of students involved, under the tutelage of a senior faculty member, in securing new trials for inmates who had been railroaded the first time around. There was a photo of them all standing on a lawn under a bright sun, eighteen students total, an equal mix of boys and girls, every one of them smiling as though they'd over-turned a life sentence that morning. Raney hunted the image for a resemblance to Sophia, but the picture was taken from a distance, the faces obscured by glare.

So Ella had inherited her mother's penchant for social justice. The aging Ferguson must be preparing to turn in his grave. Had Ella founded the club to spite him? Was he that kind of presence in her life? Imagining an antagonism between them gave Raney some small pleasure, though this pleasure in turn made him feel small. Pitting Ella against her grandfather would do nothing to bring back the years Raney had missed. It wouldn't give Ella a fa-ther.

But then she didn't seem to need one. The comparison be-tween Ella and Luisa Gonzalez had been false from the start. Yes, what happened to Luisa could happen to anyone's daughter, but there was a difference between a long shot and a near certainty. To pretend otherwise was to diminish Luisa's brief life while grossly exaggerating his own importance.

Oscar Grant had been right: Raney was too late. Were he to turn up now, he'd only disrupt Ella's life at exactly the wrong moment. Bay meant well, but whether or not Raney needed his daughter had nothing to do with whether she needed him.

He was on the road before the sun came up. He bought a combo meal at a truck stop, thought of Dunham cutting up blow on his dashboard, remembered the beating they'd given each other that night in the warehouse. Dunham, lover of music and the sweet science. Raney felt the violence of those days clinging to him, felt his own capacity for violence unabated. He was more like Dunham than Bay. He understood this now. To be good, even to wish to be good, he had to remain vigilant, had to keep a few steps ahead of himself. Stone had seen it in him. Sophia and her father, too.

He took out five hundred dollars from an ATM, rolled the bills into a tight ball and tucked them in the glove compartment. He pulled onto the highway, headed for Albuquerque.

The crew was back up and running at the Courtside Apartments. Raney parked in a resident's spot at the far end of the lot and watched them work. Their operation was cautious, exact. Teenage spotters roamed the top-floor breezeway. Foot soldiers drank soda and played backgammon in the central courtyard. No one sat or stood more than a few feet from an exit; everyone had a role to play: collect the money, fetch the product, make the handoff. The Albuquerque PD must have been riding them hard since Grant's poison hit the street.

He took the bills from the glove compartment, divided them between his pockets. Once and only once, he told himself. Under the stars, in his rocking chair by the creek. A quick respite. A chance to regroup. But he knew he'd brought too much cash for that to be true.

He caught one of the spotters eyeballing him, thought maybe the kid would send a scout. He waited, but nobody came. He opened his car door, put one foot on the pavement, pulled it back in. He started the engine, switched it off. When civilians walked by, he pretended to be reading a map.

His phone rang. He dug it out of his pocket, saw CLARA REMLER slide across the screen. He pressed Talk, held the receiver to his chest. He felt ashamed but couldn't say why.

"Are you there?"

"Yes," he said. "I'm here."

Quiet. Then:

"Where is here these days?"

"Albuquerque. Just for the morning. What about you?"

"I'm in Alamosa."

"Colorado?"

"Southern. I'm teaching at a charter school."

"Good for you."

He almost said: *Mavis would be proud.*

"It's temporary," she said. "I'm covering a maternity leave."

"How does Daniel like it?"

"He keeps asking for Mrs. Hardin. And for you."

Another pause.

"You're angry with me, aren't you?" she said.

"I'd have no right to be."

"You'd have every right. You know you would."

"No," he said. "I'm not angry with you. I'd have done the same thing. I mean, if I were you and you were me. What I told you—"

"That has nothing to do with it, Wes."

"Of course it does. There's no need to pretend."

"I'm not pretending," she said. "I'm a runner. I told you, I always have been."

"You had no choice this time."

He watched money exchange hands in the courtyard. A lanky kid with close-cropped hair disappeared into a basement apartment.

"I've been thinking about you," Clara said.

"Yeah?"

"I've been wondering if there could be something more between us. I mean something more than the way we met."

"And?"

"I think there could be."

He let it hang there.

"I want to see you again," she said. "I know it's a lot to ask."

A muscular twentysomething in a tank top and cutoffs came walking slowly toward Raney's car, hands in his pockets. The kids on the breezeway leaned over the railing.

"It isn't," he said. "It isn't a lot."

He turned the key in the ignition, backed up, headed for the main road. The foot soldier watched him go.

"You're driving," Clara said. "It's a bad time. We could talk later."

"No," he said. "It's all right. I want to see you, too."

"Yeah?"

"How far is Alamosa from Albuquerque?"

"You mean tonight?"

"I had a lousy evening planned. I'm glad to get out of it."

"Flattering," she said.

"That's not what I meant. Are you free?"

"I'm free. I'll have Daniel."

"So how far?"

"Depends on how fast you drive."

ABOUT THE AUTHOR

Christopher Charles is the pseudonym of Chris Narozny, author of the novel *Jonah Man*. Narozny received an MFA from Syracuse University and a PhD from the University of Denver. He has lived in Normandy, Paris, and Brooklyn and currently resides in Denver, Colorado.